THE THINGS
THAT SECRETS
CANNOT HIDE

THE THINGS THAT SECRETS CANNOT HIDE

A VIC LENOSKI MYSTERY

PETER W.J. HAYES

LEVEL
BEST BOOKS

First published by Level Best Books 2022

Quote from Back in the Ring by Chris Pureka, from the album, Back in the Ring, copyright 2016, Sad Rabbit Music (ASCAP)

First edition

ISBN: 978-1-68512-154-9

Cover art by Level Best Designs

This book was professionally typeset on Reedsy.
Find out more at reedsy.com

To the JDMB. Thanks for the friendship, camaraderie, loyalty and trust for all these years. It has made me a better person and willing to believe that— just possibly—there is hope for Rangers and Bruins fans.

The temptation for greatness is the biggest drug in the world.

—(Iron) Mike Tyson
World Heavyweight Champion 1987-1990

Years, come down, cut like an anchor
Through the mud and stone
Just dragging behind
Oh my god
Get up, get up, get up
Put the gloves back on, back in the ring
Get up, get up, get up
put the gloves back on, get back in the ring
Hit the ground, nothing comes easy
Gloves back on, back in the ring, hey, hey...

—From the song *Back in the Ring* by Chris Pureka

Chapter One

G eno pulled his car to the edge of the entrance road into Allegheny Cemetery and stopped, his way blocked by a wrought iron gate. He turned off his headlights, leaned toward the windshield, and searched the eastern sky.

A milky glow edged the gothic clock tower and two-story gatehouse. Near the tower's parapet, the clock promised ten more minutes until the cemetery opened. With luck, he thought, he would still see the dawn. He'd watched it every day since his release from prison six months earlier, and didn't want to miss it. He liked how the first light came to him each day. Sometimes it was a promise, and others, a demand, like a long-held secret aching to be told.

He sat back and thought about the three hundred grass-covered acres beyond the gatehouse. It was such an unlikely oasis of green for the center of Pittsburgh. He'd played there with friends as a boy, and in high school, helped teenage girls over the wall on hot summer nights. He still remembered sitting on the cool stone slabs, beer cans sweating in their hands, the city lights glittering in the distance. The flush and excitement of it all.

Geno shifted in his seat. He was eighty-three now and his joints ached when he sat too long in one position. Prison had done him no favors. The salty, processed food and lack of exercise had scarred his heart, nudged his body into a gentle slide his medications rarely slowed.

He thought of his friends resting on the other side of the gate, and it weighed on him. Today at nine o'clock was the funeral of another. He gripped the steering wheel and reminded himself he would drive the narrow,

1

winding cemetery roads through the dips and up onto the hills. Perhaps catch a little of that airy, high school magic. The slab where Suzy let him slip his hand under her T-shirt, to find she had undone her bra for him. That August before senior year and the hot tug of Leslie's hand as she guided him on top of her. Somehow, it was those memories that sustained him in jail, not the carousel of women he dated in his thirties.

But none compared to Mary, his secret wife. She was his one truth. Mary and the child she bore him, their immaculate son.

He needed the cemetery to center him, as its peacefulness did when he was in high school. To give him direction and time to think. Seeing people at the funeral was a start, but he was really there to meet someone. He'd spent months looking for him, only to discover he was working for old friends in Pittsburgh.

It was the last thing he'd expected.

He only needed a few minutes with him. It wouldn't be easy, but a lifetime was too long for secrets and the horrors they bred. He owed it to Mary, to those early days, before it all went wrong. There wouldn't be many more opportunities, and if he didn't do it now the truth would slip away, become nothing more than the rustle of summer trees.

The tap on his side window startled him. He turned his head to see a gloved hand motion to lower the glass. He pressed the window toggle, vaguely aware his car must still be running. The hand disappeared and a face materialized in its place.

"Geno," the man said. "I got something to say to you."

Geno thought he saw something in the man's face. His heart skipped. There, in the cast of his nose and forehead. It was him, he was sure of it. The years fell away. He opened his mouth and his words ran together in excitement. "I need to talk to you as well. Really. I was going to catch you after the funeral. There's something I have to tell you."

"Mine's a message from my dad."

Geno strained to understand. "No, wait, yes, that's what I want to talk to you about."

The face lifted away, replaced by a second gloved hand. For a moment

2

Geno didn't understand what he was looking at, and then he did. He even understood the reason for it. His heartbeat turned to scattershot and pain radiated from his chest to his left shoulder. He gasped a breath, desperate for the right words. "Stop. You don't understand." He couldn't take his eyes from the round black hole.

"Sure I do." The voice from outside the car was disembodied, soaked in the predawn peace. "My dad would say payback's a bitch, Geno."

The sound was a balloon pop and hammer striking wood, the flash a splinter of brilliant light. Geno's head jerked sideways as if yanked with a rope. He came to rest on the passenger seat.

He knew nothing of that. Unknown to him, his heart labored out a few more beats. He didn't feel the second shot, or the tug on the sleeve of his left arm.

The muted click of the camera. Once. Twice.

Didn't hear the hurried footfalls receding from his car.

Seven minutes later, Evan Gelhorn turned his car into the cemetery entrance. On his way to the gatehouse, he passed a blue Lincoln pulled to the side of the road. It was in a no parking zone, but people often parked there before the cemetery opened. It annoyed him, but he let it go. They were usually gone before too long. Evan unlocked the gate, latched it open, and parked on the far side of the arch. Entered the administrative building.

Thirty minutes later, as he left for one of the maintenance buildings, he noticed the Lincoln was still there, the driver's side window open. His ear caught the sound of the motor running, something he hadn't noticed when he drove by.

Angry, he walked to the car and looked in the window.

Later, he wondered why every police officer who interviewed him asked, as they suppressed a smile, if he was the one who threw up next to the Lincoln.

He'd been clear from the start it was him.

Chapter Two

Vic Lenoski settled onto the only open bench in the playground and nodded to the clutch of young mothers surrounding the two benches nearest the playground equipment. Two of them smiled and waved, their take-out coffee cups dipping in the air. Behind them, large-wheeled baby carriers stood in a haphazard jumble, as if parked by a drunk valet crew.

A year earlier, when Vic started his daily ritual of shepherding his granddaughter, Lettie, to the playground, the group had cast furtive glances in his direction, their heads bent to one another. He knew he and Lettie were the topic of conversation. The second day, the tallest of them approached and asked about Lettie, her questions gruff and direct, not even bothering to hide her suspicions of why an out-of-work middle-aged man was caring for a four-year-old girl. Vic hadn't minded. As she talked, he noticed the rest of the women watching, two with phones in their hands, poised to dial.

He decided right then to call them the Watch Mothers. He knew it would be wise to stay friendly with them.

When the woman finished, he dutifully explained that he was Lettie's grandfather, and that he and his wife—Anne—were raising her. That Lettie's young mother, his daughter, had died unexpectedly.

The tall woman, whom he now knew as Amy, blinked and let out a small 'oh.'

He followed that by explaining he was a police detective who'd taken early retirement. He showed her the photo ID all retired police officers carried. She'd squinted at it, straightened, and tried to smile.

"We just thought it was unusual," she said. Vic heard a note of apology in her voice.

He told her he appreciated her concern, and that crimes were solved by people like her, who took a careful interest in their surroundings. When she returned to the others she walked very straight, and led the conversation for the next few minutes.

As she did, Lettie, with her usual energy, clambered up the slide and down the steps, so he walked over and explained how to properly use it. He demonstrated, his knees almost bumping his chin, skootching down the full length of the slide on his rear. He knew he looked ridiculous, but he wanted to. He guessed the Watch Mothers would find it hard to be suspicious of any fully-grown man willing to make a fool of himself for a four-year-old. When he returned to the bench, the women were smiling at him. As Lettie attacked the slide the right way around, he waved to the group, and received a full complement of waves in return.

Today, Lettie first chose the swings. She was soon arcing backwards and forwards, grinning, the chain stretched to the limit and the top bar creaking. Vic opened his newspaper and skimmed the headlines. He knew he was an anachronism, sitting on a playground bench reading an actual newspaper, but he didn't care. He liked the feel of the paper in his hands and searching each page to find the story he wanted to read, rather than being prodded with articles in an on-line feed. He even liked the daily ritual of buying a paper from the corner shop he and Lettie passed on their way to the playground. Even the store was a leftover. There were so few of them in neighborhoods any more he felt he needed to support them.

He searched for another article about Hana Richards, Pittsburgh's first female District Attorney. He trusted Hana and respected her, especially the way she handled her rise to DA. They'd met while investigating his last official case, the murder of a public defender. The victim died as the result of her own crimes, and Hana helped him prove it. What neither of them expected to find was a link to Frank Marioni, the existing DA. When he and Hana discussed that development, Hana told him to let her handle it.

Had she ever.

Within a year of Vic leaving the force, a newspaper article reported that Frank Marioni's office was being audited for expense violations. Soon afterwards, buried on an inside page of the newspaper, a story appeared about the DA's office defending itself from a conflict-of-interest inquiry. By then, Hana had transferred from public defender to prosecutor, reporting directly to the DA. Eighteen months later, the conflict-of-interest story moved from the back pages of the newspaper to page one, the story now linked to the murder of the public defender.

In retrospect, that public defender case altered both their lives. It led Vic to find Lettie in North Dakota and discover the truth of what happened to his missing daughter. It paved the way for Hana to reach the DA's office.

As the next election loomed, the conflict-of-interest inquiry stuck to the DA like a radioactive burr, and the mayor and county executive withheld their endorsements. Discussion of censure followed, even the possibility of the DA's disbarment. And finally, five months before the election, Marioni resigned. Two days later Hana announced her run for DA.

She didn't bother with a planning committee. She didn't put out feelers or gauge interest. She held a press conference to announce her run on a Wednesday and ran her first television advertisement on Friday of the same week. A string of endorsements followed, ending with a startling performance at the candidate's pre-election debate. Her opponent, a white-haired ex-cop, made the mistake of calling her "honey" in his opening remarks.

Hana's responses were sharp and factual, and she appeared motivated and unflappable. She demolished him. Within three days the mayor and county executive endorsed her.

Vic watched it all unfold on the pages of the newspaper. He didn't know what was needed to run a campaign for the DA's job, but it was clear to him Hana's planning started well before the conflict-of-interest inquiry reached the newspapers. Her messaging was seamless, her endorsements a steady string of dominoes falling. Vic knew it took time, planning, money, and preparation to make that happen, to create that sense of inevitability as it all played out. On Election Day, suburban women in the bedroom communities around Pittsburgh gave Hana a lopsided win.

She had Vic's vote from the start.

"Papap?" Vic blinked his way back to the present day. Lettie was looking up at him.

"What is it, honey?"

"Seesaw?" She pointed.

A small boy was standing with one end of the seesaw between his legs, holding it so Lettie could climb on the opposite end. Vic had seen the boy before, first spotting him as he made his way home from a school bus every day around three-thirty. He lived across the street from the playground entrance. The boy frequently visited the playground after school, always by himself.

The Watch Mothers, he'd noticed, kept their children away from him.

Vic studied the boy. His jacket was zippered tight to his neck and one point of his shirt collar stuck out, as if he had dressed in a hurry. His cheeks, like Lettie's, were pink. He watched Vic, but in a way that avoided direct eye contact. "Sure," Vic said.

Lettie flashed a wide grin and dashed to the seesaw. The boy kept it stable until she climbed on, and a moment later the two were rising and falling. The boy kept the motion regular and gentle. Vic wondered if he had a younger sister he was used to caring for.

"You sure about that?"

Vic glanced over as Barb plopped onto the seat next to him. She was one of the regular Watch Mothers, her son always orbiting her, as if scared to be too far away. Vic saw the boy climb onto a swing nearby, watching them from the corner of his eye. Vic liked Barb. In the days following Amy's inquisition, each of the mothers had come over and talked to him. Barb returned the most frequently. She asked him about cases he had worked, and he knew she must have searched newspaper archives for mentions of him. She was interested in crime, but she was polite about it, instinctively understanding Vic might be unwilling to talk about his past career. Vic appreciated her willingness to respect his boundaries.

"The whole situation with that boy is a little odd, don't you think?" She asked the question softly, without looking at him.

"I haven't seen a parent around, if that's what you mean. Not even a grandparent." He gave her a small smile, but she ignored his humor. Or didn't catch it.

"Well, that, but see how skinny he is? And he's always wearing the same shirt."

That was something Vic hadn't noticed. They sat in silence, the wind pressing around them. Graveyards, soccer fields, and playgrounds, Vic thought. For some reason, in Pittsburgh, they were always located on hilltops.

"He also doesn't talk. Some of us have said hello to him. He just ignores us."

Vic wanted to say that as a group, the Watch Mothers—with their yoga pants, sleek hair, technical jackets, and high-tech baby carriers—were a bit intimidating even for an adult male, but he let it pass. "I could talk to him," he offered. "Maybe it's a guy thing."

"That's a good idea." Vic noticed she was staring at the house where the boy lived. It was set back from the street above a series of steps. The large window overlooking the front porch and the playground was blocked by a closed interior blind. Curtains were drawn against the half window on the front door.

On the seesaw, the boy stopped mid-swing and held the board steady so Lettie could dismount. Vic rose and crossed to them, taking Lettie's hand and helping her to the ground. He turned to the boy, who let the seesaw drop and stood waiting.

"Thanks," Vic called. "That was very nice of you to let Lettie on and off. I'm Vic, Lettie's granddad."

The boy turned slightly and angled away, as if ready to run. One corner of his mouth twitched and Vic thought he might speak, but his lips set and he started for his house. Vic watched him go. He shifted his gaze to the house and saw a small crack between the slats of the blind in the front window. When the boy reached the road, the gap in the blinds disappeared.

Lettie tugged on his hand and pointed at the slide with her free hand.

"Go for it," Vic said. He went back to the bench and sat down.

"See? You got nothing out of him, either," Barb said carefully.

"I'll try again." Vic wasn't sure what to do about it. There was no reason to think something was wrong with the boy, yet his silence and the lack of supervision around him seemed odd. Neither of his parents even met him at the bus stop. He remembered his statement to Amy on that second day, about people paying attention. He made a note to take his time with the boy and see if familiarity opened him up.

"Did you hear about that shooting?" Barb asked.

Vic heard a note of excitement in her voice. He knew which one she meant, but he decided to appear uninterested. "Which one?"

"Just outside Allegheny Cemetery. You need to read the online story about it, not that thing." She nodded at his newspaper with a suspicious look. "Do you like Newsburgh? The news site? They had the details. Shot in the face, I guess the inside of the car was a mess. The man who found the body threw up." She shivered briefly. "Is that the kind of thing you would have investigated?"

Vic suspected Barb relished that shiver. "If it was my turn in the rotation, it's likely."

"Do you still find it interesting?"

"Not so much."

He was lying, but he didn't want Barb asking more questions. He'd read the newspaper story of the shooting twice, the second time slowly and carefully, memorizing the details. He'd recognized the victim's name right away. Geno Varelli. Geno had to be in his eighties by now, and he had a spectacular history with the police. Vic started hearing stories about Geno almost as soon as he first put on a uniform.

Newsburgh, of course, would focus on the blood spatter and violence, because their readers loved that. Barb was the proof. The print newspaper, he hoped, would look into Geno's past. Back to the nineteen-eighties, when Geno was one of Pittsburgh's crime kings. When Geno built his reputation.

But there was a problem with reputations, Vic knew, and that was what interested him about the shooting.

Destroying someone with a reputation was how some people chose to create their own.

Chapter Three

The First Day

Ears ringing from the shots, the gun heavy in the pocket of his hoodie, heart racing, he forced himself to keep to a walk as he crossed the grass at the cemetery entrance. In the murky dawn, a car's headlights surged toward him along Butler Street and he pivoted slowly, so his back was to the car as it passed. Geno's blue Lincoln gleamed in the murk. An old man's idea of a luxury car, he told himself. A shit car for a shit man. He turned and crossed to his own shit car, parked farther along Butler Street facing Pittsburgh.

He didn't know if the city's gunshot warning system stretched this far from downtown, and he wasn't going to find out.

Thirty seconds later he executed a U-turn and drove east on Butler Street, a bothersome rattle behind the dashboard. But he'd borrowed this car just because it was a clunker. The kind of car no one noticed. His hands tingled, the gun heavy in his lap.

He'd wondered, as he planned this, if he could actually do it. Not follow Geno around and learn his habits, but pull the trigger.

That turned out to be the easy part.

He turned left onto the Route Eight bridge. A minute later he was across the river and headed north, just another vehicle in the swirl of rush hour traffic. Forty minutes later he pulled into the parking lot of a mall and parked some distance from the northernmost doors. He left the car keys sitting on the rear driver's side wheel. Inside, the shops were almost deserted, clerks still in the process of unlocking storefronts. He made his way to a men's store, and after a joke with the clerk about being the first customer, bought a windbreaker. As he returned to where he had parked his car, a niggling doubt wormed into his mind.

The clunker was gone, his own car parked nearby. His smart key was under the bumper next to the tailpipe. He opened the trunk, exchanged his hoodie for the new windbreaker, stuffing the gloves and hoodie into the carrier bag from the store. After a quick glance around, he jammed the pistol inside the bag as well.

He settled into the comfortable leather of his driver's seat. His phone was right there, in the center console, plugged in, and turned on. Exactly as planned. But the niggling doubt was now a buzz in his brain. He needed to see the two photos he'd taken. He drove as he always did, carefully, just a few miles over the speed limit. Fifteen minutes later he pulled into a residential plan of townhomes. He parked in front of the one with the clunker he'd driven earlier sitting in the driveway. He got out and rang the doorbell. He had a key and was expected, but he knew women liked it better when he rang the doorbell. He might own the house, but she lived here, and he was fine with letting her believe she had some control in their relationship.

If she thought that way, the day he kicked her out the look on her face would be almost as good as the sex.

She opened the door wearing little more than a smile, grabbed his shirt, and pulled him inside. They kissed, crushed against each other. She'd been the most trainable of the women so far, he thought, clutching her against him. When they broke apart, her gulping, he said he needed a shower. She offered to join him but he declined, making a joke about it being better to wait. Showered and shaved, he shouted that he wanted something to drink. In the kitchen, he took the small camera out of his robe and downloaded copies of the two photographs onto her laptop. He stared at them.

On Geno's pale skin was a string of eight numbers, below that a word and underneath that another set of numerals. The eight numbers and the word were all he needed, but he wondered about the numerals. He hadn't expected or known about them. The woman called to him from upstairs. He tapped the tabletop with his fingertips. It didn't matter, but from habit, he counted the numerals in the string.

Ten. A bank account?

But everything was clear and readable. That was all that mattered. He flushed in excitement, deleted the photos from the laptop, and placed the camera in the pocket of his robe.

Today was the first day, he told himself. In all, he would need seven days. Well, two or three weeks in total, depending how things played out, but he had six more tasks to complete. He would pick a day for each one. Then he would take what he was owed. What belonged to him.

It was coming together. Finally, after all these years.

As he climbed the steps to the bedroom hot blood rushed to his groin. He felt sharp and alive, ravenous.

And ready.

Chapter Four

By four-thirty Vic and Lettie were home. Sitting at the kitchen table with paper and crayons, Lettie industriously drew what looked like the playground as Vic lined a sheet pan with aluminum foil, plopped an entire chicken on top of it, and surrounded it with quartered potatoes seasoned with olive oil, salt, and rosemary. He placed the tray in the oven.

For a time he watched Lettie, impressed at her concentration. He couldn't remember if Dannie, Lettie's mother, had the same focus at Lettie's age. That produced a familiar, bothersome doubt. Before he died, Lettie's father was a career criminal. More than once, Vic had worried that someday her father's hand might reach out and guide Lettie astray. She was too young to have mimicked his traits, but Vic believed people carried two kinds of secrets: the things they chose to keep secret and the secrets they didn't know they carried. Either type was dangerous, but the unknown ones were always more damaging.

He shook his head. It was the kind of worry that wore you to nothing. He couldn't let it bother him.

Anne arrived home at six-thirty, lugging her briefcase, her face strained. Twice promoted in the marketing department of the Pittsburgh Penguins, she now brought her work home with her. He'd been careful not to mention it, to add yet another concern to the pressure she faced each day. She disappeared upstairs and changed, then joined him in the kitchen and started a story about a fulfillment company and the mistake they made with the annual mailer to season ticket holders.

Vic took the sheet tray from the oven and added vegetables to the potatoes and chicken. Flipped the potatoes and replaced the tray in the oven.

"Wait," Anne said. She stopped brushing Lettie's hair. "What's going on with that chicken?"

"What do you mean?" He knew what she meant, but wanted to have some fun.

"It's flat."

"Right. I spatchcocked it."

She stared at him for a few seconds and went back to brushing Lettie's hair. Her movements were considered and precise. "You just like the word."

Vic spread his hands in innocence. "It evens out the roasting process. Cooks faster."

She shook her head. "Men. Do you ever grow up? What's next? Bendover Bettys in the front yard?"

"Now you're talking."

She shot him a look. "It took me a while to decide to move back in. Don't push your luck."

He crossed the small kitchen and put his hands on her shoulders. Massaged them slowly. "I won't make that mistake again."

"Good," she said, working out a tangle in Lettie's hair.

After dinner, rereading the newspaper story about Geno Varelli, Vic half-listened to the murmur of Anne reading to Lettie upstairs. He liked the gentle sound of her voice, the distant warmth of it. He knew it was more than that. Somehow, the regularity and rhythms of their meals together and the focus on Lettie's schedule, all made it easier when he thought of Dannie. It salved the pain of her loss. Made it almost bearable.

It was a little after nine o'clock when Anne came downstairs from putting Lettie to bed. Vic renewed his interest in the newspaper.

"Vic," Anne said, sitting in the loveseat across from him. "I was thinking about something on the bus home tonight."

He placed the paper on the table next to his armchair. "What about?"

"It's been almost four years since you retired."

"Yes."

15

"Don't you want to go back to work sometimes?"

Vic recrossed his feet at the ankles.

Before he could say anything Anne pointed at the newspaper. "You've read that story about the shooting how many times tonight?"

"I guess a few."

"Did you know the victim?"

Vic let out a slow breath. "I didn't know him, but I knew *of* him. He was before my time. He was one of the guys we talked about."

"Why is that?"

"Do you know that big armored car robbery from the nineteen-eighties?"

Anne pursed her lips and shook her head.

"Biggest heist in the city. Ever. One of the biggest in the country. Two guys, they just walked into an armored car depot and made off with about two and a half million dollars in cash. Probably worth fifteen million today. Never caught, money never recovered. And it was a smart robbery. Very clean. They were wearing suits and said they were FBI agents, flashed identification, pretended they'd heard a tip someone was going to rob the depot. The guard relaxed and bam, they took his shotgun, tied him up. Done."

"How does that connect to the man who was murdered?"

"Maybe ten years after the robbery, our detectives caught a guy connected to one of the local mobs. They had enough to give him twenty years. The detectives got him to flip on his boss for a lighter sentence. One of the things he mentioned was that Geno Varelli was one of the guys who robbed the armored truck. And now Geno ends up dead. I bet the paper will make the link by tomorrow."

"You think he was killed over that?"

"No. I'm sure the money is long gone. I just thought it was interesting. All those gangs from the nineteen-eighties and early nineties. I heard a lot about them when I joined the force. Then Pennsylvania legalized gambling, the lottery came along, the war on drugs, banks pushed credit cards, and started doing more electronically, which meant people used less cash. It got too hard for the gangs to make a living. It was the end of an era. The crooks all went to jail, died, or went legitimate."

Anne smiled. "Are you getting sentimental?"

Vic shook his head. "No, it just crossed my mind that Geno getting shot might mean those days aren't quite over."

"See what I mean? This is what I was thinking about on the bus. I want you to consider this. You're only a short way past forty-five. It's been great having you take care of Lettie. It's let me keep working, which I'm really happy about. I want to keep doing it. But she's getting to the age where she could go to daycare. With my last promotion, we can afford it, especially if you're getting paid. That way we could both work. If you want." She smiled, her blue eyes serious.

Vic didn't hear any accusation in her voice. She was being honest with him. And, in a way, worried about him. Wanting him to be happy. He appreciated that.

Vic stared at the ceiling. "Mmmm, mall cop. Secret wish of mine."

"I was thinking more along the lines of chef." She rose, crossed to him, and slid into his lap. "I mean, right now, I'd love to know more about your spatchcocking skills."

Chapter Five

The next evening, Vic made spaghetti for dinner, adding a couple of Italian sausages to sauce from a jar. He threw some frozen peas into the spaghetti water just before draining the pasta. His personal addition. Anne eyed the concoction when he served it, and said nothing. Most of the meal involved keeping Lettie on her booster seat and the sauce off her chest.

An hour later, Anne was getting Lettie ready for her bath when the doorbell rang.

"Who's that?" Anne shouted down the stairs.

Vic answered that he didn't know. He went to the front door and turned on the porch light. Hana Richards, the new district attorney, was standing outside.

Vic opened the door, unable to keep the surprise off his face.

Hana smiled when she saw him. "*Mr.* Lenoski, I guess now. Sorry to just show up. Do you have a minute?"

"Well, *District Attorney* Hana Richards, I think I can find time." He stepped back and she entered, glancing about. Her long brown hair was pulled back in a ponytail and she wore yoga pants, sneakers, and a windbreaker. She was dressed just like the Watch Mothers, and yet nothing like them. Vic couldn't reconcile the difference given they were wearing the same type of clothes.

Vic shut the door, and after a glance at the scatter of toys on the living room floor, turned to her. "Maybe let's sit in the dining room?"

Hana flashed a palm at him. "Lead the way."

As Vic turned, Anne shouted down the stairs, "Who is it?"

18

"DA Hana Richards," Vic called upstairs. He waited for Anne to respond, but not a sound was returned.

Vic led Hana into the dining room and turned on the light. The card table was gone, replaced by the dining room table and chairs that once belonged to Anne's mother. When Anne moved back in after Vic returned home with Lettie, she'd brought the table and chairs with her. Vic waved Hana to a seat.

"Coffee or tea?" he asked, as she sat.

She shook her head. "No, I just came from the gym. Drank a ton of water on my way here."

Vic wondered if that was the difference. The Watch Mothers wore activewear as a fashion statement. Hana put hers to use. He sat across from her. "So, what can I do for you?"

"Good question, Vic." The slightest of frowns flitted over her forehead, but her eyes had the humor he remembered.

Vic was surprised at her hesitation, and filled the silence. "Congratulations, by the way. First female DA. And I like how you handled Frank Marioni. Got him out without hurting the integrity of the office."

"That was the plan." She clicked her nails on the table. "It needed some finesse. The office can't look bad or have its authority diluted."

"Finesse. So that's why you told me to leave it to you." He smiled to show he wasn't offended. "Probably a good move on your part."

"No, actually there were a couple of times you would have been a big help. Early on I didn't know enough, that's when finesse was needed. Later on, I did need someone hardheaded."

"I guess that means you can do both."

"When I need to. Does that bother you?"

"Never has."

She nodded. Vic knew she was stalling and it surprised him. He'd always known her to be direct and fearless. He was distracted by a patter of feet on the hardwood of the hallway. Lettie appeared in her pajamas, cheeks red from her bath. She stopped in the doorway and gazed at Hana.

"Hello," Hana said kindly. "What's your name?"

"Lettie."

"I'm sorry." Anne appeared, scooped Lettie up, and planted her on a hip. "She got away from me." She stepped into the dining room and extended her hand to Hana. It crossed Vic's mind that Anne had changed her top and brushed her hair. "You got here faster than I thought you would," Anne added.

"No point in waiting." Hana smiled.

"Um, sounds like I've been set up," Vic said quietly.

Hana turned to him. "I called Anne at work yesterday. I tracked her down on the spouses list. I was wondering what you were up to these days."

Vic remembered Anne's comment from the night before about Lettie being old enough for daycare. He was being maneuvered. He'd have to decide if that bothered him.

Anne hiked Lettie higher on her hip. "Well, let me get this one to bed."

"Goodnight, Lettie," Hana called, smiling at her.

Lettie, suddenly abashed at the attention, burrowed her face into Anne's chest.

"Goodnight, Lettie," Vic said. Anne made to turn for the doorway, but Lettie held out her arms to Vic. Anne walked her over and Vic gave Lettie a kiss on the forehead. Lettie gurgled happily. After Anne and Lettie left, Vic and Hana sat in silence, listening to Anne's footsteps on the stairs.

Hana fixed her gaze on Vic. "Well, isn't this nice. The family man. But let me get this straight." Small lines flickered at the center of her forehead as her eyes sharpened. "You go off to North Dakota, come back with a granddaughter. Anything else I need to know?"

Vic maintained eye contact. "Sorry, you were saying something about how good you are at finesse?"

"It's my middle name. And yet, a state police investigator I talked to out there, Karl Sorenson, said just before you came home a house burned and several people died. But you alibied out. It's all just a fabulous coincidence."

Vic stayed quiet. In his mind, he saw the windshield of a police cruiser splattered with blood. He smelled acrid smoke, as real as the moment it happened. He had to remind himself to breathe. She wasn't telling him what she really thought, or knew. He was sure of it. And she must have a reason for that.

A careful smile spread on Hana's lips. "Vic, do you remember that last time we met for coffee?"

"I do."

"You gave me a suggestion. You told me how to make a deal with that Bauer woman. Said if I did, Marioni might keep me around next time he reorganized the department."

"I remember."

"And you made the point that a new DA always reorganizes the department."

"I don't think that's a surprise."

"Right. And now it's time for me to do it."

Vic leaned back. Now he knew where Hana was going. "I'm guessing that's not for public consumption, yet."

"Exactly. Which explains me here tonight, in workout clothes. And why you didn't get an invitation to my office."

"You want your ducks in a row before you make your announcement?"

She smiled. "You and I always did see eye to eye, Vic."

"I'd agree with that."

Hana unzipped her jacket a few inches and Vic saw the collar of a technical t-shirt. "I'm trusting you to keep this to yourself."

Vic nodded.

"There's some things I want to do with the prosecutor's office, you don't need to know about that yet, but I'm also going to restructure the Allegheny County Police. They already get most of the county's major crimes, and to be blunt, their close rate isn't great. As far as the detectives go it's a bit of a mixed bag and they need more experience. Which means you."

"Okay." Vic hesitated. He'd sensed this coming, but it still stunned him when she said it. He scrambled for something to say. "Have you decided on the commander for the detectives?"

"Why, do you want the job?"

Vic huffed. "No. Since when was I the administrative type? Just trying to understand where you might be leading me."

"That's fair. For starters, not Crush."

Vic was surprised Hana knew his previous commander's nickname, and in the same moment realized he shouldn't be. "Ah," he said slowly. "Although it turns out Crush isn't as bad as I thought."

"How very polite of you, Vic. You're evolving. That's good."

"Thank you, I think?"

"I've talked to several people, but I'm leaning toward Carter Lee. Do you know him?"

Vic leaned back. "I do. He's solid. We crossed paths years ago. He'd been a detective maybe five years when I tested in. I never worked a case with him, but I heard his updates in meetings. Very logical and detailed. Thinks things through. Easy to work with. I thought he went to the FBI?"

"He did. But his wife is from here and I guess her mother has health issues and she wants to move back. He put a feeler out to me through the local FBI office. I like the idea he has contacts in the FBI, and he's worked complicated cases. He understands all the moving parts. He has about twenty agents reporting to him right now. Bit of a lateral move for him, maybe even a step down, but it checks the boxes with his family."

Vic smiled at her. "You sure you don't want Crush?"

She slid her hands into the pockets of her jacket. "After I was elected, he sent me flowers as congratulations. Flowers. Then he showed up twice at my gym. Told me he was just checking it out. I don't think so."

"The way he works out, I'm surprised he isn't a member of every gym in the city."

"Think about it. How did he find out where I went? He had to ask around. I mean he was researching me." She held up a hand with her thumb and forefinger an inch apart. "This far from stalking."

"He never met a career opportunity he didn't like."

"Anyway, that's it. Do you want to think about it or can you give me an answer now?"

Vic considered the offer. "I need some time. I'd like to talk to someone."

"Maybe your old partner, Liz Timmons?"

Vic watched her. "Yes."

"How's she doing?"

"Pretty much recovered. She's got some scarring and she wears long sleeves all the time. Her lungs took the longest. Smoke inhalation does that to you. She's been working her old job the last couple of years."

"Well, just don't take long. I want to move fast. And when it happens, several detectives at County will be taking retirement. I expect Carter to sign on the dotted line tomorrow."

"When you say fast, how fast?"

"Monday."

Vic stared at her. "It's Tuesday. That's less than a week."

Hana smiled at him and rose. "So don't dilly dally, *Mr.* Lenoski. When I announce, the offer is off the table. And doesn't *Detective* Lenoski have a better ring?"

Vic rose and led her to the front door. "Nice. Put me under deadline."

"That's how you work best, Vic. We both know that."

Vic reached out to open the door but dropped his hand. "Just out of interest, who's got the Geno Varelli case?"

Hana stared up at him. "Why do you ask?"

"There's history there. It means a lot of people might want a piece of him. Even after all these years. Makes it interesting. But it's strange. The newspaper had the story of the shooting yesterday, but no follow-up today about Geno's past. I figured they'd give him half a page. That guy was certifiably the best thief Pittsburgh ever saw."

Hana was silent for a few beats. "Well, just another reason to get this reorganization announced on Monday, isn't it?"

Vic opened the door for her. Hana stepped outside and turned to face him. She held out a business card. "My cell is on the back. Sooner the better, Vic."

"I heard you." He watched her walk to a small SUV and climb in. As she pulled out Vic closed the door. When he turned around Anne was standing in the hall, watching him.

"Well? Did she offer you a job?"

He nodded slowly. "She did. I have to tell her in the next couple of days."

"Are you leaning one way or another?"

"Hard to say. Do you want some tea?"

Anne followed him into the kitchen. "The new DA comes all the way to your house to offer you a job, and all you can say is 'hard to say'?"

Vic stood in the center of the kitchen, thinking about it. "She's different, somehow," he said slowly.

"Of course she is. She has one of the most important jobs in the entire county."

Vic filled the kettle and placed it on a burner. "I need to think about it."

Anne huffed in frustration. "You know you want to work again. You wander around the house like a lost puppy. You asked her about the Varelli case. For goodness' sake, yesterday you spatchcocked a chicken. And every day you work out downstairs. You're doing that for a reason."

"Maybe I am," Vic said slowly. He turned on the stove and gazed at the kettle.

"A watched pot never boils, so make up your mind," Anne said tartly, and left the kitchen.

Chapter Six

The next afternoon, as Lettie clambered over the jungle gym, a nondescript blue sedan pulled up at the edge of the playground. A few moments passed and the driver's door opened. Liz Timmons climbed out and strode into the playground toward Vic, the Watch Mothers shifting into high alert, several of them unabashedly staring at her. It crossed Vic's mind that in all the days he'd brought Lettie to the playground, Liz was the first Black person he'd seen there. Liz seemed to read his thoughts at the same moment. She stopped, pivoted to face the Watch Mothers, parted her jacket, and settled her fists on her hips. Her badge glinted from her belt, the stock of her service weapon jutted outward. The women all took an interest in the ground or each other. Liz crossed to the bench where Vic waited.

"Nosy, aren't they?" she said, sitting next to him. "They dress each other? They look like some damn white gang."

Vic smiled. Lettie had spotted Liz and was clambering down from the jungle gym. Vic held his breath as she missed a rung, but she caught herself and dropped safely to the ground with a smooth dip of her knees. He turned to Liz. "I call them the Watch Mothers."

"They're definitely a bunch of *mothers*."

"And thanks for stopping to look at them. I'll be hearing about that for the next two days."

Lettie ran over and climbed into Liz's lap. Liz gave her a hug and Lettie let out a happy squeal.

"Any weekend you want to babysit again, let me know." Vic grinned at her.

"You just like your babysitters packing heat." She helped Lettie climb back down to the ground and watched her run to the swings. "Okay, so what's this about? I got to drive over here in the middle of the afternoon?"

"I think you'll decide it was worth it. Before we get to that. Geno Varelli, you guys get his case?"

"No. Went to the county detectives. There's something hinky with it. We had it for about fifteen seconds and then a couple of their detectives showed up and took what little we had. Real closed mouth about it. Why?"

"Want a chance to work on it?"

Liz pulled back so she could get a good look at him. "What are you talking about?"

"Hana Richards stopped by my house last night. Offered me a job with the county detectives."

"What's that got to do with me?"

"I decided not to take it unless you come too."

Liz cocked her head. The light caught the rippled skin near her left ear. Vic remembered the small golden star she always wore in that ear, before the fire scarred her cheek and ear lobe too thickly for pierced earrings. "Okay," she said slowly. "Don't be a pain in the ass and try to guilt me into this. You can join without me, you working over there has nothing to do with me. Although…" She stared at him, her dark eyes piercing. "Without me, you couldn't solve your way out of four left-hand turns. So yeah, I can see why you'd want me as part of the package."

"Exactly."

"Huh." She fell silent.

For several seconds, they both watched Lettie, her shoulder-length blond hair streaming behind with each downward arc of the swing. Vic wondered how Liz was doing at work. After her medical leave, she'd returned to her old job, but he had no idea if she liked it. He realized he should have asked.

"She's fearless, that one," Liz said softly, her eyes following Lettie.

"How's Jayvon doing? Freshman year at college, right?"

"First semester grades were okay. But now he keeps talking about this girl." She shifted on the bench. "Of course, boys are hopeless without a girl, so maybe this will help him. Assuming she's smart enough not to get pregnant."

"I guess I should have asked," Vic said. "How's it going in the hole?" Automatically he lapsed into the slang they used for the detective pool.

She frowned. "Crush is still Crush. Instead of paying us more, he brought in some consultant to *reengineer* the department. Fulfill our *potential* as a department. We had to spend two months presenting and discussing efficiency ideas. Now we're a *learning* department with a bunch of bullshit quality standards." She fell silent, her eyes returning to Lettie. "That's something. Are we talking more money if I join county? Jayvon's college is expensive."

"They have better pay grades. And I can see arguing we both need a promotion. If she called Anne the day before to find out what I was doing, and then came to my house, she's hungry to have me. Us."

"Calling Anne doesn't count. That's just smart. Half the time you don't know what you're doing."

"Did anyone ever mention you can be a pain in the ass, sometimes?"

"Oh, and who are you, Grandpa Snuggle Hugs?"

Vic grinned and looked away. One of the Watch Mothers took a sudden interest in the sky. Barb briefly met his gaze before turning to someone else. "Well, think about it. But it has to be fast. She wants an answer next day or two." He turned back to her.

"I'm interested," Liz said. "Why don't you see what kind of money we can get. Do I need to interview?"

"I would bet, but it won't be about whether to give you the job. Hana will want to understand how you tick. She already knows you a little from visiting you in the hospital, but she likes to understand the people she's dealing with. I think you guys will get along great. She likes people who talk back to her. Just don't overdo it."

"She still got that country club hair?"

"Couldn't say. Last night she had it in a ponytail. She was on her way back from the gym."

Liz shook her head slowly, and Vic knew what she was thinking.

"She's not like Crush. He does it to look good. I'd say she does it to stay healthy. And maybe to think. Exercising is good for that, and she's a thinker."

"Yeah, that girl is smart. I'll give her that." Lettie waved and Liz waved back.

"I'll call her tonight," Vic said.

Liz rose. "I got to get back. We have these end-of-shift reports we have to write now. Like I said, we're a *learning* department, which means I've learned to write more reports."

Vic stood as well. "Say hello to Levon for me. How's it going with him?" Vic and Levon were friends, but Vic hadn't seen him in a couple of months.

"I'll say hello. None of your business how it's going. I mean when he's actually in the country. That man does fly off to other parts of the world. Never tells me why, but that's the job." She gave Lettie another wave and headed for her car, glaring at the Watch Mothers as she passed.

Vic sat down and watched her go. He thought about her last comment. No matter their age, Liz always referred to males as boys and females as girls. That was the first time he'd ever heard her call a male a man.

He decided things between her and Levon must be going quite well.

Chapter Seven

That evening, Vic called Hana's cell. She called back an hour later and they talked through Liz being hired and their money and grade requirements. Hana agreed to it all so quickly Vic wished he'd asked for more.

"I'm glad Liz wants to come over," Hana said when they finished.

Vic wasn't surprised. It was Hana who brought up Liz's name originally. Vic remembered the questions about the lack of diversity in the DA's office during the election debate. Liz was a twofer, an African-American and a woman. He didn't dwell on it. Liz was an excellent detective, he liked working with her and trusted her judgment. That was what mattered to him.

"You guys will have to agree on her salary," Vic said quickly. "And she's worth every penny."

"I'm sure we can work that out."

"When do I start?" Vic asked, thinking he needed at least a week to find daycare for Lettie.

"Like I said, Vic, I announce on Monday. So Tuesday. Carter Lee signed up yesterday, he'll be with me at the press conference."

"I'll need to recertify on the range. Liz may need to give two weeks."

"That's okay. I'll see what I can do about your recertification."

An hour later his phone dinged with a text message. Hana's administrative assistant had scheduled his firearm recertification for Saturday. He and Anne were sitting in the living room.

"I guess we need to find a daycare for Lettie," he told her. "I didn't think

Hana would move this quickly."

Anne looked up from the papers she had brought from work. "No problem, I called a bunch of places near here during lunch. We have meetings set up for Friday. I told them we need to place her on Monday."

Vic folded his newspaper. "I feel like you and Hana are working together on this."

Anne cocked her head. "Maybe this is why men worry about women in the workforce. We can out-organize you guys by lunchtime."

Vic smiled. "Sure feels that way."

Twenty minutes later his phone dinged again. This time an email from Carter Lee. He looked up to find Anne staring at him. "What?"

She smiled. "Kind of fun to be back in the game, isn't it?"

Vic shrugged that he didn't care, but in truth she was right. The connection to something moving, being on the hunt again, it made him feel good. "Just Carter Lee, my new boss. He wants to meet for brunch Sunday morning."

Anne stared at him so long he knew she'd seen through him. The smile still on her face, she slowly lowered her head and returned to reading.

Carter Lee was waiting for Vic at a table when he arrived at the diner Sunday morning. Carter stood and they shook hands, eyeing each other. Carter was shorter than Vic, but stocky. His black hair was cropped close to his head, his dark blue shirt tight on his thick shoulders. He was electric with energy, as if he was mid-movement diving headlong into a problem. As Vic sat he wondered how many generations had passed since Carter's relatives immigrated from China.

"Thanks for doing this on a Sunday morning," Carter said briskly. He pushed a menu across the table. Vic didn't need to look at it. He'd eaten at this diner hundreds of times over the years and knew what he wanted. A waitress appeared, poured coffee and they ordered.

As the waitress headed for the kitchen, Carter grinned. "Haven't eaten here in years. I missed it. The pancakes? One of the reasons I wanted to meet here. My wife worries about me gaining weight so I had to say we're going someplace else."

"I almost lied to my wife as well. Just the opposite reason. She loves this place. I thought she might want to tag along."

Carter laughed easily and took a sip of coffee. When he put the mug down he said, "I hear you've been on sabbatical,"

"Four years. Early retirement, technically."

Carter nodded and hesitated. "Well, let's get this part over with. I was kind of pissed when Hana said she wanted you on the team. I like to pick my own players."

Vic didn't hear annoyance in Carter's tone, it sounded as if he was over being angry. He even thought he saw a glint of humor in Carter's eyes. "I can see that," Vic answered, waiting for the punchline.

"So I called around. Talked to your old commander. Tompkins?"

"Peach of a guy."

"I remember him being a bit of a dick. But he only had good things to say about you. Said he was sorry to lose you. He also told me about your daughter, and you finding your granddaughter in North Dakota." Carter hesitated. "I'm sorry about that, Vic. I have two daughters. I'd never get over it."

Vic thought Carter's statement was absolutely genuine and he was surprised at the knot that tightened in his stomach. He also found he wasn't surprised by Crush's remarks. That was at least three times Crush had supported him. It was getting to be a habit, and it felt good.

Vic sipped his coffee. "Then I guess you really didn't like it when I said I wanted to bring Liz with me."

"You, I remember. I don't know her. I talked to her last night. We went over some of the cases you guys worked. She mentioned one murder case, you ran into a couple of old-time gangsters that have gone straight. Bandini and Thuds Lombardo? I guess they're getting on in years."

"We did. Interviewed them related to a murder case. Bandini was the father-in-law of the victim." Vic thought of Geno Varelli. "Are you mentioning that for a reason?"

"I am, but I'll get to that. I like Liz. Right to the point and she has great experience. Did you know the commander I'm replacing?"

"Yes and no. I might have shaken his hand once. Mostly I saw him on television when he ran for DA. He debated Hana. Called her 'honey.'"

Carter chuckled, a low rumble in his chest. "How'd that go?"

"Pretty much as you'd expect. His ass is still sore, I bet."

Carter sat back. "Yeah. I see that. That's one of the things I want to change. He liked his detectives a certain way." He hesitated, and Vic knew he was supposed to supply his own words to fill the silence. He guessed those words were 'male' and 'white.'

"And that," Carter said slowly, "is why I like to pick my own team. But Hana said you were part of the package. I guess I had three interviews with Hana before she offered me the job. I learned a lot about her during that process, and there's one thing I know for sure. She's legitimately three pay grades smarter than me. I doubt she makes many bad calls."

"She's definitely smart. And tough. And she thinks the right way about the DA's office."

Carter nodded. "Agreed." He smiled. "And so I'm over you being part of the package. And Liz. I'm actually looking forward to it."

"We'll do our best."

Carter waved his hand as the waitress arrived with their food. "This isn't a job interview."

As the plates clattered onto the table Vic thought to himself, yeah, it kind of is.

Neither spoke while they spread butter and poured syrup onto the thin, crepe-like pancakes. Vic avoided getting syrup on the crunchy edges. Carter stuck a large forkful in his mouth and closed his eyes for a moment. Chewed.

"Yeah," he said, after swallowing. "That's what I remember." He cut one of his sausage links into segments, rolled a piece in part of the thin pancake and popped it in his mouth. Chewed and swallowed again. "Okay," he said, and pointed his fork at Vic. "Geno Varelli. I know you haven't seen the file, that's for Tuesday, any thoughts?"

"Lousy way to go. Convenient he was close to the cemetery."

"There's that."

Vic realized he might get along with Carter. Jokes like that annoyed Crush, but apparently Carter was okay with it.

Carter circled his fork in the air in a 'get moving' motion. "Tell me what you know."

"Geno was old school. He was about the best thief Pittsburgh ever had. We're pretty sure he pulled the big armored car job in the eighties. There was also a bank in Washington that was supposed to be his work. They went in through the roof on a holiday weekend. Not quite as much money as the armored car job, but close. At least two or three others. All of them were big paydays, we never caught anyone for them."

"How did he get nabbed?"

"I don't remember, exactly. He was before my time. I'll have to go through the old case files."

"Right." Carter sliced the last of his pancake into squares and rolled another section around a piece of sausage. "That's why I asked about Bandini and Lombardo. Figuring out who shot Geno, I bet it has something to do with the old days. It might be relevant to something today, but to unravel this thing you need a good picture of him back in the day. Known associates, his bosses, you know the drill." Carter frowned. "That armored car job. It was just him and some other guy, right? Anybody ever figure out who his partner was?"

"No. I remember the two guys were described as one white, one Black. And they said they were FBI agents."

"Okay, you and Liz, you start that case. There's a couple of guys working it now, but they'll be gone two weeks after you start. Retirement, so to speak. Shadow them and get up to speed."

Carter rolled the last square of pancake around the last segment of sausage, daubed it in syrup, and popped it in his mouth. Vic glanced at his plate; he was barely half-finished. Carter was one of those full-speed guys, he decided. Not a bad thing for a boss.

Carter swigged his coffee. "They said they were FBI agents, huh?"

"They did. Claimed they had a tip the place was going to be robbed. They were wearing suits and ties, as you'd expect. It made the depot guard relax. Bad for him."

Carter grinned. "Well, I worked with the FBI for ten years. I've met a couple of agents with the balls to do something like that. Maybe it wasn't Geno, maybe they *were* FBI."

"Too bad Geno can't tell us."

Carter tapped his fork against his empty plate. "Good case for you to knock the rust off. Can't imagine there's any kind of hurry on solving it, not something that goes back as long as that."

"Unless it's connected to something going on today." Vic spoke carefully, but that was to cover a thought rising inside him. He'd been off the job for four years. Did he still have it? He put a forkful of food in his mouth, but it was tasteless. In the sudden appearance of Hana and the excitement of landing the job, he hadn't asked himself that simple question. Hadn't stared in the mirror and asked if he still had the dedication and skills to chase down a killer. He chewed. Carter started talking about the Penguins hockey team, and Vic barely heard him.

Chapter Eight

The Second Day

D ay two of seven. He left the condominium ninety minutes later.
He'd planned to leave sooner, but dear Terri was so compliant
and enthusiastic, he couldn't resist. He hadn't thought they would
stay together this long, but she kept surprising him. He wasn't sure of
the mechanism that made her so willing to live with their arrangement.
Several years ago, he'd noticed that while most women wanted a romantic
relationship that was recognized and public, a small subset thrived on secret
romances. At first, he thought it was driven by notions of forbidden fruit,
but he came to suspect that some women gained a sense of power and
superiority from the secret itself. And perhaps another handful just liked to
be kept, but didn't want others knowing that. Yet another secret. Slowly, he
taught himself to spot those women. He now understood what was meant
by the meaningful glances he sometimes received at work, especially if there
was no requirement for him to act. Somehow, a woman who looked at
him that way, and let him see she was looking, gave the impression she was
waiting for him. It was a message that said you have me. And when he did
suggest they go somewhere, she always immediately went along, almost
wordlessly. As if that was the arrangement from the start.

But he needed to get home, to pat his two daughters on the top of their
heads. They were his firmament. Well, his wife and kids, and Terri. Of
course, he'd lied to his wife the night before and told her he was on a business

trip to Wheeling, to visit one of their businesses. And that's where his car spent the night, before Terri drove it back in the morning for the exchange in the mall parking lot. Terri had even checked into a Wheeling motel under his name, using the app on his phone, so she could use the electronic key and not visit the front desk.

And the beauty of last night? Somewhere, buried and waiting in the national hotel chain's database, was a record of him reserving and sleeping in a room in Wheeling. Of him checking out and opening and closing his room door at a time that made it impossible for him to drive back to Pittsburgh in time to shoot Geno Varelli. And Terri had asked no questions, as he knew she wouldn't.

When this was over and he'd recovered what was stolen from him, he'd repay Terri. Give her enough that she would never talk about that night.

A warm feeling came over him. Or not. There was a second option he hadn't considered until now. Killing Geno had been a cinch. Maybe that was the safest way. Invite Terri somewhere near one of the rivers. Put a bullet in her head and throw her from the bank. It would take some planning, but none of the patience Geno's shooting required.

He smiled as he drove. The planning for Geno was brutal. The tiny apartment building where Geno lived wasn't suitable for the killing, there were too many neighbors. He'd followed Geno around for days, looking for the right opportunity. Twice he thought he had him, and twice he'd called it off. Then he'd heard about the funeral. He was sure Geno would go, so he'd staked out Geno's apartment well before dawn. Followed him to the cemetery. He hadn't expected Geno to park outside the gate. That was luck. But you made your own luck. He knew that.

He parked in his driveway and let himself into his house, lugging his overnight bag behind him. He was late enough that his oldest daughter had already left for school, but his wife and youngest were still at home. He ate breakfast with them, telling his wife a made-up story about the problems with the Wheeling restaurant. How he'd solved them.

Forty minutes later he was driving south. This time, when he reached Route 28, the main artery just north of the Allegheny River, he turned east.

Before long he exited onto a two-lane road that ran parallel to the river. Another fifteen minutes and he turned right onto an asphalt road barely wide enough for two cars. He passed several houses and a decrepit pump station for the local water authority. Twenty yards further was a long stretch of road without houses. He pulled to the side and got out. The river smell was strong, the river just a few feet away through a gap in the trees.

He opened the trunk. He pulled the gun from the carrier bag and replaced it with the prepaid phones he and Terri had used to stay in touch. The gun went under the trunk carpet just above the spare wheel well. He added a brick to the bag, rolled it up, and secured it with duct tape. A quick once-around to confirm he was alone, and he stepped through the gap in the trees to the river's edge. A strong underarm pitch and the bag landed in the river with a flat plop. It disappeared immediately.

He slid behind the wheel and started the car. That was it, the second day finished. He'd lay low for a week, see what the police said about Geno. Read what popped up in the newspapers. And by next Tuesday, if everything looked good, he'd restart the countdown with day three.

As he drove, he knew his mind was made up. Terri being dead would save him a few bucks when everything was finished. It was his money, after all. Well, money stolen from his father, but it was owed to him. His father was dead but his will remained as specific as the day he found it in his mother's closet, along with his real birth certificate and her marriage license. In that moment he'd learned, finally, who his father was, and that his father's fortune—his fortune—had been stolen.

It was time to get it back from the people who stole it.

And yeah, the payback had already started.

As he drove toward Pittsburgh, he thought about that. He laughed to himself. Poor, stupid Geno. His father and Geno were partners, once, and rich. When prison loomed they needed an agreement, a way to trust each other when trust was impossible, a method to reclaim their property—together—upon release. So, each tattooed half of an address on their forearm, without knowing what appeared on the other's arm. Only together could they reconstruct the address and reclaim their wealth. But

Geno tried to shorten his sentence by ratting out his father. It worked, and his father went to prison as well. But what was so funny, so priceless, was that when his father died, Geno thought the tattoo died with him.

But it hadn't.

His father had written down the words and numbers of his tattoo in his will. And with the photographs of Geno's arm, he now had the entire key.

He would have it all.

Payback really was a bitch.

Chapter Nine

Vic caught part of Hana's Monday press conference on the local television news. She was smooth and specific. She introduced Carter and he said a few words about living up to the tradition of the department and the high standards established by his predecessor. Vic had no doubt that Hana coached him on the wording.

The next morning, Vic dressed carefully, buttoning his shirt and taking time to make sure his tie was straight and the right length. He was nervous and keenly aware of how quiet the house was. Anne had taken Lettie to daycare early, worried about her silence on Monday after her first full day. Vic had a different view, but hadn't mentioned it to Anne. He didn't think Lettie was worried or sad about her first day, but preoccupied. He guessed she was processing the change in daily routine and the more structured activities of daycare. He didn't see that as rejection or unhappiness, more that Lettie hadn't made up her mind yet. As much as a four-year-old could make up her mind.

Still, the house felt oddly quiet and hollow as he made his way downstairs. He stood in the hallway for a few moments, gathering himself. He had a knot in his stomach as large as the one on his first day as a patrolman.

He knew the reason. He'd barely slept the night before, his concern about returning to work compounded by a second thought. Just suppose he really had lost it, that he couldn't handle the job anymore? That somehow, over the last four years, his skills had ebbed away. What then? What would he do? He wouldn't be able to stay in the job. He'd be a danger and a liability to Liz and the force if he wasn't one-hundred percent.

THE THINGS THAT SECRETS CANNOT HIDE

He didn't have an answer to that. All he could do was start and see how it went. He took a deep breath and went downstairs to the basement. He gave the heavy bag in the corner a long look and went into the garage.

The offices for the detectives of the Allegheny County Police was a single-floor bullpen of low-walled cubicles surrounded by offices and conference rooms. As soon as he entered, a voice called out from his right, asking if she could help.

Vic turned to a desk manned by a thick-set, round-faced woman with shoulder-length curly hair streaked by different coloring attempts.

"I'm Karen. You got the new kid look. You Lenoski?"

Vic stepped to her desk. "I am. Call me Vic. I'm supposed to meet Carter Lee?"

Karen nodded in the direction of a center aisle between the cubes that led to an office. "End of the aisle. Don't worry, we cleaned up the blood from yesterday."

Vic wasn't sure what she meant. "Okay, thanks." He followed the aisle to the office door and knocked on the door frame. Carter was on the phone but waved him in. Still talking, he pushed a manila envelope across the desk and gestured for him to check it. Inside was a sheaf of human resource papers. Carter tossed his phone back on its cradle. It slid off and he grabbed it with a low curse.

"Damn new phones. The old ones were tanks, you could throw them against the wall and they'd bounce back and give you five stitches." He carefully replaced the handset and pointed at the envelope. "Go through the paperwork, sign where you need to, and give it back to me. The photo they took yesterday is on your ID, that's in there too." He gave Vic a deadpan stare. "Don't give me that back." He popped out of his chair and gestured for Vic to follow. Carter led him back down the aisle, turned left halfway along. This aisle was narrower. Some of the desks were empty, others contained people working. Vic noticed a lot of sidelong glances in his direction.

Carter stopped and swept his hand over an empty cube. "This is you." He nodded toward the empty desk across the aisle. "That's for Liz. You can show her around when she gets here."

40

"She texted me last night, said Crush just wants her for three days to offload her case files and make sure no one drops the ball. She'll start Thursday."

"Yep, she emailed me." Carter pointed at the computer on Vic's desk. "It's a standard set-up, you'll recognize the databases. I asked a tech guy to come up at ten and make sure you can access everything."

"Sounds good. And the guys who were working the Varelli case? Maybe I could talk to them while I wait for the tech guy."

"Yeah. Well, that would be nice, but no go. They seemed…" Carter stared at the ceiling as if searching for the right word, "pissed off about their impending retirement. They walked out yesterday afternoon after I told them. I guess that's their prerogative. I offered them two weeks."

Vic stayed quiet. Now he understood Karen's comment about the blood. He was also fairly sure that walking out was designed to make it look like they were fired, which might give them enough leverage to bring a case against the department. Or at least use the threat of legal action to get a better retirement bonus. He was glad that wasn't his problem. Still, he was sympathetic to the detectives.

"Okay," Vic said quickly. "After the tech guy leaves, I'll dig around and find their case notes. I'm guessing those are online?"

"Yes. You'll find it under active cases. I checked this morning. Tech guy can show you all that." Carter slapped him on the upper arm. "Glad to have you here, Vic." He grinned. "Let's catch us some bad guys. Department staff meeting at eleven, I'll introduce you." He turned and headed for his office.

Vic tossed his manila envelope on the desk and checked inside the cube for a hook and hanger. He slid out of his jacket, hung it up, and lowered himself into the chair.

Okay, he thought. Back in the saddle. The thought didn't calm his nerves.

He looked around the desk. It was clear the last occupant left in a hurry. Different colored Post-it notes stuck to the edge of the monitor made it look like a weird petalled flower. The desktop was littered with yellow pads and pens. Vic opened the side drawers of the desk to find a couple of wrinkled ties and several stained mugs. He checked the center drawer and stared. Attached to the inside front edge was a row of built-in compartments for pens, paper clips, and other office paraphernalia. One was filled to the brim with nail clippings. Vic closed the drawer, rose, and after introducing himself to one of his neighbors, found the storage room. He salvaged a cardboard box.

Ten minutes later everything in and on the desk, except the Post-its, were in the box. Even the nail clippings. Those he'd scraped into one of the mugs and taped over the top to keep them in place. If someone had kept them this long, he reasoned, they would want them back. He found disinfectant wipes in the kitchen and cleaned the drawer compartments. He then found the men's room and washed his hands for several minutes.

By ten-thirty he was online and reviewing the Geno Varelli case file. Or what little there was. The file existed, but there were no notes. Either the detectives working the case hadn't started, which wasn't true, or they hadn't transferred their notes onto the online system yet. Vic knew that was more likely. He was the same way and always relied on Liz to update the online system. For the first time, he understood the value of keeping the system recent. Given the apparent bloodletting the day before, he was quite sure if he tracked down the detectives working the case they would claim their notebooks were missing. It annoyed him, but he guessed he might lose his own notebooks if he was unceremoniously tossed into early retirement.

He would have to start from zero. The thought chilled him. Murder investigations needed to move quickly. Every day meant eroding leads and witnesses less confident of what they'd seen or heard.

He took a deep breath and studied the Post-it notes surrounding the computer monitor. He found nothing obvious, just phone numbers, a couple with names included, and what looked like a grocery shopping list. He tossed that. As he rubbed the back of his neck, his eye was drawn back to one of the Post-its. He recognized the name but couldn't place it.

A quick internet search produced a string of results. He did know him. It was Justin Day, a reporter who once worked the crime beat at Pittsburgh's largest daily newspaper. Vic remembered a tall, rangy man with a motor mouth. But Day left the newspaper during the last buyout, an old-timer discarded by the new regime. Yet the Post-it looked new, and the prefix was a cell phone. From what Vic remembered, Day was a walking encyclopedia of Pittsburgh crimes and criminals. He wondered if the now-retired detective responsible for the Varelli case had considered Justin useful for background. Vic certainly saw the possibility.

His cell phone rang and he slid the button.

"They actually let you into the place?" Liz asked.

Vic squinted at the desktop. "Wait. Are you making a joke?"

"Your Momma never taught you not to answer a question with a question?"

"Okay, I'm not answering that with another question. We'll be here all day. Yes. I'm at my desk trying to figure out what we have on Geno Varelli. I'm also looking at your desk. When you come in, bring disinfectant wipes."

"You're kidding, right?"

"Unless you like a drawer full of nail clippings."

For three solid seconds, Liz didn't answer, then, "What is wrong with white people?"

"Hey, how do you know it was a white guy?"

"Does county have any Black detectives?"

Vic didn't know. Liz would. That meant he now knew as well. "Anyway, we're starting from nothing. No one updated the case file system. I've got a staff meeting at eleven, then I'm going out to the crime scene and to Geno's apartment. I found that listed in his parole documents."

"Good. I'll meet you at the cemetery."

"I thought you weren't coming in until Thursday?"

"I've got nothing to do. You know I always keep the system updated. I told the detectives taking over my cases to read my notes and I'd come in tomorrow morning to answer questions. I got the afternoon free."

Vic let out a slow breath of relief. He could go over the scene himself, that wasn't a problem, but a second pair of eyes was better. Especially if they belonged to Liz. "Good. I'll call the coroner and forensics, find out when we'll see their reports. One o'clock? Entrance to the cemetery."

"See you then. And Vic?"

"Yeah?"

"Don't be late."

Chapter Ten

Vic wasn't late. He ate lunch at one of the restaurants in Lawrenceville and parked across the street from the cemetery entrance fifteen minutes early. He crossed the street to the sidewalk and walked up the driveway to the location where the reports said Geno parked his car. He did some quick math. A week since the shooting and the scene had been released. He was just as likely to find Native American relics as anything related to the murder.

A few minutes later Liz arrived and started up the driveway toward him. "Let me guess. Shooter dropped his driver's license and you found it."

Vic was studying the stone gatehouse. "Right. And it fell into the holy grail. We're good to go, this life and the next."

"Amen to that." She stopped next to him. "Did you find out when the forensics report is coming?"

"Tomorrow. Vic pointed at the grass triangle between the Butler Street sidewalk and the angled driveway leading to the gatehouse. "I hope they fine-toothed over that."

Liz followed his outstretched finger and stared for a moment, then looked at the gatehouse. "Yeah. Shooter didn't go into the cemetery, the gate was locked. They either crossed the grass or went back down the driveway to the street."

"Right. And if they crossed the grass, we might have a shoe print."

"If forensics thought of that. With the tape gone we can't figure out what they inspected."

"That's what's worrying me."

Liz frowned. "You'd think the detectives running the case would have told them to look."

Vic sighed. "Let's hope. Or that's really why Hana wanted them to retire."

"So many mysteries." Liz nodded at the odd, stiff gait of a short man walking toward them from the gatehouse. He was pinch-shouldered and pale. "He looks like he wants to talk to us."

"I asked him to," Vic said. "Called him earlier."

The man reached them and stuck out a hand. "Evan Gelhorn."

Vic shook his hand. "You're the one who found the body?"

"Yeah. And before you ask. Yes, I was the one who threw up next to the car."

He sounded angry, and Vic realized some of the officers must have kidded him about it. "Wasn't going to ask." He tried to make his voice sound reassuring. "I know you've done this probably ten times, but we were just assigned to this case. Could you walk us through how you found the body?"

Evan gave a terse account of driving by the parked car, and how half an hour later he saw the driver's window open and realized the engine was running. That he dialed 911 after looking inside the car.

When he finished, Vic looked up from his notebook. "It's pretty standard to see cars parked here?" He pointed his pen at one of the No Parking signs.

"Pretty much. People park there if they want to go for a run before the cemetery opens. If we see the driver we ask them to move, but the cars are usually gone not long after we open."

"So you let it go when you first saw the car," Liz said evenly.

"Yeah. And that's why I walked over to it when I saw it was still here."

"Where exactly was the car?" Vic asked.

Evan pointed to a spot a few feet from them. "Right there."

"Did you recognize the victim?" Liz asked. "Ever see him before?"

Evan shook his head. "He was a mess and I didn't look carefully. Just saw it was an elderly gentleman."

"Had you ever seen the car before?" Vic asked.

"No." Evan accompanied the word with a sharp shake of his head, certain of himself.

Vic glanced at Liz, but her eyes were blank. He knew what she was thinking. There was no information to be had from Evan. He gave it one last shot. "When you first got here, you didn't see anyone hanging round here, or anything odd? Anything at all?"

Vic saw a flicker of impatience in Evan's eyes. "No. I was just getting the cemetery opened up, like I do every morning."

"You opened up the cemetery," Vic repeated, more to himself. For a moment he was overwhelmed by the memory of Dannie's grave, he could picture it, he knew exactly which turns to take once he was through the gatehouse. He remembered the service they'd held after her remains were shipped back from North Dakota. He blinked, his breath shallow in his chest. He'd missed the obvious. He glanced at Liz and settled his gaze on Evan. "Maybe he was here to exercise, but maybe for another reason. Were there any funerals that day? I mean perhaps he was here early for a funeral."

Gravel crunched as Liz shifted closer, interested in Evan's reply.

"Beats me," Evan said. "I'd have to check. Why does that matter?"

"You never know what matters," Liz said sharply.

Evan looked from Vic to Liz and back, a frown on his face.

"Could you check?" Vic stared at him in a way he hoped turned the question into a command.

Evan breathed out in exasperation, turned, and stomped toward the gatehouse.

"Good point," Liz said softly. "Maybe you still got it."

"I'm out of practice." Vic watched Evan duck into the administrative building behind the gatehouse. "Should have thought of it right away."

"I hadn't got there either."

That surprised him. It was unlike Liz to admit mistakes. He turned so his back was to the location where Geno had parked. He and Liz hadn't worked together for almost four years and he wondered if things would be different, now. He was already unsure if he still had the skills for the job, he hadn't even considered how Liz might have changed, and whether that might alter the alchemy of their partnership. He pushed the thought away and studied the row of businesses facing the crime scene, scanning for security or doorbell cameras. He pointed at the buildings. "I sure hope someone canvassed the street. I'm not seeing any cameras, but you never know. And maybe someone lives above one of the businesses and heard something."

"And you gotta wonder which direction the shooter went afterwards."

Liz was also staring at the far side of the street. Vic understood what she was saying. Parking was only allowed on the side of the road nearest the businesses. That meant all the stationery vehicles pointed west toward Pittsburgh.

"Driving into Pittsburgh during rush hour," Vic said thoughtfully.

"Wouldn't be my choice for a getaway," Liz answered. She looked east and frowned.

Vic agreed with her. They were just guessing. He heard a door thump and looked at the gatehouse to see Evan walking toward them, a large book under one arm. When he got to them he shifted it to the palm of his left hand, opened it, and used the fingers of his other hand to find the right entry and stop the wind from blowing the pages closed.

He took a slow breath. "We had two funerals, first one at nine o'clock." He squinted at the entry. "That was for a Mr. Art Rizolli. The second was two o'clock. Woman named Evelyn Rooney."

Vic made eye contact with Liz and saw no recognition in her eyes. Of course, she wouldn't know, he realized. She was from New Orleans and had moved to Pittsburgh after Hurricane Katrina.

He turned back to Evan. "Thanks, Mr. Gelhorn. I appreciate you talking to us again."

"No problem." He didn't sound like he meant it. "Is this going to be it for you guys? Most people already don't like the idea of a cemetery, being reminded that someone was shot right here doesn't help."

"I think so," Vic answered. "We should have the forensics report tonight. If we have any more questions we'll call, that way you don't have to put up with us." Automatically he reached for a business card and realized he didn't have one yet. He dropped his hand. "Thanks for your help."

Evan's gaze skated from Vic to Liz and back to Vic. He seemed to relax, and when he did his eyes grew friendly. "Thanks, that works. Call me if you need me." He turned and lugged the book toward the cemetery entrance.

"He seems happier," Liz said gently, as Evan disappeared under the gateway arch. "Art Rizolli? That means something to you?"

Vic glanced at her. "Yep. Ragman Rizolli. I bet Geno was here for his funeral. Rizolli was one of the crime bosses when Geno was doing his thing. I'll tell you about him later. We need to know who showed up for the funeral. Carter Lee thought we'd find the solution to this back in the eighties. Maybe he's right."

"Still real thin."

"Yes, it is." Vic understood how she felt. Even if the funeral attendees was a lead they could reel in, it was on a fishing line so low-test a bluegill could snap it. "Well, at least we nailed down that Evan was the one who threw up beside the car."

Liz gave him a sidelong glance. "Let's go look at Geno's apartment."

Vic thought he saw the trace of a smile on Liz's lips. Together, they set off across the grass toward the street. As they walked, they automatically scanned the grass, checking for any kind of clue.

As far as Vic was concerned, at that moment, pretty much anything would do.

Chapter Eleven

Geno's apartment building was in the northern suburbs. Half a block long, it was four stories of red brick and peeling white trim hulking behind a brown lawn scarred with bald spots.

Vic parked and got out in front of the building. As Liz wrestled her car into a spot several spaces away, he stared at a downspout that teetered from its bracket halfway between the roof and the ground.

"Who says crime doesn't pay?" Liz said, joining him.

"After prison, this probably looked like heaven."

Liz huffed. "Might want to see the apartment before you say that."

Inside the front door, an elderly man with an impressive belly looked up from a bench. "You the cops?"

"We're the cops," Vic answered. "Thanks for meeting us."

"I'm Lou."

Vic gave the man their names, but Lou's focus was on standing up, which took several seconds. Immediately his belt disappeared under his belly and his green T-shirt strained with the weight of it. Without another word, Lou led them to the elevator, a large ring of keys in his hand.

As the small elevator creaked to the third floor, Vic saw Liz furtively check the maximum safe weight sign.

The elevator was in the center of the building, and on the third floor, Lou led them to the right and halfway down the hall. He tried at least fifteen keys in a door before one slid back the deadbolt.

"Can you stay in the hall?" Vic asked as Lou swung open the door.

Lou glanced up and down the hall. "There's nowhere to sit."

"We'll bring you a chair. Just give us a moment," Vic added.

The apartment door opened into a small living room. A tight kitchen was to the right and a short hall with two doors to the left. Vic waited as Liz snapped photographs of the layout and furniture from the doorway. When she finished, he crossed to the small kitchen table and carried one of the two chairs into the hall.

"There you go," he said, placing it next to Lou.

Without a word, Lou sank into it. As Vic turned for the apartment, it crossed his mind that if Lou was the building's superintendent, that explained the building's disarray. He closed the door behind him.

"Lou's a real go-getter," Liz said.

"I bet he's a peach. You take out here and I'll do the bedroom and bathroom?"

"Got it."

It took Vic half an hour to work his way through all the drawers in the bedroom and the bathroom's medicine cabinet and under-sink cupboard. There was little to find, except a collection of heart and blood pressure medications in the medicine cabinet. Geno had few possessions and didn't have a hobby he could spot. The only personal item was a faded photograph in a cheap frame. It sat on the bedside table next to a digital alarm clock. Vic took a photograph of it and picked it up for a better look. It showed a woman and baby, the child no older than a year. From the woman's hairstyle, and the photo's fading colors, he guessed it was taken in the nineteen-eighties. The woman was strikingly pretty, with deep brown eyes. She was holding a newborn, but it occurred to Vic that she wasn't just holding the child, she was presenting the child to the camera. Or, he thought slowly, the person taking the picture.

"You find anything?" Liz asked, from the doorway.

He handed her the framed photograph. "Just this. Otherwise, it's like anywhere a broke ex-con lives. Can't even find an address book."

"Yeah. Half the kitchen cabinets were empty. Bunch of canned soup and stews. No alcohol." Liz studied the photograph. "She's pretty."

"That's what I thought."

Liz turned the frame over and unclipped the back. With a quick movement, she dropped the backing, frame, and glass into her free hand and tossed them onto the bed. She checked the back of the photo and pursed her lips. "Nothing written here, but see the edges? Pin holes and bits of tape. I bet that photo was in jail with him."

"I wonder if the woman's still around. Or the child."

"We can check birth and marriage records. Maybe Geno was married to her."

"We need something."

Liz handed the photo to Vic and returned to the living room. Vic weighed it in his hand, staring at the frame, glass, and backing on the bed. It felt wrong to leave the frame in pieces; it was the only personal item in the entire apartment. Geno might be dead, but this was his universe. What mattered to him. To leave it scattered wasn't right. From the direction of the kitchen, a drawer slammed. Quickly, Vic reassembled the frame with the photo inside and placed it on the bedside table. He stared at it for a moment, feeling better somehow, and followed Liz out of the room.

Liz was waiting for him by the front door. As he approached she turned the handle, and they found Lou in the hallway still sitting in the kitchen chair, his chin on his chest, eyes closed, his breath a gentle wheeze. Vic cleared his throat. Lou blubbered awake and repeated the slow process of standing. Vic returned the chair to the kitchen and the three of them took the elevator to the ground floor.

Outside, he and Liz stopped at the end of the front walk and turned back to look at the building. Seeing it again, and knowing what the apartment looked like, Vic was overtaken by a sullen feeling. He tried to separate the strands of anger and gloominess to understand his thoughts.

Liz interrupted his contemplation. "Tell me about this Art Rizolli, the guy whose funeral Geno was going to attend?"

Vic took a slow breath. "I remember a few things." He took a moment to sort them out. "He was one of the guys active when Geno was doing his thing. He ran a garbage pick-up business. Bribed and extorted his way into a bunch of municipal and business contracts. But the rumor was that he could make anything at all disappear. That's how he ended up working with Bandini and those guys. Want to get rid of bloody clothes? A body? He was your guy. And he had a nasty mouth. You made a mistake working for him and he'd rag you out in front of everyone. That, and people used to call anyone who collected the old rags people threw out a ragman. Get it? That's the Ragman nickname."

"Huh. And Geno would need a guy like him?"

"You knock off an armored car or a bank and you've got marked bags, clothes, and maybe some weapons you want gone, you called Ragman."

Liz squinted at her car, thinking. "Who do we talk to next?"

Vic had the feeling Liz already knew the answer, she just wanted him to say it.

"Well, Bandini. I know you don't want to hear that. But before we do let's talk to Justin Day. He's an old crime beat reporter. Day might have some background on Geno and Bandini we can use," he said slowly.

Liz sighed. "I guess we can't get around Bandini. And I bet he was at the funeral." She turned to him. "But I warned you last time about him, Vic. We need to watch out with those guys."

"This is a murder investigation. We have to talk to them."

Liz shook her head. "You know that doesn't work with boys like that. They don't do conversations. Everything is a trade or a favor. They always want something back."

Vic thought about how he and Liz saved Bandini's daughter from a murderer years earlier. "We might still have some credit with him."

"Not after he gave you those photographs. The ones that led you to Lettie? In his mind that wiped the slate clean. A granddaughter for a daughter. That's how he'll look at it."

Vic was careful not to meet her gaze. He knew she was right, but he didn't want to admit it. "Maybe. Maybe not. But we still need to talk to him. And Thuds." He looked at her and growled, "It's a murder investigation, dammit."

Liz smiled. "And there's the Vic I missed." She turned and walked to her car. "I'll phone you tomorrow," she called over her shoulder. "I might be free in the afternoon."

"Thanks."

Driving home, Vic's mind drifted back to the photograph. There wasn't even a date on it. He decided to show it to Anne. Anne was good about identifying hairstyles, she picked up on things he often missed. And the woman in the photograph had high frizzed hair that surrounded her face like a halo. Maybe Anne could tell him when hair treatments like that were in style. He wasn't sure why, but he felt like that photograph still had something to tell him.

Chapter Twelve

The Third Day

For seven days he floated to work each afternoon and evening and spent the remaining time with his family. He'd arranged a couple of hours with Terri one morning, telling his wife he needed to go into work early. As always, she hadn't questioned him.

Sometimes he wanted her to, just so he could tell her the brutal truth. About Terri and the string of women before that. Watch her face collapse. He got excited just thinking about it. What would she do? Accept it? The thought made him breathe deeply, taste the headiness of how it felt to hold her entire world in his palm. Her life revolved around their daughters, the neighborhood they lived in and the fantasy she carried about the sanctity of their marriage. And he could end it all with a few sharp words. Maybe he'd give her an ultimatum. Accept Terri and whoever he chose next. Or leave.

She didn't have the courage to move out. To take the girls. He was sure of it. And if she did, he would cut her off. She wouldn't have a chance. She didn't know that soon he'd have the money to pay lawyers who could decimate her in divorce court.

Only he had the patience and intelligence to see all this. He was certain of that. And today it was time to start things moving again. He'd drifted with the tides for the last week, reading the newspapers every day, watching the news. Waiting to see if the police somehow found a current that carried them to him. That was the only thing that might force him to change his plans.

But the news stories about Geno stopped almost immediately, overtaken by breathless reporting about a reorganization in the district attorney's office. The forced retirement of a number of detectives. A shakeup among the prosecutors. Geno Varelli's murder was lost in the riptides and swirl of new hires and angry retirements. He read all this and saw a sign that he was doing the right thing. At the right time.

Solid ground ahead.

It was as if he was chosen. As if it was all for him. A gift. As he'd known all along he deserved.

It was almost three in the morning, now. He'd been home for thirty minutes. A whiskey sat at his elbow. Upstairs, his wife and daughters slept, oblivious in their stupidity. He'd used a work computer to print out the best photograph of Geno's tattoos, and he placed it on his desk. From a hidden slot inside his briefcase, he removed the letter he had found with his father's will. He flattened it out next to the photograph. Flipped to the second page and found the correct paragraph. Aligned the numbers and words.

His father had explained that two items were tattooed on his forearm. The first, a short alphanumeric, the second, a set of three pairs of digits, separated by dashes. Geno's tattoo was a number and a word. Now, between the letter and the photograph, he put everything together. From Geno, a street address. From his father, the alphanumeric identifying the right door. The three pairs of digits were the combination to the lock.

And now he had all of it.

Where to find the storage locker and how to open it.

He wrote it all down on a Post-it note. Folded it and slid it into his shirt pocket. Tomorrow, at work, he would do a map search and identify the location of the storage facility. Then, in a few days, if the police were still trapped in the whirlpool of their reorganization, he would visit the storage locker. Gather what was his.

From the explanation in his father's letter, he knew how Geno and his father worked together. The contours of their partnership. Geno was the money, his father the brains and vision.

That was before Geno's betrayal. He sipped his whiskey. In all of this, in everything he had reconstructed from his father's papers, that was the one thing he couldn't understand. Why Geno ratted out his father. Doing so meant Geno couldn't recover the money and documents at the heart of their partnership. It made no sense that he would throw all that away. And Geno's sentence wasn't shortened. It was lengthened.

He'd meant to ask Geno that question before he pulled the trigger. But the excitement of the moment had proven too much.

And one, last, niggling question. Logically, someone else knew the same details he now possessed. It was the only way the tattoo artist could know what to ink on each man's arm.

Maybe, just maybe, someone had already ransacked the storage locker.

He swigged the last of his whiskey. He doubted it. His father was too smart for that. Certainly, at one time, someone else knew all the details. But they were gone, one way or another. It had to be. Otherwise, his father wouldn't have bothered to explain the agreement and the tattoos. Wouldn't have taken the time to write the letter to him as he lay dying in prison. His father knew the storage unit was safe.

It was all there. His inheritance. The proof he needed to take back what was his.

Killing Geno for betraying his father was just a bonus.

Chapter Thirteen

Vic was barely inside his house when his cell phone rang. He didn't recognize the caller's number but answered it anyway.

"Mr. Lenoski?" asked a tentative voice.

"Yes?"

"This is Barb. You know, from the playground? I'm sorry to call you but I thought you should know something."

Vic wondered how Barb knew his cell number, then remembered a day several months before when she'd asked him to briefly watch her son at the playground. She'd needed to pick up a prescription at the drugstore—and with none of the other Watch Mothers about—Vic was the only choice. They'd exchanged phone numbers. While she was gone, Vic had wondered if the errand was a ruse to get his number, but Barb never called or texted him afterwards. He'd forgotten about the incident, until now. "Sure. What can I do for you?"

"Well." Vic heard a long intake of breath. "It's about that boy that lives across from the playground. He and Lettie were on the see-saw not long ago?"

"I remember."

"The day after that he didn't come to the playground. In fact, I didn't see him walking back from the bus or at the playground until today." She paused.

Vic realized Barb was the type of person who needed continual affirmation from the person she was talking to. He gave her a quick "okay," and willed her to get to the point.

"He's got a cast on his arm."

When she didn't say anything more Vic realized that was the reason for her call. She saw the cast as significant. "Um. Maybe it just means he broke his arm and needed a few days at home to rest?"

"Right." Her words tumbled out. "I thought so too. But when he came to the playground today I asked him if he was okay and what happened. He didn't say anything. He just turned and almost ran home."

"Well," Vic drew out the word, wanting to slow her down. He saw the looming problem. She wanted him to look into it as a detective, despite there being no indication of a crime. And if he looked into it, chances were good she would ask him to check other things as well.

She cut him off. "I remembered you said you were going back to work as a county detective. Maybe you could check on the boy somehow?"

"Barb, I'm sorry, I need evidence a crime was committed."

"But it's suspicious, you know it is. There's never a parent around. He always plays by himself and runs off if we talk to him. He's underfed. He doesn't have many clothes. And now his arm's broken."

"There could be perfectly good reasons to explain all of that." Vic closed his eyes. Barb suspected abuse, he was sure of it.

Barb huffed out a breath in frustration. "Maybe you could at least look up the address? See if police were ever called to the house? That might tell you something."

Vic squeezed his eyes closed. He knew he was going to regret his next words. "Okay, what's the address?"

She gave it to him quickly, as if she was making sure he didn't have time to change his mind.

Vic took his time writing it down. When he was finished he said slowly, "Barb, please understand, I can't do this right away. And so we're clear, I'm not supposed to use our systems for personal business. I'm not going to make a habit of this."

"Well, it isn't personal business if something is wrong, is it? And thank you. I wouldn't ask if I didn't think something bad was going on."

Vic didn't think anything bad *was* going on, but he promised to check and call back. He ended the call and discovered a text from Anne, telling him she'd picked up Lettie at daycare. He texted back that he would start dinner.

Ten minutes later a pot of water was heating on the stove. Next to it were a box of spaghetti and a tub of store-bought pesto. He stared at the meager ingredients and decided two things. Spaghetti with pesto and a few vegetables would have to do for tonight, and he and Anne needed a better method to plan dinner now that they were both working.

With a few minutes to kill until the water boiled, he checked the daily newspaper's website and found no mention of the Geno Varelli murder, just an ongoing analysis of the reorganization in the DA's office. On a whim, he clicked on the Newsburgh news site. He froze.

In large type, an angry headline accused the DA of fumbling the investigation into Geno Varelli's death. The accompanying story questioned why Hana pushed seasoned detectives into retirement and replaced them with unproven investigators. Vic flushed with anger. He might be rusty, but he wasn't unproven, and Liz was at the top of her game. He scrolled down the article, skimming, to find a color photograph of Geno sprawled across the front seat of his Lincoln, blood and brains splattered across the inside passenger window, dashboard, and windshield. Alongside the story were two more photographs. One was a close-up of Geno's face, his mouth open, eyes blank. The second was a distant shot of the entrance road to the cemetery showing the parked Lincoln and the gatehouse.

Vic stared. Crime scene photographs were never released to the media. Worse, he hadn't seen them before, he was still waiting for the forensics report. He stared at the images. It dawned on him that none of the items used by the forensics team to tag evidence and indicate perspective were there. No rulers or measurement gauges. No yellow numbered tags. These were shots taken before the forensics team arrived.

With a sinking feeling, he knew the most likely culprit, but he forced himself to consider all the options. There were four possibilities. Evan Gelhorn was one, but Evan had thrown up after looking inside the car. It was unlikely he then walked around taking pictures.

The second was someone passing by, but the photos were shot in daylight, well after police had secured the scene. Any passersby would have been chased away before they took any photos.

On the stove the pasta water started to bubble, steam wafting from the pot. The third possibility was one of the officers protecting the crime scene. That didn't feel right to him. If one of the uniformed officers provided the photos, the story would be about the crime and the content of the photographs. But the article was an attack on Hana and her reorganization.

That left the first detective on the scene. The photographs even looked like the type he and Liz routinely took before the forensics team arrived. He reread the story, the pasta water bubbling hard now, steam rolling from the pot.

He texted Carter Lee, mentioned the Newsburgh story, and asked who was assigned to the Varelli case before he arrived. Thirty seconds later Carter replied with two words: Gabe Chilton. A second text identified Gabe as one of the detectives pushed into early retirement.

Now it fit. Gabe most likely took the photos. He could see Gabe offering the photographs to Newsburgh on the condition the reporter attack the DA's reorganization.

Vic weighed the phone in his hand and another thought came to him. He texted Carter and asked which desk Gabe had used.

"The one assigned to you," was the immediate reply.

Vic put down his phone, feeling clammy and hot, as if he had leaned too close to the boiling water. The sympathy he'd felt for the detectives forced into early retirement disappeared.

He couldn't understand how anyone in Gabe's situation could be so angry they felt justified in releasing crime scene photographs. It was petty. He remembered the fingernail clippings in the drawer and suddenly understood the pathology of it. Gabe was so convinced of his own importance and value, so wrapped up in himself and blinded by his own sense of value he couldn't even throw away his fingernail clippings. It would be incomprehensible to him that Hana chose him for early retirement. That Hana would even think to do it.

Releasing the photos was revenge.

CHAPTER THIRTEEN

Vic reduced the flame under the pot and watched the water slow to a rolling boil. Another thought came to him, and he didn't like it. If his analysis was correct, then Gabe's ego was in charge. And that meant Gabe would only stop when someone made him.

Chapter Fourteen

The next morning, Vic arrived at work to find a message from the forensics team sitting at the top of his email list. He didn't recognize the name of the sender, but the note was clear. At Carter Lee's request, he was forwarding everything Forensics had prepared so far. Vic counted six attachments. The email went on to say the final report would follow when the toxicology screen results were complete.

Vic smiled. He was starting to like Carter Lee. After their brief text exchange the night before, Carter had obviously reached the same conclusion about Gabe. Carter's solution was to push the case forward quickly so Gabe would no longer have anything to offer the press.

"What do you know. Vic Lenoski. I heard it was true but never believed it. Had to come and see."

Vic looked up to find Dave Norbert staring down at him. Vic rose and they shook hands.

"I guess you survived the reorganization," Vic said.

Dave shrugged. "So far. New job now. I'm liaison to local departments."

"Not major crimes?"

Dave shook his head.

Vic thought that whoever made that decision was wise indeed. He'd last seen Dave while working on the public defender case. When it was moved from the Pittsburgh Bureau of Police to the Allegheny County Police, Dave was given the lead. But Dave had already admitted to Vic and Liz that he knew the victim so well he'd frequently visited her bed. It was an egregious conflict of interest. As the public defender's lover, Dave was a likely person of interest or material witness. Somehow, political animal that he was, Dave kept the affair secret.

"I heard Liz is coming over as well." Dave looked around. Vic thought he was worried Liz might walk up behind him. Liz never hesitated to insult Dave about his sleeping around.

"She starts Thursday."

Vic glanced at the documents on his screen. He wanted to get started, but another thought came to him. "Can you answer a question for me?" Vic waved his hand at his desk. "Gabe Chilton sat here, right? What was he like?"

"Pretty good detective. He solved his share."

"How was he to work with?"

Dave pursed his lips. "Not sure he was a guy people actually worked with. He liked to be the lead, and he wasn't much on taking suggestions."

"Pretty impressed with himself?"

Dave shrugged again, his gaze sliding down the aisle, as if he didn't want to be overheard. "He sure didn't like being told to retire, I can tell you that."

"Not sure anyone would."

"Yeah, well, they had to call security and walk him out of here. He was supposed to have a two-week wind-down period, but he was so pissed that didn't happen."

Vic gestured at the desk again. "Yeah, I'm still cleaning out his desk."

"Good luck with that. Well, great to have you on board Vic. I heard you found your granddaughter in North Dakota."

"I did."

Dave nodded. He was smiling but his eyes were flat and calculating. Vic knew Dave couldn't be happy with his transfer to a staff position, but there was more to it than that. Vic had needed Dave's help when he was trying to find his daughter, and had threatened to reveal Dave's affair with the public defender to get it. Dave was being polite, but they were never going to be friends.

Vic was just fine with that.

"Okay," Dave said, shifting from one foot to the other. "If you need anything, let me know."

"Same here." Vic gave him a smile and watched Dave turn and head down the aisle.

As soon as he was gone, Vic printed out every document sent to him by Forensics. He still preferred working with hard copies over electronic files. He collected the pages from the office printer and sat at his desk, arranging the reports into the order he wanted to read them. Before starting, he considered the Post-it notes on the frame of his monitor. He still wanted a conversation with the crime beat reporter, at least for background. But first, he needed to see if Forensics had found any hard evidence.

He started reading the physical description of the crime scene but stopped at the end of the first paragraph. He hesitated, reread it, and stopped again. He couldn't retain the words, they slid away like water through sand. He blinked, gathered himself, and read the paragraph a third time, slowly, concentrating.

This time the words stuck. He stopped reading and wondered about what just happened. Granted, it was more than four years since he had read forensic reports. But that wasn't it. It was how the report was written. In the last four years, his reading had widened. He'd read a newspaper every day and books out loud to Lettie most nights. But the big change was his nose-dive into poetry.

Two years before, he'd taken Lettie to buy a new book for her bedtime reading. Wandering the store shelves, he'd found a table of books written by Pittsburgh authors. A name jumped out at him: Jimmy Cvetic. He knew Jimmy from Golden Gloves. Jimmy was a boxing trainer and owned several gyms, and for years was a Pittsburgh detective. Vic hadn't known he also wrote poetry.

Out of interest, he bought the book.

Jimmy's poems were instantly recognizable to him. Many were stark stories recounting Jimmy's police cases and Vic instantly recognized the hopelessness of what he'd also seen every day as a cop. Vic recognized the mineral veins of humor in the poems, and the hard need that ran through the lives of the people Jimmy talked about. He read the book three times, and then Jimmy's other collections.

Wanting more, he reached out to Jimmy Pronghorn, a friend he'd made in North Dakota. He knew Pronghorn was an avid reader, and once Vic explained Jimmy Cvetic's writing to him, he'd recommended Charles Bukowski. Then Gary Snyder and some Polish poet named Herbert. With those books behind him, Vic was hooked on the form. Now he was reading T.S. Eliot. He liked the economy of language, how the turns of phrase surprised him, and the way a line could carry multiple meanings, if he took the time to think them out.

And that, he realized, was why he found the report difficult to read. The stilted language, inconsistent tenses, and potholes of jargon had thrown him. He needed to readjust. He shook his head, smiling to himself. He'd worried about losing a step and not being able to do the job. Who knew he'd stumble over the fact his reading comprehension had improved?

He started over, and when he finished, knew the reports weren't very helpful. Geno was shot twice, in the head and in the abdomen. The car window was down, the engine running, the transmission in Park. Given blood spatter, he'd been shot by someone standing next to the car on the driver's side who fired through the open window. No shells were found on the scene, suggesting a revolver was used. A canvass of the area found no footprints, no murder weapon, or anyone who heard the shots. There was no CCTV of the scene.

Vic sat back. The biggest problem was the autopsy report. The autopsy was completed a few days after the murder, but the report was missing the photographs of the body. It was clear the coroner was waiting for the toxicology results before finalizing the report. Vic couldn't wait that long. He fired off an email to the coroner's office asking for everything they had, and returned to his computer to examine the photographs of the scene. After ten minutes of zooming in and out on each picture, he decided to get coffee. As he rose, Carter Lee appeared beside his desk.

"You got everything?" Carter asked.

"Just went through it. We still don't have everything from the autopsy, just a preliminary summary. And no photos."

Carter waited.

Vic realized he wanted a report. "I did notice one thing."

Carter raised an eyebrow.

Vic turned back to his computer and pulled up one of the photographs. "I saw it last night when I looked at the leaked photographs. It's clearer here. Might be nothing. Okay, from the description of the scene, Geno's sports coat was lying on the back seat. He was in shirtsleeves." Vic pointed to the position of Geno's left arm. "But see that? Geno is on his right side and his left arm is extended straight along his body. Kind of an odd position, but weird things happen in shootings. Now, see the cuff of the sleeve?"

Carter squinted at the screen. "It's above the wrist."

"Right, and unbuttoned. See how it's spread out? Compare it to the other cuff." Vic pointed at Geno's right forearm and hand, which peeked out from underneath him.

"Someone pulled up his sleeve?"

"Kind of looks like it, which is an odd thing to do. The preliminary autopsy report mentions a tattoo on Geno's body, but just says it's on the left arm and doesn't say what it looks like. That's why I need the photos of Geno's body. I want to know the exact location of that tattoo and what it looks like. I also asked Forensics to test the left cuff for gunshot residue. That might tell us if the shooter undid the cuff. If the tattoo is on the left forearm and we find a decent amount of gunshot residue on the cuff, then the tattoo might be material."

"Maybe Geno just forgot to button that cuff when he got dressed."

"It's possible, yeah." Vic knew that was the most likely explanation, and hearing his argument out loud for the first time didn't help. He decided to change the subject. "Oh, and I have another question. Geno's criminal record isn't there, and neither are his incarceration records. I get those files are from the days before we were online, but there's nothing. Has anyone asked for it from the archive?"

The hint of a smile appeared on Carter's face and Vic realized that Carter was waiting to see if he noticed the lapse.

"I had the same thought," Carter said. "I asked for them my first day and they couldn't find them."

"They've got to be somewhere. Geno was a legend."

"That's what I thought, too. But the archives don't have them."

They stared at each other for a few seconds until the realization hit Vic. "You think the DA's office has them?"

"I've put out a feeler. We'll see."

Vic warmed. "Geno was a CI?" Vic knew that in the old days, the DA's office only maintained criminal records under a few circumstances. The most important one being the person was also a confidential informant.

Carter shrugged. "We'll find out. But something is going on. Just glad I worked here years ago, or I never would have remembered CI files are kept separately. Every city handles it differently. Anyway, I contacted Hana and she has someone looking."

It crossed Vic's mind there could be another reason the file was missing. Someone had stolen it. Before everything went online, all it took was a quick payment from the criminal to a friendly police officer.

Carter nodded. "Good. Keep at it, Vic. When I hear from Hana about the file I'll let you know."

"I have another question," Vic asked.

Carter nodded for him to ask.

"The photos posted in Newsburgh last night? Any idea who leaked them?"

Carter tapped Vic's desk with his knuckle. "There's one obvious possibility."

"Maybe someone should warn him off?"

Carter gave him a tight smile. "Hana and I talked about it this morning. We both agreed to leave it alone for now."

Vic wanted to disagree but caught himself. Something hard had crept into Carter's smile.

"For starters," Carter said casually, "Gabe can't know much more than he leaked last night. But really, we'd rather give him enough rope to hang himself." Carter flashed him a wicked grin and turned for the conference rooms along the back wall.

Vic watched him go. He liked the exchange, but the discussion also told him Carter had reviewed the forensics and preliminary autopsy files himself. There was a message in that.

Carter didn't trust him yet.

Vic was okay with that. He didn't mind proving himself. But he'd just learned something else. If Carter's approach to Gabe's leaked photos was to let Gabe hang himself, he didn't want to be on Carter's wrong side, either.

Chapter Fifteen

Not long after he returned with his coffee, a text arrived from Liz saying she would stop over after lunch. Vic gingerly pulled the Post-it note with the retired reporter's name from his monitor and dialed the number.

On the second ring, a gruff voice said, 'Talk to me."

"Is this Justin Day?"

"Who's this?"

Vic ignored his annoyance at Day's sharp retort. He was two steps slow on Geno's case already and didn't have the luxury to get angry, even if the person could only help him tangentially. "Detective Vic Lenoski with the Allegheny County Police. I wanted to talk to you about Geno Varelli. Just some background. I figured if you're the Justin Day who did the crime beat for the newspaper, you'd know him better than anyone."

Silence lengthened between them, but Vic sensed an intensity on the line. "Vic Lenoski," the voice repeated. "Last I heard you retired."

"I did. And then I didn't."

A sound part phlegm clearing and laughter came down the line. "Yeah. Didn't take you for the retiring type. Allegheny County now, huh? Okay, so what can I do you for?"

"I said. Geno Varelli. I'm looking for background. I figured you might have some history."

"Christ, history is all I got. I'm a retired asshole now. Dumb-ass new owners of the paper kicked me out. They like these sweet young things right out of journalism school. They pay them shit and tell them what to write.

These days everybody who owns a newspaper has an agenda. Although I got to say, those young'uns make the newsroom a lot prettier than in my time."

Vic started to think he'd made a mistake.

"Okay. How do you want to do this?" Day asked, and Vic decided to stay on the phone a bit longer.

"Any chance we could meet this afternoon? You tell me where and when and we'll come to you, although the sooner after lunch the better. Does that work?"

"Sure. One o'clock." He gave Vic an address. "You said 'we.' Who else is coming?"

"I work with Liz Timmons."

"Good. Always wanted to meet her. I hear she's a tough nut. I mean that respectfully. Actually, one-thirty okay?"

"See you then." Vic hung up. Now that he'd made the call he had the feeling talking to Day was going to be a roller coaster. But at least it was checking a box.

Day's home address was a nineteen-forties clapboard house in the Squirrel Hill neighborhood of Pittsburgh. The house needed paint, the driveway potholes patched and the porch roof propped up. Vic didn't need to look at Liz to know what she was thinking.

Day answered Vic's knock almost immediately and waved them inside. It was like walking into a wall of stale cigarette smoke. The entry was small and they were jammed together as they shook hands. Day was thin and badly hunched, his eyes bright in the low light. He waved them into a living room overwhelmed by a couch of dark wood and rough upholstery that should have belonged in the house of someone's great-grandmother. The spindly IKEA chairs and tables surrounding it looked like a flotilla of support vessels for an aircraft carrier.

Day gestured beyond the living room to the dining room. One end of the long dining table held a desktop computer and a laptop, as well as several piles of files and a teetering column of newspapers. A printer and scanner were hunched on the breakfront, the wires connecting them to the laptop a jumble on the floor. Day took a seat at the opposite end of the table and indicated they should sit in the nearest chairs. Vic was keenly aware that Day had not stopped staring at him the entire time they walked to the dining room. It was starting to annoy him.

Once they were seated, Day leaned toward him. "You were the one figured out that public defender's death, right?"

"Both of us." Vic gestured to Liz.

"Yeah, yeah. There's a story I'd like to get into. There's meat on that bone. You know how I know?" He looked from Vic to Liz and back again. "Nobody wants to talk about it. Dead giveaway. You guys did all the legwork, the DA's office cut a deal with the suspect so we don't know any of the details. Then three years later the DA resigns and we have a new DA, who just happened to be on the suspect's prosecution team, and you show up working for her. Yeah. There's a story there. And I know it because I actually talk to people. I can see when someone is scared to talk. It's in their eyes. I'm not one of those hot-shot-new-age-freaking-digital-economy-on-line news sites that do everything from an F-ing ergonomic chair and Google. I get out and look people in their sockets. That's the problem with newspapers today. They're staffing like they're running websites. They don't hire anyone who wants to dig up news." He sat back.

Vic gave Day a moment, wondering if he might need to catch his breath. He could tell from Liz's posture that she had decided he could take the lead.

Coward, he thought, glancing at her. "Okay, that's all interesting," Vic said slowly. "But we really wanted to talk about Geno Varelli. You were the crime reporter for years, we thought you might have some history."

Day glanced from one to the other. "Yeah. Look at that dumb-ass excuse for a newspaper now. A measly fifteen column inches on the shooting, that's it. No storyline follow-through, a guy like that, and all he gets is fifteen inches? Garbage. They could have done three days of stories just waiting for your first press conference." He lifted his hand and straightened a nicotine-stained forefinger. "One, recap his career." A second finger shot up. "Two, thought piece on how crime in the city has changed." A third finger joined the first two. "Three, overview of all the crime bosses back then. Geno knew 'em all. Worked for most of them. It's all just sitting there. And I'm not even trying hard to come up with stories." He dropped his hand. "So what do you want to know?"

Liz took a notebook from her jacket pocket. "His career. People he knew and worked with."

Day nodded, his eyes gleaming. "And what do I get out of it?"

As they drove to Day's house, Vic and Liz had discussed Day asking exactly that question. They didn't have much to offer.

"What do you want?" Liz asked. That was how they'd decided to handle it.

"All the inside dope when you catch the killer. You can tell the papers what you want, but I want the inside dope. The TV and radio stations just want a sound bite, they're not even in this game. You see what that dumb-ass online Newsburgh thing is doing? Playing mouthpiece for some pissed-off detective. Gabe Chilton, am I right?"

That interested Vic. "Why would you want inside dope? You're not writing for anyone, are you?"

Day thumped his fist on the table. "Writing for myself. Doing a book. Pittsburgh crime. Nineteen-twenties to today. We've had it all. The country's first-ever armored car robbery was here. First time an IED was used to rob an armored truck? Right here. And that was just the nineteen-thirties. I got a million stories like that. And Geno? Biggest armored car heist this country's ever seen. All right here. Pittsburgh boys play for keeps. And Geno getting shot? That's my last chapter, because he's the end of it. End of an era. End of the Golden Age. We were The Constantinople of Crime." He moved his hands in the air as if imagining a movie marquee. "How's that for a book name? I wanted to interview him, but I didn't track him down in time. You guys will have to do. That's why I want the inside dope." He grinned, and the smile was the type people give when they taste a good whiskey. "Actually works out better, him getting shot. I can end the book with a bang."

Liz shifted in her chair, her face tight.

Vic forced himself to take a breath before he spoke, to ignore Day's last line. "Maybe. But what can you tell us?"

Day leaned over the table toward him. "Yeah. I heard you'd drive a tough deal." He spread his hands. "What do you want to know?"

"Who Geno worked with, who he made deals with. Who he worked for. Everything you can give us." Liz's voice was tight. Vic wasn't sure if it was anger or disgust.

"Yeah, okay." Day reached behind him and grabbed a pack of unfiltered Camels and a plastic lighter. He offered a cigarette to Vic and Liz. When they declined, he lit up, waved away the smoke, and hunched lower, if that was possible. "I can answer all that. Do we have a deal?"

"You talk. If I hear enough, we have a deal," Vic said slowly. "But anything we give you later, it wasn't from us. No attribution. You never heard it from a couple of cops."

"Deal. Okay." Day took another drag on his cigarette. "Geno was a rain-maker. Back in the eighties, they still had numbers, rackets, loansharking, insurance fraud, drugs, that was how most of those boys made money. All nasty stuff, but Geno was a thief and that made him a cut above. Plus, Geno was a freaking tremendous thief."

"How did he get started?" Liz tapped her pen against her notebook.

Day turned his bright eyes on her. "Yeah. Good question. That's the key to it. I don't know where he was born, but he grew up here, in Lawrenceville. I bet he played in the cemetery when he was a kid." He stopped and drew on his cigarette. "Got to remember that." He grabbed a pen and scratched some words on it. "Geno started and ended at that cemetery. Nice symmetry. Anyway, then he was in the Army. Korea. When he came back, get this, he got a job with an armored car company. Drove the thing around, made deliveries. He was maybe three years with them. You see, I think that taught him the best times to hit banks and armored cars. You got to remember that, back then? People used cash all the time. Credit cards were a new thing and people didn't trust them. And from working for the armored car company, he learned stuff like how banks stocked cash a couple of days before payday, so they could cover payroll checks. Then take that back up the chain. If the bank needs a big cash delivery on Thursday, let's say, then the armored car company needs the cash on hand in their depot a couple of days before that. Geno learned the pipeline. He was smart that way. After he left his job, I always figured he kept a couple of guys greased inside the armored car companies. They'd tell him when big deliveries were being made, that kind of thing. Geno hits the bank right after the delivery. He gets a big payday and gives his inside guys side cash. Cops never thought to talk to the armored truck company because it was the bank got hit. That was how Geno worked. Smart."

He paused and took a long drag on his cigarette. Tapped the ash into a nearby saucer.

Vic was itching to ask some questions, but decided to let Day talk. He could circle back to them at the end.

"Anyway." Day tapped the end of his pen on the table. "I'm pretty sure Geno started small. Jewelry stores, that kind of thing. Smash and grab. But he realized that was high risk. Hardly anyone had video cameras in those days, but the decent jewelers were wired to the local precincts. Someone in the shop hits a button and the cops show up in a couple of minutes. He decided to do something better." He drew greedily on his cigarette and blew the smoke toward the ceiling.

Vic waited. He noticed Liz was watching Day, interested.

"You see," Day said slowly. "Back then, a lot of mob bosses stole semi-trucks. They'd drive it to a warehouse, unload it, then dump the truck. Ragman Rizolli had a whole side business getting rid of the trucks. I bet there's a bunch of them in the rivers around here. But guess what. After a while, the warehouses where they kept the stolen truck cargo started getting hit."

Liz leaned forward. "Geno was stealing from the mob?"

Day grinned yellow teeth and stubbed out his cigarette butt. "Can't prove it, but I'm pretty sure. The key was this guy he started hanging out with. No one knew him. Black guy from out of town. Someone told me they were both in Korea. Anyway, right about the time this guy shows up, Geno stops hitting jewelry stores and puts together a crew. They move to warehouses and steal from guys who can't complain to the cops."

Vic couldn't stop himself. "Who was the black guy?"

"I said. I don't know. I heard he was called Priest, but that makes no sense." Day's gaze flicked to Liz and back. "I just saw him and Geno together a few times. And they were tight, you could see it. It was like they were one guy, really. Watching each other's backs."

"You saw them?" Liz asked. "You hung out with them?"

Day waved his hand. "Not really. I'd just started at the paper. First job. But there were a couple of bars in town the mob liked, and I'd go there to see if I could hear something. Geno showed up a lot in those days. He liked to party. He'd walk in and the whole place turned electric. He'd be slapping backs, buying drinks, leaning on the ladies. He was a live wire."

"And Priest was there when that happened?" Vic thought Priest would be good to talk to, if they could find him.

"Later on. But he'd sit in a booth by himself, kind of watching Geno. But I noticed that if Priest nodded to Geno, Geno would pack it up and they'd leave. Like I said, they were tight."

Something didn't sound right to Vic. "I don't follow. Go back. You said Geno started robbing the gangs of the merchandise they stole from the trucks, and then he parties with them?"

Day gave his throat-clearing laugh. "You got to understand. Geno had balls. He liked living large. I don't think he ever saw himself as a thief, more like a pirate. Swashbuckling, you get my drift?" He poked the table hard with a finger. "He was a damn romantic."

Vic didn't look at Liz. He could guess what she was thinking.

Day slid a cigarette out of the packet but didn't light it. He held it between two fingers, caressing it with the knuckle of one of the fingers. "But he did stop robbing the warehouses."

"What happened?" Liz asked.

Day grinned. "See, this is where it gets really good. Back then there were maybe four mobs in the city. Remember I said Geno was a rainmaker? All the bosses knew that. They started bidding for him. They figured if they hired him to steal for them, then he wouldn't rob their warehouses. Turn a loss into a gain. It got nasty between the crime bosses. And Geno took his time choosing. And get this, I think that was the plan he and Priest had all along."

"But he did go with someone?"

"Yeah." Day waited, a gleam in his eye.

"Okay," Vic said. "I'll bite. Who was it?"

"Let's review," Day said gruffly. "When this is done I get the inside scoop? I get as much of your time as I need to get my last chapter right?"

"This isn't a bargaining situation," Liz said sharply.

Vid laid his hand on Liz's forearm but kept his gaze on Day. "I'll give you one interview with me, and you'll get everything I can legally give you. After that, you're on your own. But no attribution."

Day's gaze skidded from Vic around the room to his computer. He stared at it for a few seconds and turned back to Vic. "Okay. Fair enough." He wiped his mouth with the back of his hand. "The guy he started working for was Paul Zielinski."

Vic felt something click into place. He didn't understand how or where, but it did. "Hammer Zielinski?" he said carefully, aware of Liz turning to look at him.

Day finally raised the cigarette to his lips, clicked the lighter, and drew in. He savored the smoke for a few moments then blew a stream toward the ceiling. He lowered his gaze to Vic. "Yep. The one and only. The Hammer."

Chapter Sixteen

Vic had several thoughts at the same time, but Liz cut in before he had time to sort them out.

"You need to explain this," she said quickly, her words clipped. Vic knew she was annoyed. He and Day knew of Hammer Zielinski. This was likely the first time she'd heard the name, and didn't like being excluded from the conversation.

Vic glanced at Day, who stayed quiet. Vic realized Day wanted to hear what he had to say. That meant Day had his own store of information and was interested to see if Vic knew something more. If Vic did, Day gained information without asking a single question. He suddenly understood why Day was so good at his job.

Vic gathered his thoughts. "I just heard this second hand. I never met the guy and he was in jail before I finished the academy. But the story was, he did two things better than anyone else. If you crossed him, he came down hard. That was the Hammer nickname. And he was very smart. He saw what was happening with the war on drugs, and by the end of the eighties, politicians were already talking about legalizing gambling. That didn't happen until later, but the writing was on the wall. He was one of the first to bet on going legit." He took a slow breath. He knew Liz didn't want to hear what he said next. "And back then there were two young turks who worked for Zielinski. Thuds Lombardo and Vince Bandini. That's how they both got started. It's how they met."

"Figures," Liz said, not quite keeping her disgust out of the word.

Vic knew what she meant. Whether she liked it or not, now they absolutely had to interview Thuds and Bandini.

Day tapped his forefinger on the table. "Exactly. And that's why I think Geno hooked up with Zielinski. It was that whole going legit thing. If Geno went with the other bosses, they would protect him, but he would take all the risk and only get a percentage of what he stole. I think Zielinski told Geno he wanted him to steal for a reason. He wanted Geno's robberies to fund legitimate businesses. I bet they made a deal. Maybe Geno would get a percentage of the legit businesses, or maybe they were going to be partners. That would be a much smarter play for Geno, and Geno was a smart guy. That's one of the things I wanted to ask him. I think Geno and Zielinski were in business together."

"Do you have any proof?" Liz asked.

"No. That's why I wanted to interview him. But some of these guys weren't just dumb crooks. They ran organizations of fifty or sixty guys. They knew how to invest and manage risk. And you have to remember, in those days there weren't a lot of choices. Mills were closing and jobs were drying up. That meant all the businesses that supplied the mills were disappearing. Whole towns were dying. Crime was one of the few ways to put food on the table."

"Yeah," Liz said sharply. "Like there was no other way."

"Get off your high horse," Day shot back. He waved his hand and left a trail of smoke in the air. "I'm just telling you what happened. You came here to find out what I know. I'm telling you. And you guys need to respect our deal. I've done my part." He leaned across the table. "So, you gonna interview Bandini and Thuds? They started out working for Zielinski, and they're still around. I heard you two saved the life of Bandini's daughter a few years back. He doesn't give interviews, not to guys like me. But I can give you a few questions to ask him. That might help both of us."

Vic stared at him across the table. "You forgetting our deal already? I said when we're finished with the investigation, not before." He stood. "But this was helpful, Day. We won't forget that."

Liz stood as well.

Day ground his cigarette into an ashtray and rose. "Well, I'd sure ask

Bandini if Geno and Zielinski were in business together."

"Thanks," Liz said sharply.

Day stretched his lanky frame but immediately hunched into his usual question mark of a posture. "Keep this in mind. When Zielinski went to jail, he already had four legitimate businesses. He left Bandini to run them. Today, Bandini and Thuds have a freaking empire of restaurants and other businesses, all legitimate. But a few years ago Zielinski dies in jail, then six months ago Geno gets out of jail, but someone puts a bullet in his brain. Maybe someone doesn't want Geno around. Like maybe Geno's owed something and someone doesn't want to pay up. And you got Thuds Lombardo hanging around in the background like Ted Bundy. You know how Thuds got his nickname?"

"I know exactly how he got it." Vic remembered the dead Columbians on the concrete floor of the warehouse. How afterwards Lombardo was christened with the nickname Thuds. A name that sounded a lot like a dead body hitting a stone floor.

"Maybe Dom Bandini has Thuds cleaning up a little old business. Just making sure everything runs smooth for them." Day opened his palms, all innocence, but his eyes were burning as if he was following a blood trail.

Vic met Day's gaze and held it. "I can tell you're out of newspapers and pretending to write a book. Because now you're just making shit up."

Day smiled, and his eyes softened. "Yeah. That must be it."

Vic gestured to Liz and they headed to the front door. Outside, the sky was overcast. They walked to the car in silence.

Seated inside, Liz said, "My clothes are going to stink for a week."

"Yep." Vic slid the key into the ignition. He only turned it far enough to operate the windows.

Reading his mind, Liz lowered hers halfway. "He's right, you know. If there was a deal between Geno and Zielinski, we need to look at Bandini and Thuds."

"If there was a deal." Vic started the engine and pulled away from the curb. If anything, he felt farther behind the case than when he walked into Day's house. He couldn't remember working a crime like this, where the best leads were forty years past, the people involved dead or dying. He had a sinking feeling. He knew what time did to memories. How people convinced themselves of the exact opposite of what happened, just to forgive themselves or to hide things. How they decided some things should remain secrets. Welcome back, he thought to himself. You asked for it.

Liz raised her window. "All this old-time crap." She said it quietly, more to herself.

Vic pulled up to a red light. "Yeah. It's unreliable. But we have to keep digging at it. Something we can use might break."

Liz was quiet for at least a minute as Vic negotiated traffic.

"Or maybe we're thinking about this backwards."

"How's that?" Vic asked.

"I mean, why now? I get Varelli only got out of jail six months ago, and maybe someone's been waiting all these years to get him. But that would make the shooter the same age. Have you ever heard of someone waiting thirty years to get even?"

Vic thought about it. "There's a point, there. That's a long time to wait."

"Maybe we should think of it backwards. Maybe this isn't about something that happened in the past. Maybe it's about something that's *going* to happen."

"But why would they need Geno dead to make something happen?" He glanced at her and added slyly. "Or maybe it's both."

Liz shot him a sidelong look. "Don't be a jerk. I'm serious. And thanks for dragging me out to meet Day." She raised her forearm to her nose. "Now my clothes stink as bad as this case."

Chapter Seventeen

It took Vic forty minutes to negotiate the tunnel and parkway traffic back to their offices. Liz spent the remainder of the afternoon cleaning up her desk area and working with a computer technician to gain access to the county software systems. She wanted to be ready for her first full day. At four o'clock Carter Lee asked for an update, and they spent half an hour giving him the results of their conversation with Day.

Back at his desk, Vic kept an eye on the clock. He needed to pick up Lettie at daycare and knew the rush-hour traffic into Pittsburgh was a logjam. He decided to stop at the playground afterwards, so she could run around. That reminded him of Barb's request about the small boy and the house across from the playground. He did a search and found no record of police visits. He knew that, to be sure, he should talk to the officers at the local precinct, but he didn't think it was worth the time.

Liz had left and Vic was just about to follow when an email appeared. Finally, the coroner had sent the photographs and other materials he'd requested. He printed them all out, stuck the pages in an envelope, and took it with him on his way to pick up Lettie.

It was only his second time visiting the daycare, and he was still unfamiliar with the layout. He found the room where Lettie spent her day, but it was empty, and he had to remember they consolidated the children in a single room as they neared closing time. Lettie spotted him as soon as he walked in, dropped her drawing pencil, and ran over. He nodded to the teacher monitoring the room. She smiled back at him in a dazed way, her eyes never leaving the other children. She did manage to say goodbye to Lettie.

THE THINGS THAT SECRETS CANNOT HIDE

When they reached the playground, Vic unstrapped her from the car seat. She slid by him like an eel and ran for the slide. They were the only ones there, which relieved Vic. He didn't want to explain to Barb that he came up empty checking on the boy. He knew Barb would urge him to do more.

He left the coroner's photos and documents in his car. He wasn't about to read it in the park. Lettie ran to the slide, shooting down the metal and running back to the steps, her eyes squinting in determination. Lacking a newspaper, Vic swiped through his phone and found the Newsburgh news site. Three stories down was another article about the Geno Varelli shooting. He opened it and read quickly. Within a few paragraphs, he was angry at himself. He'd forgotten to ask Day if Gabe Chilton had already talked to him, and he knew Day was too clever to mention it himself. The story read like an abbreviated version of his interview with Day that afternoon, and quoted an unnamed source. But it was how the article ended that really annoyed him. Like the previous article, it was an open attack on Hana, pointing out that her decision to fire several of the most seasoned detectives meant Hana and her team lacked the experience to navigate a case so complicated by Pittsburgh's criminal past.

Vic thought the attack was off-base, but effective. DAs didn't lead murder investigations, they handed them off to their detectives. Within the department, everyone knew that. But the attack did make Hana look bad to voters. He thought about that. Hana had eighteen months remaining on her term. Possibly, Gabe Chilton was laying the groundwork to run for DA. Hana would be at her most vulnerable during the next election. Four years just wasn't enough time to establish a solid record of accomplishments in office. But Gabe Chilton? Vic had met him once or twice and he didn't seem the political type. Although he certainly seemed to be angry enough at Hana and clearly had the ego for it. Carefully, he forwarded the link to Liz.

He looked up. Lettie was on the roundabout, being pushed by the boy from across the street. He'd been so absorbed in reading he hadn't noticed him arrive.

The boy pushed the merry-go-round with his right hand only, the bright white of a cast peeking from the left sleeve of his jacket. Vic watched. The boy was keeping the rotations slow enough that Lettie was in no danger of flying off. Again, Vic thought the boy must have a younger sister he was used to playing with. Lettie was grinning and hanging on. Liz was right, she was fearless.

The boy stopped pushing and hopped onto the merry-go-round himself. He rode for a few revolutions before jumping off, still holding on, and ran alongside to slow it to a stop. He helped Lettie down and walked with her toward the swings.

Vic rose and crossed to them. "Thanks," he called as he neared them. He took his time, not wanting to spook the boy, and stopped some distance away. "Remember me?" He grinned. "I'm Lettie's grandfather. What's your name?"

The boy circled behind Lettie, ready to push the swing. Vic saw how the movement was designed to keep Lettie between them. All he could see were the boy's nose, eyes, and the top of his head over Lettie's hair. His grey eyes were steady, calculating.

"Oliver," he called.

Lettie said something to him and he gave a gentle push to start the swing. He backed up a few steps.

"Oliver? Great name. I'm Vic."

The boy was silent, but Vic saw a quick flash as he broke eye contact and checked the house. Vic maintained the distance between them.

Lettie swung back and the boy pushed again, broadening her arc.

Vic nodded at where he thought the boy's arm should be. "I saw your cast. That must have hurt."

"It's okay." Oliver's words fell away. Just as quickly, he turned and headed toward his house. The movement was so quick Lettie didn't realize he was gone and squealed when the expected push didn't arrive at the end of her backswing. Vic watched him cross the playground. He walked quickly. Vic looked past him to the house and saw a man standing on the front porch. Even at that distance, Vic registered the man as mid-height, perhaps five feet eight. His hair was dark and it looked as if he wore rimless glasses.

"Time for home, Lettie," he called. "Nana is bringing dinner home with her." Lettie frowned, unhappy, but dug in her heels and dragged herself to a stop. She hopped off the swing, took his hand, and together they followed the boy.

As they reached the sidewalk, the boy topped the steps onto the porch. The man held the door open for him, and as Oliver whisked past the man leaned down and said something. Vic saw Oliver's shoulders tense, but he didn't stop. The man straightened and turned to Vic.

"I'd appreciate it if you don't talk to my son."

Vic stood looking over the car roof at the man. "He was being nice to my granddaughter. They like to play together, and he's careful with her. He's making an effort not to hurt her. I appreciate that. All I did was say hello and thank him."

"Yeah, well. You've been told. Don't talk to him. I don't know who you are."

Vic made a split-second decision not to say he was a detective. "My name's Vic Lenoski. We live about four blocks up that way." He tilted his head in the direction of their house.

The man was silent for a few beats. "Like I said, you've been told."

He started to turn into his house but Vic called across the road to him. "How'd Oliver break his arm?"

The man stopped, his back to him. Finally, he pivoted and looked at Vic. "He fell. He's clumsy. He's fine now." He turned and was inside the house before Vic could say anything more. The front door thumped shut.

Vic took his time strapping Lettie into her car seat and closed the door. As he walked around the back of the car he gave the house one last look. He wasn't sure, but he thought someone was watching him from an upstairs window. As he climbed into the car he wondered if it was Oliver

He relived the encounter as he drove. The man wasn't from Pittsburgh. He'd heard a slight southern accent, but he wasn't familiar enough with dialects to place it. Oliver hadn't said enough to reveal if he spoke the same way.

But one thing was certain. He'd watched Oliver on the merry-go-round. Seen him jump off as it spun. He'd been fluid and balanced, nimble, even with a cast on his arm. He wasn't clumsy at all. Far from it.

He didn't like to admit it, but Barb might be on to something.

Chapter Eighteen

It was almost nine o'clock before Vic finished reading to Lettie. As he made his way downstairs it occurred to him that he and Anne were more disciplined about Dannie's bedtime than Lettie's. He corrected himself. In those days it was Anne's responsibility to put Dannie to bed. They were sharing the task this time, and Vic knew Lettie always squeezed one or two more stories out of him than Anne agreed to read to her.

Anne was perched on one end of the living room couch under a standing lamp, her legs curled under her, a report open on her lap. She looked at him.

"All set?"

"Yep."

A small smile curled the corners of her lips. "How many times did you read The Giving Tree to her?"

"Apparently not enough. She wanted it one more time but I shut her down."

Her smile widened. "Oh, that's it. You shut her down. How could I not know?"

Vic knew defending himself wouldn't work. "I'm going to use the dining room table. I have work to get through."

"How's it going?"

He thought about it. "Slow. I'm out of practice and this case has all these weird connections, most of which took place forty years ago. It's not a cakewalk."

She gave him a warm look. "Then have at it."

Vic spread his papers on the dining room table and stared. Half were photographs of Geno's body, the remainder a transcription of the recording made by the medical examiner as he conducted the autopsy. He started there.

It took Vic thirty minutes to work through the report. The summary contained references to specific photographs, which he studied at length. When he finished he sat back and rubbed his eyes. The transcription was more thorough than he was used to, and he liked that. From the living room their television started up, the volume dropping, and he knew Anne had turned it down so he wouldn't be bothered.

The majority of the transcription was exactly what he expected. Geno was suffering from a variety of ailments, including arthritis of the hip and knees. His heart and circulatory system showed damage from high blood pressure and a past heart attack. The medical examiner determined that the bullet trajectories and location of the body placed the shooter outside the driver's door, shooting through the lowered window. Geno was still upright in the driver's seat when the first, fatal shot was fired. The entry wound and trajectory of the second shot indicated Geno was already slumped onto the passenger seat when the bullet entered.

The transcript also speculated that Geno had a heart attack moments before the shooting. The medical examiner noted they should test the blood samples for enzymes indicating a heart attack.

Vic thought about that. The shooter standing outside the car. Fear might have induced the heart attack. If Geno saw the gun, that might be enough. Or, he'd seen the person holding the gun and had known that particular person wouldn't hesitate. Or both.

The lowered window suggested Geno knew the man who pulled the trigger. Or the woman, he thought, hearing Liz's voice in his head. He tried to place himself inside the car in Geno's place. Geno would find it hard to see who was outside the car without scrunching down. The angles were wrong. And it was barely daybreak, making it hard to see.

He decided that analysis was faulty. Geno could have lowered the window for any number of reasons. He was hot. He was listening for something. He expected to meet someone. Perhaps someone asked him to lower it.

He considered that and arrived at another possibility: someone was in the passenger seat when Geno parked. Someone Geno had brought to the cemetery. Perhaps someone got out of Geno's car, walked around to the driver's side, and shot through the open window. He made a note to ask the forensics team for any indication of someone sitting in the passenger seat before the shooting.

There were too many possibilities.

Knowing the correct sequence of events during the shooting was impossible. But the more he thought about it, the less he believed it mattered. The only line of investigation that might come from those facts was if Geno transported the shooter to the cemetery with him. It might be possible to trace the person.

With a sigh, he turned to the photographs showing Geno's body. With a small blip of excitement, he saw that the tattoo was indeed on Geno's left forearm. He studied the tattoo itself. The ink of the numbers and single word were too even and precise to be a jail tattoo. It looked like they were done professionally, which meant they were already on Geno's arm when he entered jail. He made a note to confirm that from Geno's incarceration records. He wrote down the numbers and the word, followed by the ten digits below them and stared at them. They meant nothing to him. They were a key in search of a lock, or the reverse.

He found a short document on the state of Geno's clothes. As requested, the coroner had sent the shirt to the forensics team. Their single-page report confirmed substantial gunshot residue on the unbuttoned shirt cuff of the left arm, more than might have appeared from random activity. As Vic read the sentences, he finally felt the first stirring of something positive in the case. A positive GSR test. In other words, following the firing of the gun, the shooter reached into the car and unbuttoned Geno's cuff with the same hand used to pull the trigger.

The only likely reason was to look at the tattoos.

Liz might be right about the shooting being about something in the future. If the shooting was revenge, why check the tattoo? Looking at the tattoos meant something was important now. Today.

Excitement flickered inside him. Something else, he realized. He had the start of a profile of the gunman. He put the facts together. Male or female, the shooter fired twice. Quickly enough that Geno couldn't raise his hands to defend himself, and before his heart attack affected his posture. If the logic followed that Geno saw the gun, his heart capitulated, and the shooter pulled the trigger, then the shooter didn't hesitate. And afterwards, the shooter had the presence of mind to pocket their weapon, reach inside the car, unbutton Geno's cuff and check the tattoo.

His excitement sobered. This wasn't an ordinary killer. In deadly force situations, with adrenaline and fear slamming through your veins, most people lost their fine motor skills. He'd heard stories of police unable to reload revolvers, and knew that was why military weapons were designed to reload and fire from simple movements. Yet this person had shot Geno and unbuttoned a cuff? Manipulated a button through a buttonhole? In the dark and mostly by feel? That was the actual definition of fine motor skills. This wasn't a spur-of-the-moment shooting or a gangbanger. This was someone who knew exactly what they were doing. They were committed enough not to hesitate, and cool enough to stay utterly in control.

A sense of urgency overtook him. He gathered the papers and slid them back into the envelope. A shooter like that, calm and task-oriented, could do it again.

And likely would.

Liz was right. He was sure of it now.

Something was coming and he had no idea what it was or how to head it off.

Chapter Nineteen

Liz was reading a report when Vic arrived at work the next morning. Seeing her hunched over the monitor, her short leather jacket hanging against the side wall of her cube, gave him a small charge of familiarity. He felt like he was back at work, finally.

He'd sent her an email the night before outlining his thoughts, and she'd come in early to review the coroner's materials herself. He said good morning and she turned slowly on her chair to face him.

"You get points for last night. Tattoo was a good catch. And we got the start of a profile on the shooter."

Vic couldn't remember the last time Liz complimented him. For a second he was speechless, before he pulled himself together. "And another reminder how far behind we are."

"What else is new. I was looking at the tattoo. The long number might be a bank account number. Those are ten digits. I guess we could ask the major banks to check for an account with that number, but if we find it they won't tell us anything without a warrant."

Vic nodded. It was a long shot at best. The account could be anywhere in the world.

She held up a photo of the tattoo. "The number and word? Might be an address."

"How do you figure?"

She gave him a long look. "I Googled it."

Vic tried not to look annoyed. Not with Liz, but at himself. He'd never thought to plug the word and numbers into a search engine. He really was out of practice. "Anything interesting?"

She smiled, which was worse than if she'd made fun of him. "Yeah, actually. It's a storage facility in the northern suburbs."

Vic thought about what they knew of Geno. "Wait, how long has the facility been there?"

Liz blinked.

"His tattoo," Vic continued. "It's too clean for jailhouse ink. If the tattoo references that storage facility, it needed to be built before he went to jail."

"Huh." Liz turned back to her computer.

Vic knew the exchange didn't cover the fact he'd forgotten the simplest way to check the meaning of the tattoo, but it did dull the mistake. "You searched on the ten digits?" he called across the aisle to her.

"Yeah. Nothing that made sense," she called back, without taking her eyes from her monitor.

He didn't reply, knowing she was down the rabbit hole of finding the age of the storage facility. He picked up his telephone and dialed a number from memory.

The person who answered didn't say hello. "Allegheny County Police Department? Really? Must be gramps Lenoski." Vic knew Levon Grace must have read the caller ID on his phone and guessed it was him.

"Could be your girlfriend," Vic said, referring to Liz.

"She trusts me enough to call my personal cell. What's up with the new job?"

"I'm out of practice."

"Ah. You never forget how. It's like falling down stairs."

"There's that. I will say..." Vic leaned back in his chair. "Makes it easier having Liz here. And so far so good with our new commander."

"Makes all the difference. So what's up? Never known you to make social calls."

"Right." Vic gathered his thoughts. "I need to meet with Bandini. It would be good if Thuds was there as well."

"Okay." Levon fell silent.

Vic knew he was thinking through the best way to approach Bandini.

Bandini was unlikely to answer if Vic called, he liked to keep the police at a distance. But Bandini knew the value of maintaining a back channel. Understanding that Vic and Levon were friends, he'd suggested an arrangement when Vic was investigating the murder of Bandini's son-in-law. If either Vic or Bandini needed to speak to the other, they called Levon and asked him to set it up. That way no records existed of direct calls between them, something Vic appreciated as well.

"He'll want to know why," Levon said, finally.

Vic thought about inventing an excuse, and realized that was the worst thing he could do, even if there was a possibility Bandini was a suspect. "I think we go in open and clear about why we want to talk to him. He'll know Geno Varelli was shot. Just tell him Liz and I got the short straw and we're investigating Geno's death. Bandini's smart. He knows someone from my side of the fence is going to show up at some point. He might even be glad it's us."

"That makes sense. Do you have a time frame?"

Vic thought about being pushy, but decided Bandini might take it the wrong way. He could lawyer up faster than handcuffs clicking shut. "Tell him I respect his time, but as soon as we can do it."

"Mighty polite of you. He might get back to me in a week."

Vic had another thought. "Tell him this. We have a theory about the shooting. We don't think it was revenge. We think it was the beginning and there's more to come. That might get him moving."

Levon chuckled, his deep voice rumbling. "You're the boss."

"Pretty sure Liz is," Vic replied, and hung up before Levon could say anything more. He turned around to find Liz standing at the entrance to his cube.

"Liz is what, exactly?" she asked.

"I was talking to Levon. Just reminding him you're the boss."

She eyed him. Vic saw she didn't find it funny.

"Your real boss—Carter Lee, remember him? He wants us in a meeting as soon as you're off that call."

Vic thought the faster he changed topics the better. He rose from his chair.

"Lead the way."

They found Carter at the head of the table in the floor's largest conference room. Ten other detectives were scattered around the room. Vic already knew some of them and he nodded greetings or answered them when offered. A well-dressed young woman Vic didn't know made a point of ignoring him, which Vic took as a nervousness at being in a room filled with middle-aged and mostly male detectives. He guessed she was a prosecutor. He and Liz took seats. Within a few minutes, two more people joined them, both from the forensics unit.

"Okay," Carter said when everyone was seated. "Mark this day and time on your calendars, this will be our weekly staff meeting. I've asked someone from the crime scene unit to be here, as well as the prosecutor's office. Just in the interest of better communication. If you don't know them, Brian Frost there is forensics, and Evelyn Trent is from the prosecutor's office."

Vic liked Carter's approach. Crush, his last commander, had handled the links to the CSI team and the DA's office personally, keeping himself as the lynchpin. It looked like Carter couldn't be bothered with that kind of grandstanding.

Despite how well Carter kept the meeting moving, the sheer volume of reports dragged on for two hours. At least two detectives slipped out early, claiming appointments. By the time they were all dismissed, Vic had decided the idea was a good one, but needed a better format. Two hours was just too long. As he and Liz reached their desks, Carter walked up.

"Sounds like progress," Carter said, referring to the update he and Liz had given in the meeting.

"It's something," he answered. Liz stood in her cube, watching them.

"What's the strategy from here?"

"Track down the tattoos. We've also reached out to Dom Bandini and Thuds Lombardo." Inwardly, Vic cringed. He hadn't had time to tell Liz the reason he was talking to Levon was to set up a meeting with the two former gangsters. "Dom and Thuds worked for the same gangster Geno Varelli did," he added quickly. "That might give us some insights." He avoided looking at Liz.

"Okay, get at it." Carter turned to Liz. "Liz, good to have you on board." He nodded and strode away, leaving Vic and Liz standing.

"Yeah, I guess we do need to talk to them," Liz said slowly.

"Sorry, I didn't get a chance to tell you. That's why I called Levon. You know he sets up the meetings with Bandini."

Liz was about to say something but instead sat down. She didn't look angry, but from the heavy way she dropped into her seat, Vic knew she wasn't exactly happy, either. They hadn't worked together since Liz moved in with Levon. It occurred to Vic that because they lived together, Liz might have a proprietary feeling toward Levon and wanted to be the one to call him. He pushed the thought aside. He and Levon were friends and met before Liz started dating him. He didn't see why he had to walk on tiptoe when he wanted to call Levon.

His phone dinged. He checked the text message and smiled. He called across to Liz. "Guess what. Bandini wants to meet tonight."

Liz swiveled around on her chair and looked at him across the low wall of her cube. "Too fast. He's worried about something."

Vic smiled at her. "Exactly what I was thinking."

Liz pointed at her screen. "And look at this. That storage facility? It opened a year before Geno landed in prison."

"Now we're getting somewhere."

"We're just getting started," Liz added quickly, her eyes bright. "Ownership is a holding company. And guess who registered the holding company?"

Vic stared at her. It couldn't be that easy. "Dom Bandini?"

She shook her head. "Nope. Even better. Vincent Lombardo."

Vic stared at her. "I thought Dom ran everything and Thuds worked for him."

"Looks like Thuds has his own little empire. And that holding company owns six more businesses. A couple more storage facilities, and, get this, two ice cream franchises and two jewelry stores."

Vic laughed, he couldn't help himself. "Ice cream? Big bad Thuds owns ice cream shops?"

Liz shrugged. "Maybe he has a sweet tooth." She blinked slowly. "And isn't it convenient ice cream shops are mostly cash businesses."

Vic knew that was really the point. If your sweet tooth had to do with laundering cash, ice cream shops, and jewelry stores were a great way to do it. "You've got that right," he agreed. "And we need to visit that storage facility."

"And stare at a bunch of storage lockers? Not sure how that helps us."

Vic knew Liz was right. It was a long shot at best. "True. Low priority."

Chapter Twenty

The Fourth Day

He made a simple excuse to his wife that morning, something about a basement leak at one of the businesses, and followed his eldest daughter out of the house when she left for the school bus. It was so easy. His wife never questioned him. There was a time she did, early in their marriage, but no longer.

When he and Terri went to bed, she was willing but reserved. He knew what that meant. And sure enough, afterwards, as he made coffee for his travel mug, she nonchalantly mentioned the pitiful state of her car. How she really needed a new one. That he should know that from driving it.

He wondered if there was a suggestion of a threat in that last statement. There was certainly blackmail. Perhaps there was both. It gave him a little shiver of excitement.

He promised they would talk about it seriously the next time they met. He even asked what kind of car she wanted. Almost immediately her enthusiasm returned. He then lost six or seven minutes, his back to the front door, watching the top of her head bob back and forth at his waist. He didn't mind that his coffee was lukewarm by the time he reached the highway.

Why was it always this way, he wondered, as he drove. The pattern was so predictable. It didn't matter the type of relationship. When he and his wife first started dating, it felt like that was enough. Then a promise of love was required, to be confirmed by an engagement ring. A wedding came next.

Afterwards, a child. To him, each step was a toll booth requiring payment. She saw it as growing commitment, he saw it as a racket. What was it all for? A promise of eternity and security? Did she really believe they would become the sun at the center of their universe? That the gravity of their union would keep their daughters orbiting like moons? The stars shine only to guide them at night? Did she actually believe he would spend the rest of his life with her?

Terri and the other women were no different, but the currency required at their toll booths made more sense to him. Assignations in his car were fine early on, until the new requirement became a hotel room, and finally, the condo. Along the way, a sprinkling of jewelry was needed. Now a new car. He actually didn't mind those things. They only cost money. The difference was that he and Terri both knew it would end. Terri's toll booths were simply designed to provide her with something when it did. She'd have the money saved from not paying rent. Baubles for her neck and ears. A new car. He got what he wanted and she did too. To him, that was honest business, nothing more. Marriage was the real con. Each of those toll booths was a pound of flesh, another lost opportunity, and a foundation stone removed from his own world. He knew better. He'd grown up moving with his mother from town to town, forced to remember a new name at every school. His mother's marriage was a sun that burned their skin. His only orbiting moon was her fear whenever a dark sedan crept near them in the night. The stars were pinheads of terror.

Marriage guaranteed nothing.

Eternity was for the dead, the idea of security a mirage.

The road stretched ahead, and in the distance, a faded sign identified the storage facility. He shook off his thoughts. When he reached the entrance, he slowed and turned.

The driveway led him past the end of the first row of storage units, where the large plate glass window of an empty office stared at him. A poster taped in the corner offered a phone number to call for anyone interested in renting a unit.

He slowed at the end of the next row to read the sign indicating the range of numbers for the next row's units. Not yet. He continued to the next row, spotted the number range he needed, and turned his car. The number once tattooed on his father's arm was on the left, one from the end. He parked and stepped out. He was alone, the sky blue and high overhead. A light wind pressed against his face. In the distance, traffic hummed along one of Pittsburgh's northern expressways.

The lock on the unit's door was a combination lock. He glanced up and down the row, studying the roofline. A security camera stood at each corner, staring at him. He doubted they worked, reasoning that a small storage facility like this, well away from urban areas and rarely used, didn't use 24/7 security. It would be too expensive to maintain.

He lifted the combination lock. The black dial was weathered and faded to gray, the shank pinpricked by spots of rust. With his free hand, he removed the Post-it note from his shirt pocket and stuck it to the door above the lock. He gave the dial a spin and listened to the gentle clicks as it moved. His muscles sang. When was this lock last opened? Thirty years ago? Longer? He checked the combination, and after two full spins of the dial, worked through the sequence of numbers.

The lock clicked. The shank was stiff, but opened with a quick pull. He removed the lock, reached down, and grasped the handle on the miniature garage door. He lifted. As the door clattered open the inside of the unit flooded with light. He stood and stared. The space was about eight feet by eight feet square. In one back corner stood a shovel and pick-ax, next to folded sheet plastic. In the opposite corner were two worn duffel bags. But it was the footlocker directly in the center of the unit that drew his attention. He stepped over to it. It was old-fashioned, black, with brass trim. A small padlock was threaded through the hasp, locking it. He crossed to the duffels and unzipped them. Tools. Just about every kind he could think of, all of them scratched and dirty. Well used. Those were Geno's, he guessed. He selected a crowbar, returned to the footlocker, and with a quick jerk broke open the small padlock.

He lifted the lid to find two equal cinderblock-sized bricks of dollar bills wrapped in plastic and duct tape. From the end, he saw denominations of hundreds and fifties. He guessed they belonged to his father and Geno, shares from some long-ago heist. He ignored them. Instead, he picked up a large brown envelope and slid out a sheaf of papers. They were held together by two brass split pins at the top. He turned each page, smelling the mustiness of the document, until he reached a signature page at the end. There was his father's scrawl, Geno's childish signature, and one other name in a flowing, confident hand.

Dominick Bandini.

Smiling, he folded the document and returned it to the envelope. Stuck it in his back pocket. He went outside and opened his trunk. From the well for the spare tire, he removed the pistol he'd used to shoot Geno. He carried it inside and placed it in one of the duffel bags, collected the two bundles of cash, and placed them in the trunk. Closed the lid. He kept his head down as he did all this, to minimize his time in the cameras' line of sight. A minor precaution. Then he closed the footlocker and the door to the unit. From his pocket, he removed a new combination lock and snapped it into the hasp of the closed door. Slid behind the wheel of his car.

As easy as that.

He reversed up the alley between the rows of storage units and backed into the access road. He took his time. A minute later he turned onto the two-lane road that led to the highway.

He hadn't expected the cash. The letter with the will said nothing about that. But it didn't matter. The legal document was the prize. Its power wasn't complete, but it was enough to scare, to create leverage. That document was his sun. It would give him the moon and stars.

As he pulled onto the highway, he mulled over Terri's request for a new car. She'd wanted something small and sporty, not a high-end luxury car. That was something else he liked about her. She was clever enough to know his limits. She didn't overreach.

And, depending on how much cash was in those bundles, she might just get it.

Chapter Twenty-One

As the afternoon wound down, Vic called Anne. She answered on the third ring.

"Hey," he said, "I'm leaving to pick up Lettie, but I wanted to let you know that I have to meet someone after dinner."

A moment of silence. Vic guessed she was less concerned about his meeting than how this signaled a change in their lives after the last four years.

"Well, I guess I should have known this would happen when I told you to take the job."

"Sorry. I was hoping it might be longer before it started."

She took a slow breath. "Vic, just understand, we can't go back to the way it was before. You always out doing what you do. I can't handle Lettie *and* my job."

"I won't let that happen." Anne had quit her first job to be a stay-at-home mother when Dannie was born, and had kept the house and cooked as Dannie was raised. He didn't want her to go back to that. She was right, she couldn't do everything. And shouldn't. "I'll make this work."

"Let's see how it goes," Anne answered.

Vic heard a tired *here we go again* tone in her voice. He didn't want that to take hold. "No, seriously, I won't let it happen. You deserve a career now, after everything you did."

"Just keep in mind that when hockey season starts, I'll need to be at the arena for most of the games."

"We'll figure it out. Maybe we need a babysitter on the string."

"We do. But that's been Liz. If you're off chasing a case, she'll be with you." She paused. "How about my sister? She never had kids. She might like it."

The image of Anne's sister conjured in Vic's head. Her grey helmet of hair, her aggressive distaste toward him. That time when he and Anne were separated and she called the police on him because he'd arrived unexpectedly—smelling of booze—to talk to Anne.

"Um, let me think about that."

Anne's laugh silvered through his phone. "I was kidding. You'd shoot her before the night was out."

Vic sat back and stared at the ceiling, his phone plastered to his ear. "Am I that bad?"

"Both of you are. As I said, let's see how it goes, but finding a babysitter is a good idea. There will be a day."

"I'll see if I can think of anyone. Thanks. I'm going to pick up Lettie and dinner."

When he put down his phone he glanced at Liz. She was watching him.

"Fun, isn't it?" she asked.

"Yeah, I don't know how you did it with Jayvon. There was just the one of you."

"Well, that was after we moved up here. He was ten or eleven by then. When he was small it was still the three of us. And my mother-in-law helped out."

Vic noticed she didn't use her husband's name. He didn't press it. Liz's husband, a patrolman for the New Orleans Police Department, disappeared in the aftermath of Katrina, there one moment and gone the next. His body was never found. Vic wanted to say something, but Liz turned to her computer screen, ending the conversation. He called to her profile, "Levon says Bandini wants to meet at his daughter's apartment. Seven-thirty."

She turned back to him. "Have you been there before?"

It was a loaded question. Some years earlier, he, Liz, and Levon had saved the life of Mary Monahan, Bandini's daughter. Liz knew how startlingly intelligent and good-looking she was. At the time, Vic and Anne were separated. Liz was fishing, to see if there was something more between Vic and Mary.

"I have," Vic said, keeping his voice casual. "I met Bandini and Thuds there once. That's the only time." He added the last to answer Liz's implied question. "That was the meeting Bandini gave me the lead on the strippers who went missing, which is what led me to Dannie."

Liz acted as if she was unaware her question had a subtext. "Meet up beforehand?"

"Sure. The parking lot of Mary Monahan's office building. You can leave your car there. It's maybe ten minutes away."

Liz nodded and started tapping on her keyboard. Vic checked the clock, collected the files open on his desk, and dropped everything in a desk drawer. Locked it.

"See you then," he called, as he headed for his car.

Liz just nodded. Later, as Vic drove to collect Lettie from daycare, he thought about that exchange with Liz. She'd actually revealed something about her life before Pittsburgh. Something personal. He couldn't remember the last time she did that. He hoped that was a sign that she was coming to terms with the loss of her husband.

Vic picked up a pizza on the way home, and when Anne arrived they ate a quick dinner before Vic left. Liz was already waiting in the parking lot of Mary Monahan's office building when he arrived. She slid into the passenger seat of his car and they drove the seven blocks to Mary's apartment.

They parked down the street, in the first open spot Vic found. Walking back to Mary's building they passed a black Cadillac Escalade. Vic glanced inside, knowing it was Bandini's preferred transportation. It was empty, and he wondered why. Bandini always had a driver who doubled as a bodyguard, who usually stayed in the car when Bandini had a meeting.

Surprisingly, the front door to the apartment building was unlocked. A small sign reminded tenants the door was only locked from sunset to sunrise. Somehow, Vic had assumed that Mary would live in a more secure building. They took the elevator to the top floor and Vic knocked on one of only two apartment doors for the entire floor. Mary answered the door, stepped into the hall, and placed a hand on Vic's bicep. She reached up and kissed him softly on the cheek. Her shoulder-length brown hair swayed and Vic caught the whiff of a perfume that somehow felt like a promise.

"Vic, it's been too long." Her brown, evenly spaced eyes were warm. She turned to Liz. "And very good to see you, Liz. I'm so glad you're working together again." She smiled, her teeth a flash of white, and gestured for them to enter her apartment.

Inside, Mary closed the door and led them into a large living room. Vic drew up short, Liz shifting to his right so she didn't bump into him. Bandini and Thuds were sitting in armchairs overlooking the Allegheny River. Hovering near them were two other men. The one closest to Thuds was tall and beefy, with a chest that looked like he regularly bench-pressed small boats. His hands were so large it was a miracle they fit through the sleeves of his sports coat. Vic recognized him immediately. Mike Turcelli, driver and bodyguard. No wonder the Escalade was empty. The other was lanky and dressed like Bandini, right down to the banker's business-casual look, although their jackets carried too much of a silk sheen for that world. Thuds rose from his chair. He wore the black slacks, grey t-shirt and black sports coat that was his uniform. He was lean, weathered, the muscles in his neck as thick as hawsers. Vic hadn't seen him in five years, but he still gave the impression of being a drawn knife blade.

"Nobody's armed, Lenoski. Calm down," Bandini said from his armchair. He waved at the two younger men, who Vic guessed were in their late thirties. "You know Mike. This is Aaron Holt. Aaron started with us five or six years ago. He manages some of our businesses. You ought'a know them. They ought'a know you. One of my dumb-ass lawyers keeps saying I need a succession plan. I guess he hopes I'm dying."

Aaron nodded to Vic, his brown eyes flat and almost disinterested, as if he took prescription drugs to alleviate stress. Mike's eyes were brighter, and he still carried the confused look that usually inhabited his face.

Vic crossed to the men, Liz in tow, and they greeted one another and shook hands all around. From Liz's movements, Vic knew she was on edge, but her voice didn't betray it. Bandini waved at the empty seats across from him. Vic chose an armchair and Liz settled into a loveseat.

"Drinks?" Mary asked. She was still standing, her dress somehow elegant for something so fitted and brightly colored.

His back to the windows, Vic was distracted by the facing wall of bare brick and the two large and angrily-colored abstract paintings hanging there. He focused himself and glanced at the coffee table between him and Bandini. A glass of scotch or bourbon in a cut crystal glass sat in front of Bandini, a bottle and glass of imported water in front of Thuds. Vic asked for a beer and Liz requested water. Mary disappeared in the direction of what Vic took to be the kitchen.

"Geno Varelli," Bandini said, settling deeper into his chair. Behind him, Aaron remained standing, but shifted back a step. He seemed interested in what was going on outside the window.

"It's a hell of a thing," Bandini continued. He picked up his glass, glanced at Thuds, and swirled the brown liquid.

Vic thought Bandini had aged over the last five years. He still radiated energy, but the skin around his eyes was creased and puffy and his round face more jowly. Thuds was largely unchanged. Bandini had added to his paunch, Vic decided, while Thuds had lost weight, if that was possible.

Vic noticed that Turcelli was watching him, his brow still knotted in confusion. He recognized the hitch in Turcelli's nose from the time Thuds thought he needed a lesson. Vic waded in. "Thanks for meeting. Levon probably told you, but Liz and I got the Varelli case. We were hoping you guys might give us some background. We know you worked with Geno back in the day. Anything at all would be helpful."

"Allegheny County cops, huh?" Thuds interrupted.

Vic turned to him and met the gaze of his pale eyes. He didn't reply.

"That's right," Liz answered.

Thuds glanced at her but talked to Vic. "I thought you were done playing cop." He looked at Liz. "I knew you weren't."

Vic decided to see if he could get a reaction out of them. "Our new DA asked me to come back."

Thuds leaned forward. "You know her? How'd that happen?"

Vic hesitated. Thuds' questions were getting them off track and his response was a challenge. He remembered Liz's warning that talking to Bandini, and by extension, Thuds, wasn't a conversation, it was a give and take.

Bandini waved a hand as if clearing the air. "Hana Richards. I voted for her. We needed a change. Anyway. What do you want to know about Geno?"

Vic guessed that Hana got Bandini's vote because he didn't think a woman could do the job, which he would see as an advantage. Even if his illegal ways really were behind him. "Anything you can tell us. You worked with him, right? Back when you guys all worked for Paul Zielinski."

Bandini and Thuds glanced at one another, just as Mary returned from the kitchen, balancing a bottle of beer and another of water on a small tray. She bent over the table and placed the beer in front of Vic and the bottle of water near Liz. She lined up a glass beside each bottle, the movements of her hand precise. From the corner of his eye, Vic saw Aaron appraise Mary as she was bent over. Vic almost laughed out loud. Mary was so far out of his league he wasn't even playing the game.

"Thanks, Mary," Vic said quietly as she finished. She flashed him a smile and straightened up. Vic sensed Liz watching them, gauging their interaction.

Vic looked at Bandini. "Paul Zielinski?"

"Yeah," Bandini said slowly. "We all worked for him." He took a sip of his drink and returned the glass to the table.

Mary slipped from the room. Mike Turcelli seemed to realize the question wasn't aimed at him and faded into a corner of the room, where he looked about as unobtrusive as a rhinoceros. It crossed Vic's mind that Mary might have chosen not to be in the room. It was an easy way to avoid legal entanglements should they arise later.

"C'mon, we all worked for Zielinski," Thuds said, egging Bandini on. Vic heard a trace of annoyance in Thuds' voice, as if he thought Bandini was stalling.

Bandini sighed as if unhappy he couldn't get out of the conversation. "Okay, yeah. I handled a lot of Zielinski's side jobs. I usually picked Lombardo to help me." He shot a glance at Thuds, and Vic wondered at him using Thuds' last name. It was a message, he just didn't know them well enough to read it. "Anyway, Paul brought Geno in and the two of them got tight real fast. Geno did jobs that minted money. Paul made the investments."

"When you say jobs," Liz cut in. "Like what?"

Bandini hesitated, and Liz added, "Most of this stuff is long past the statute of limitations. We're just trying to figure out if anyone might have it out for Geno."

Vic was surprised. It was a kind of tact Liz wouldn't have bothered with when they first partnered.

"When you put it that way," Bandini said slowly. "Look, you have to understand the times. Late eighties. The ways we made money were going away." His voice trailed off.

"Zielinski knew we had to go legit," Thuds cut in. "He and Geno made a deal to do just that. And he kept up his end of the bargain."

Bandini nodded. "By then Zielinski was only making enough to keep the organization going. We needed money to grow in a new direction. And that was the deal between Zielinski and Geno. Everyone called Zielinski the Hammer, but he was shrewd when it came to business. He understood how the city was changing. The mills were closing, people were leaving the city, the economy was lousy, figuring out where the growth was took smarts. He had them. And if Geno brought in the capital, Zielinski would figure out how to invest it in new ways of doing things."

Vic sorted out what Bandini was saying, glad it aligned with Justin Day's comments. "One thing, though. What did Geno get out of it? He just handed cash over to Zielinski? I don't buy that."

"Oh hell no." Bandini eyed his glass. "The deal was Zielinski only invested in clean businesses, and Geno got a piece of that. He was a silent partner. It even got written up that way. I mean they had a contract. That was new as well. Zielinski wanted everything legit. No more handshake deals. He got a lawyer on the string and papered all the deals, like any legitimate business. Zielinski even found an accountant, started paying taxes. Most of the other guys we knew thought he was crazy."

"Did he ever use the clean businesses to launder money for the other activities?" Liz was on the edge of the love seat, watching Bandini.

Bandini gave her a mean smile. "You'd have to ask Zielinski."

Vic cut in before Liz said something that might end the interview. She might have learned tact, but she wouldn't ignore a shot like that. "You're saying there's a paper trail on all this?"

Bandini shrugged. "Well, there was. Those early businesses, they aren't around anymore. Haven't been for years."

Aaron shifted his weight, but Vic was mostly aware of Thuds watching Bandini, his eyes hooded. Vic thought about the businesses closing, the span of years from then until now. "But you've built up a heck of a portfolio since then. You invest in start-ups, own all those restaurants, strip clubs, nightclubs, even ice cream stores." He watched Thuds out of the corner of his eye as he said the last, but Thuds didn't move a muscle. "And the FBI went through your portfolio some years ago and didn't find any money laundering. Even your taxes were up to date. We know that. When I was investigating the murder of your son-in-law I talked to the FBI about it," he said quietly, watching Bandini.

Bandini shrugged. "You know what I know."

"Okay," Vic said. "So what happened? Geno got nabbed robbing a bank and his rainmaking days are over. Eighteen months later the county nails Zielinski. How do things develop from there?"

Bandini took his time downing the last of his drink. Vic realized he had yet to try his beer, so he took a quick sip. The chill was gone and it tasted sour. He put the bottle back down and realized he should have poured it into the glass, like everyone else.

"Well, not my finest hour," Bandini said slowly. If he noticed Vic's slip about the glass, he showed no interest. "I was new to it all, and I made some mistakes."

"How so?" Liz asked.

"Zielinski tapped me to run the businesses he'd started with Geno. The clean ones. I didn't really pay attention to them much at first, I thought Zielinski would be out pretty quickly. Then the judge threw away the key and I realized I was on my own. I should have done a better job, but it was all new to me. I had to close them. Bankrupt. But I always thought Zielinski was right, the best way to go was legit. From then on, that's what I did. Learned from my mistakes and kept going. Been that way ever since."

Vic knew, without a shadow of a doubt, that Bandini was skating over the surface. He'd also said two things that didn't align. First, that Zielinski was good at picking winning businesses, yet in the same breath he'd said those businesses went bankrupt.

"What made the businesses fail?" Vic asked, carefully.

"Didn't watch the overhead. When they started to go under I tried promotions to close the gap, but it didn't work."

Vic was aware of Mike staring at Bandini. Aaron had shifted a step closer and cocked his head to listen. Vic realized this history of Bandini's empire was probably new to them, as was Bandini admitting he made mistakes. Vic wasn't satisfied with Bandini's narrative, but he had no way to push back against it. He didn't know enough. Liz settled back into her love seat, and he knew she was thinking the same thing. Bandini was providing a story that couldn't be verified. Vic gradually became aware of Thuds staring at him. He met his eyes and had the immediate feeling Thuds was waiting for him to see something, to make a connection.

Or was worried he would.

Vic turned back to Bandini. "What about Geno's circle of friends. Did he have family?"

"That are still alive?" Bandini laughed.

Liz just stared at him. She didn't seem to care about the disgust that showed on her face.

"Maria," Bandini shouted, and looked around for her. Vic didn't miss that he called her by her given name, not the one she adopted when she left home. Everyone waited, and it was a long fifteen seconds before Mary stepped into the room. Bandini held up his glass. Mary took it without a word and disappeared down the hallway. Bandini turned back to Vic. "Yeah, yeah. Sorry. Circle of friends. I can make a list."

"Wife? Girlfriend?" Vic asked.

CHAPTER TWENTY-ONE

"Not that I know of," Bandini sighed.

Vic nodded his thanks. He took a notebook from his sports coat pocket and pushed it, along with a pen, across the table to Bandini. "I would appreciate it if you could write down the names. Everyone you can think of. Then his enemies."

Bandini shuffled forward on the armchair and hunched over the coffee table. Mary appeared in the doorway, carrying his glass. She put it down next to her father and squatted next to him.

"Last one," she said softly, but loud enough for everyone to hear. "Your blood pressure."

He waved a hand at her. "Yeah, yeah."

Vic caught himself before he smiled. As she rose, Mary gave Vic a small head shake of annoyance.

"What jobs?" Liz asked. "You never said which jobs Geno did to raise money."

Thuds turned to her. "Definitely the armored car depot. The bank in Greensburg. That was a nice piece of work. There was a racetrack they hit in West Virginia that didn't make the papers here. Geno was in his prime then."

Vic prodded. "You said *they*. Geno had a crew, right? At least a black guy?"

Thuds nodded, his gaze inward. "Yeah. Priest." He smiled, and Vic thought he saw genuine warmth in it. "You know, I don't think I ever really knew Priest's real name."

"Why that nickname?" Liz asked.

Thuds shrugged. "Priest didn't drink, he wore this gold cross around his neck. Not one of those big clunky ones like the guys today. Small one, the kind someone religious would wear. And he kept Geno on the straight and narrow. Made sure he was honest, in a way."

"Disciplined," Bandini interjected. "Geno was a loose cannon until he hooked up with Priest. Priest taught him to be patient and that the work was in the planning, not the execution. I remember Zielinski talking about that."

Thuds' gaze returned to Vic. "When Priest showed up Geno even stopped dating everything that moved. He'd always had that problem. But he gave up on the ladies, as far as I could see. The two of them put it all together and for about five, six years, they were tight. Real pros. Never got caught, and every job was a huge payday. And they were clean with each other. Honest with their crew."

"Then how did he get caught on a bank job?" Liz asked. "It's out of character."

Neither Bandini nor Thuds said anything for a moment. Bandini swigged the last of his drink and looked at Thuds. "Priest was gone by then, right?"

Thuds nodded, his gaze inward again. "Yeah. Priest showed up out of nowhere one day and disappeared the same way. It was maybe four or five months later Geno got nabbed."

Liz turned to Vic. "I read the arrest report. Bank alarm went off at ten-zero-seven, police response to the location was six minutes. They found Geno a couple of blocks away on foot."

"On foot?" Vic frowned. It made no sense. He looked at Thuds. "My experience is that guys like Geno have a clock in their heads when they're inside a bank. They know they only have three minutes, tops. But most of all they have an exit plan. A driver."

Liz nodded. "His accomplice ran after two minutes. Never caught. Geno wanted one of the tellers to open a gate inside the vault to get to the real cash. She was scared and kept dropping the keys, couldn't find the right one, and when the gate was finally open Geno spent too long bagging all the cash. Then his duffel was so heavy he couldn't move fast. He gets outside, and guess what, when the accomplice ran he took the getaway car. Geno was on foot."

Nobody said anything for several seconds. Vic turned to Thuds. "Do you know the guy who ran?" He wondered if there might still be a witness somewhere.

Thuds started to shake his head but stopped. He frowned. "Yeah. Holy shit. Haven't thought of the guy in years, but at the time he pissed me off so much I'd get mad just thinking about him. Last name was Flanagan. Just cut and ran."

"He was new," Bandini said sharply, staring at Thuds. "Not the regular wheel man."

Vic glanced from one to the other. Bandini started to take a drink, hesitated when he saw his glass was empty, but upended the last few drops into his mouth anyway.

If Thuds was bothered by Bandini's retort, he didn't show it. The distant look was back in his eyes. "I remember all that now," he said slowly. "Geno was nabbed a couple of weeks before Zielinski got married." He glanced at Bandini. "Remember that? Geno was supposed to be best man. I forget who stepped in for him."

"That lawyer Zielinski liked. Mendelbaum."

Vic pointed at his notebook. It seemed to take Bandini a moment to understand what Vic wanted, but Bandini finally leaned forward and added the lawyer's name to the notebook.

"Funny," Thuds said slowly. "Right then we thought we were on top of the world. We'd figured it all out. Looking back, that was the beginning of the end of those days. Eighteen months later, Zielinski's in prison with Geno."

"What was the name of Zielinski's wife?" Liz asked, looking from one to the other.

Bandini pointed in the direction Mary had disappeared. "Mary, same as my daughter. Of course, my Mary's real name is Maria. Just to confuse things. She just doesn't think Maria is white bread enough."

"The son's name was David," Thuds said quietly. "I went to the christening."

Without being told, Bandini leaned forward and wrote the names in Vic's notebook.

When he finished, Vic asked, "And what happened to Zielinski and Geno's partnership? I mean they were both in jail."

Bandini shrugged. "Well, like I said, they went bankrupt. When that happened, the partnership was done."

A shadow crossed Thuds' face and he turned to Bandini. A question. Disbelief? But it was gone so quickly Vic wasn't sure. He looked at Liz. She was watching Thuds as well. She turned to him and their eyes met. She gave just the slightest of nods.

"Okay," Vic said into the silence, and turned back to Bandini. He leaned over the table, retrieved his notebook and pen, and slid them into his jacket pocket. "I appreciate you talking to us on short notice." He looked at Liz. "Anything else?" He already knew the answer, but did it anyway.

She gave just a small shake of her head.

Vic glanced from Bandini to Thuds, who looked tired, suddenly. "We may want to talk to you again, and if you remember anything else, let us know. Just call Levon."

He rose and Liz did the same. Mike separated himself from the wall, leaned into the hallway, and said something. Vic glanced at Aaron. His face was slightly flushed, and he wondered if perhaps Aaron didn't like being relegated to sideshow status.

"Good to meet you," Vic said to Aaron.

Aaron considered him, his brown eyes cool and calm. "Yeah," he said finally. "Interesting to hear everyone's take on the old days." He flashed a smile, but it wasn't enthusiastic.

Mary appeared, and after hand-shaking all around, led Vic and Liz to the doorway.

"He's a pain, my father," she said in a whisper when they were outside in the hall. "Doctor told him to lose weight and get his blood pressure down, and he couldn't care less."

"Just keep after him. Some people are more hard-headed than others," Liz replied.

"Hard-headed is right." She turned to Vic and smiled. "We need to have lunch. I want to hear about Lettie."

"That'll be a long lunch," Liz said quickly. "He never shuts up about her."

"That's how it should be." She gave Vic a quick kiss on the cheek and held out her hand to Liz.

Outside, Vic and Liz walked in silence until they were past the black Cadillac.

"They aren't telling us the half of it," Liz said finally.

Vic nodded as they passed under a streetlight. "We need to get to them separately. They tag-teamed us today. We should have seen that coming.

112

And something is going on with Thuds. He's not comfortable with what Bandini's saying."

"I saw that."

"Let's work the list he gave us. See what we can find out. We don't have enough to get them to talk, yet. And I just don't think Bandini was giving us a straight story about what happened to Zielinski's properties."

They reached Vic's car.

"Works for me." Liz smiled into the night sky. "Kinda funny seeing Mary give it to her father. Telling him he was done drinking. I bet she's the only woman in the world who can talk to him that way."

"Down the road, there might be a judge who does." Vic looked over the roof of the car at her. "Or a DA."

Chapter Twenty-Two

Liz was at her desk when Vic arrived the next morning. He hung up his coat and was barely seated before Liz called across the aisle to him.

"That list Bandini gave us last night? Known associates?"

"Yes."

"Pretty much a bust. Almost all of them are dead or in jail. The only one who might give us something is the lawyer Zielinski and Geno used. Mendelbaum. He still has an office. I looked him up. He's well into his eighties. Not sure how often he actually goes into work, but I left a message for him."

"I guess we start there. How about Zielinski's wife. Mary? Their son? Maybe Zielinski said something to her about the businesses he set up with Geno."

Liz shrugged. "Nothing yet. It's like they fell off the earth."

Vic sat back and squeezed the bridge of his nose with his thumb and forefinger. His mind flashed on the hitch in Mike Turcelli's nose. He'd spotted it as soon as they were in Mary's apartment. The last time he'd seen him, Mike Turcelli had a couple of black eyes and a broken nose, all courtesy of Thuds. It was Thuds' way of reminding Mike he only worked for Thuds, and wasn't allowed to freelance.

"Sleeping on the job?"

Vic opened his eyes to find Carter Lee staring down at him.

Carter smirked as he dragged a chair from a nearby empty desk. He settled himself in the aisle between Vic and Liz. "Need an update, guys. Where are you on this Varelli case?"

Vic glanced at Liz but she pointed at him to go ahead. "Still digging into his background." Vic walked him through their conversation with Bandini and Thuds.

"You got to them fast," Carter said when he finished. Carter's head was tilted in a way that signaled he was impressed.

"Bumped into them before." Vic didn't want Carter to know how close he was to Bandini's daughter Mary, and that Liz's boyfriend once saved her life. He added quickly, "It was weird, they were so fast to agree to a meeting I, we," he gestured at Liz, "thought they were worried about something. But it didn't show last night."

"Except for Mike Turcelli being with them," Liz pointed out.

Vic nodded in agreement. "Mike is driver and bodyguard to Bandini," Vic explained, so Carter could follow the conversation. "Usually he stays with their vehicle. Last night he was in the apartment with them. Made us wonder if they wanted close protection. But then again they also had a guy we've never met, Aaron Holt. I guess he's Bandini's new golden boy."

Carter nodded, the gaze from his brown eyes flicking from Vic to Liz. "Okay. I was going to tell you guys to get moving, but it sounds like you are. And who picked up Varelli's body?"

Vic and Liz looked at each other. It was Vic who stumbled out the question. "The body was cleared and someone picked it up from the morgue?"

Carter glared at him. "Absolutely. Body cleared yesterday. Coroner did the autopsy and ran all the tox screens. Took DNA. No reason to hold it. Some funeral home picked it up early this morning."

"Do we know who made the arrangements with the funeral home?" Liz asked quickly.

Carter stood and rolled the chair back into the empty cube. He looked from Liz to Vic. "I feel like that's something you guys should already know."

"We're on it," Vic said quickly.

"Thanks."

"Wait." Vic organized this thoughts. "Have you heard anything from the DA's office about Geno's file? If he worked as a CI?"

"Nothing yet." With a quick pivot, Carter headed to his office.

Vic turned to Liz. "Isn't the coroner supposed to check with us before releasing the body?"

Liz held up her hand so he could see she was holding her phone. She was dialing with her other hand.

"Why are we always a step behind?" he said, more to himself. He picked up his keys, bent over to unlock his desk, and stopped. The top drawer was misaligned. He tugged on the handle and it slid open easily. He stared at his case binder, a cold feeling rising inside him. Policy was for him to use the online system, which locked case documents inside their electronic systems. It was his own old-fashioned habit to make a binder with hard-copy of all the documents. Had he forgotten to lock the drawer? He started to chastise himself and stopped. He did lock it, he was sure. He glanced at Liz. She was hunched over her desk, talking on the telephone. Vic looked around his cube.

Both boxes of Gabe Chilton's belongings were gone.

He stood, swung on his jacket, took a step, and stopped. He returned to his desk and locked the drawer to check if there was a glitch with the lock. It didn't budge when he pulled. He turned and walked swiftly to the administrator shared by the detectives.

"Hi," he said, trying to remember the woman's name. They'd met on his first day of work, but her name hadn't stuck. She looked up. Despite the upward tilt of her head, she still owned an impressive double chin. Her brown eyes were sharp and hard.

"Karen," she said, reading right away that he'd forgotten her name.

"Sorry." Vic scrambled to be polite and keep his voice calm. He really wanted to shout. "Um, I noticed the boxes in my cube are gone. Gabe Chilton's belongings? Were they sent to him?"

"Beats me." She turned to her computer, her plump fingers tapping the keys, and a spreadsheet opened on her monitor. She squinted at it. Vic saw a pair of reading glasses on the desk but she didn't put them on. "Here." She pointed at the screen. "He picked them up himself last night."

"He can just walk in here?"

She turned to face him and interlaced her fingers on the desktop. "Of course not. That would be against policy. He was accompanied by another detective."

"Who?"

"Dave Norbert. Dave brought him in as a guest."

"Great," Vic said quickly, hearing the false note in his voice. "I was wondering what was taking so long to move those boxes. I wanted Gabe to have them."

Karen's gaze didn't shift from him. "Dave asked me yesterday if I could clear Gabe in to get them. I said sure."

Vic had the immediate understanding that Karen was someone to keep on his side. She might be the shared administrator for all the detectives, but it looked like she ran the department to the letter of each policy. "Yep. Sounds good. Thanks!" He tried to sound like he was in a good mood.

He returned to his desk, unlocked the drawer, and went through his binder a page at a time. Nothing was missing. He understood the unlocked drawer could be an innocent mistake. Perhaps Gabe still had a desk key, and had simply checked to make sure he'd collected all his belongings. But after the leaks to the Newsburgh website, and Gabe being the likely culprit, he didn't like the possibilities. He decided to check the Newsburgh site regularly over the course of the day.

"John Jefferson," Liz called to him.

Vic sat back, looking at her.

She smiled. "Coroner's office gave me the name of the funeral home. I called them, they said they were contacted by a John Jefferson and instructed to pick up Geno's body. Burial is Friday at eleven. Guess where?"

"Allegheny Cemetery?"

"Got it on one. Then I called our friend Evan Gelhorn. He confirmed it. Plot was bought by a John Jefferson. And here's where it gets interesting." Liz smiled.

"I'm not giving you a drum roll."

Liz raised two fingers and waggled them. "He bought two plots. One right next to the other."

"We'll have to ask our friend John about it on Friday."

"My thoughts exactly."

Vic turned to his monitor. "I'll see what I can find out about him."

"Yeah, be good if you did some actual work."

Vic waggled one of his own fingers at her.

"Great working with you again, Vic."

Vic turned to say something but Liz's phone rang. She snatched it up so he couldn't get the last word in.

Vic did a general search on the John Jefferson name, but came up empty. Several John Jeffersons had criminal records, but he couldn't tell if they were the right person. He didn't know how John Jefferson related to Geno. That was a question they needed to ask him.

"We're in business," Liz called to him.

"How's that?"

"That was our legal eagle, Mendelbaum. He'll be in his office until four, should we want to stop by."

Vic stood. "No time like the present."

Liz rose as well and shrugged into her leather jacket. "I knew I kept you around for a reason."

Chapter Twenty-Three

Vic and Liz found the front door to Andrew Mendelbaum Esq.'s offices next to the kitchen door of a Chinese restaurant in Pittsburgh's Squirrel Hill neighborhood. Across the road stood a coffee shop and a Thai restaurant. A brass plaque with Mendelbaum's name stood out from the list of businesses inside the building. It needed a good polish. The door opened onto stairs that led to a second-floor hallway. Mendelbaum's name was on the first door to the right. Vic knocked, and was rewarded with a distant, reedy voice telling them to enter.

The door opened into a surprisingly large waiting room with an empty receptionist's desk under a burned-out fluorescent light. To the left of the desk, a hallway with four doors led to a window at the front of the building.

From the last doorway at the end of the hall, a short, hunched man with wispy grey hair shuffled out of a doorway and waved them toward him. As they walked, Vic smelled garlic and ginger and heard a rapid clanking of metal on metal. The entry and start of the hallway were directly above the kitchen of the Chinese restaurant, he realized.

Andrew Mendelbaum was no taller than five-foot-seven, bald, his round face overwhelmed by large glasses. He looked younger than Vic expected for someone in his eighties, but his stiff movements gave away his age.

As they shook hands he waved his other arm toward the rest of the offices.

"Just me now," he said, his voice thin. "We had four lawyers crammed in here years ago. A receptionist and a couple of paralegals. Can't afford to keep them."

He led them into his office, made spacious by a fifteen-foot ceiling. Two large windows overlooked a donut shop and an ice cream parlor. The room contained a large wooden desk and a round conference table with four chairs. Mendelbaum led them to the table, pointing at seats.

Once they were comfortable, Mendelbaum looked from Vic to Liz, his eyes bright. "I'd offer you something to drink, but I don't keep anything here these days. There is a coffee shop across the street."

Liz shook her head just slightly.

"We're fine," Vic said. "We appreciate you talking to us on short notice."

"Well." Andrew spread his hands. "Geno Varelli. It's a murder case, right?" He frowned, and his face seemed to collapse around his glasses. "I represented Mr. Varelli after his arrest. Well, my office did. We had a few lawyers working on it. We could put together a good team back then." He sighed. "Time catches up to you. We just don't have the client base anymore. Not sure I can work the sixteen hours a day I used to, anyway. But there's still loose ends to tie up. And I hate golf." He smiled, and Vic was taken at the warmth that radiated from him.

Liz said slowly, "We're actually interested in how you might have helped Mr. Varelli before he was arrested."

"Oh? Like what?" He looked directly at Liz and didn't break his gaze. When he blinked his thick glasses accentuated the movement.

Liz glanced at Vic.

"We had a conversation last night," Vic said slowly, "with a couple of people who are knowledgeable about Mr. Varelli's activities in the years prior to his arrest." Vic heard the formality in his voice and wondered where it came from. Somehow the lawyer's wrinkled face and thick glasses brought it out. "They mentioned that Geno Varelli signed at least one legal agreement with Paul Zielinski. We're interested in that document. They said your office executed it."

Mendelbaum blinked, the movement reminding Vic of a wiper blade moving across a windshield. "Ah." He sat back.

They all sat in silence for a few moments, until Mendelbaum leaned forward again. He carefully placed his elbows on the table. "Unfortunately, murder investigation or not, I would need a warrant to release any documents. Client privilege."

Vic didn't understand. "Both men are dead. How can it matter now?"

"Yes, Mr. Zielinski and Mr. Varelli have passed away. However, on several of those documents, another signatory is very much alive. Therefore, I can't be compelled to release a copy of the document without an order from the court."

"Who else signed the document?" Liz asked.

Mendelbaum hunched, a defensive posture. "As I just said, I'm not at liberty to say."

"One of your clients?" Vic asked, getting annoyed.

"Of course. I'm invoking client privilege."

Vic had a good idea who the third person might be, but he didn't say. "Can you at least tell us what type of document it is?"

Mendelbaum spread his hands above the table. "I'm afraid that falls under client privilege as well."

Vic suddenly understood what Mendelbaum was implying. "You're saying the document signed by these people, two of whom are dead, is still binding in some way?"

Mendelbaum thought for a moment before answering. "Of course."

Vic straightened in his seat. They were at an impasse. It would be almost impossible to get a warrant. They just didn't have a compelling reason to see the document, at least one that a judge would agree with. But something needled at him about the way Mendelbaum answered their questions. He tried to put his finger on it.

"Okay," Liz said slowly, "Let me ask another question. This is specific only to our boy Geno Varelli, and he's dead. You said you defended him at trial. One of the things we're struggling with is why he spent so long in the bank, during the robbery that led to his arrest. Did he ever mention to you why he was in the vault so long?"

Mendelbaum nodded once, slowly. His eyes turned inward. Vic was glad Liz asked the question. He wanted time to think about another way to get at the document Varelli, Zielinski and someone else signed. Because he was pretty sure the third signatory was Bandini.

"I'm not sure," Mendelbaum said slowly. "We did talk about the timeline inside the bank quite a bit. We thought the prosecutor would bring it up, and of course, he did. He tried to make it look like Mr. Varelli was some kind of thoughtless monster, prolonging everyone's fear. Our defense, of course, was that Mr. Varelli took so long because the teller was nervous and kept fumbling and dropping the keys, and Varelli didn't want to stress her more. He tried to be patient with her."

"Right," Liz said. "But Varelli was a pro. Usually, he would cut and run at two or three minutes."

Mendelbaum slowly shook his head. "It's so long ago." He frowned. "There was one night, we were practicing his testimony for when he took the stand. It was late, after midnight. I think I asked him that question. I have to ask every question I think the prosecutor might throw at him on cross-examination. It's the only way he can be prepared. I remember he laughed." Mendelbaum shut his eyes for a few moments. "He said something like it was ironic he was caught on this job, because it was the last one. That's why he needed as much as he could take."

"Not sure that would have been helpful if it came out in trial," Liz said gently.

Mendelbaum smiled. "No. We went back to the earlier answer about him wanting to calm the teller. All we were doing was throwing him on the mercy of the court. Not that it helped much. Anyway, I wish I could be more precise on the details, it was just so long ago."

Listening to the exchange, and seeing Mendelbaum struggle with his memories, made Vic understand what bothered him earlier. "Could we go back to the agreement for a moment, the one signed by Varelli and Zielinski? And someone else?"

Mendelbaum looked at him. "I think I've said everything I can say about that. At least at this point."

"Right, but tell me something. How many of those types of agreements have you written up over your career?"

He shrugged. "Hundreds, I would guess. Perhaps thousands. Why?"

Vic leaned forward. "But you remembered the specifics of that document exactly. Despite the fact it was signed all those years ago and is just one of hundreds your office created. You knew it was still binding. It was fresh in your mind. Why is that?"

Mendelbaum blinked. "Well, yes, you have a point." He glanced at the window. "I reviewed it yesterday."

Vic tapped his middle finger on the tabletop. "And why did you do that?"

Mendelbaum's gaze skated across Liz's face and settled on Vic. "Someone called me about it yesterday. They wanted to know if it was still binding. I had to pull it from the files and review it."

"Who called?" Liz asked.

Mendelbaum blinked. "I'm not sure I can say."

Vic felt his shoulders tense. "Was it someone who signed the document?"

"Um, no." Mendelbaum squirmed in his seat.

"You told that person but not us?" Vic sat back. "I wouldn't call that charitable, Mr. Mendelbaum, *Esquire*. I might even think it flirts with obstructing an investigation."

Color rose to Mendelbaum's cheeks. "It does not."

"It could be something the bar association finds unethical," Liz said quietly.

"It was a judgment call," Mendelbaum said hurriedly. "There are mitigating factors."

"Such as," Vic growled.

"The person who called is associated with one of the signers of the document. Even has power of attorney over some of his affairs. He frequently calls for clarifications on documents associated with their businesses."

"But isn't a client," Vic shot back.

"No, not technically." Mendelbaum licked his lips. His eyes had a cornered look. He glanced at the window but didn't seem to find any help outside. "Fine, it was Vincent Lombardo," he said thickly.

Vic had to remember to breathe. "And when exactly did he call yesterday?"

"It was early afternoon." Mendelbaum took a deep breath. "He called and asked about it, and I told him I needed to review the document. I found it, read it, and called him back at about four-thirty."

Liz sat back. Vic saw her brain working. Thuds had wanted to know the content and implications of the document before they all met the night before. That was significant, he just didn't know why. Not yet.

"That's a very fine line you're walking, Mr. Mendelbaum," Vic said carefully.

Mendelbaum's eyes were liquid and he looked disappointed in himself. "Is there anything else?" he finally squeaked out.

Vic glanced at Liz. She had a small smile on her face. She shook her head.

"Not at the moment, Mr. Mendelbaum," Vic answered. "But you can expect that we'll be back."

They all rose. Mendelbaum didn't look happy and Vic thought he moved a bit more like someone feeling their age. He and Liz were almost to the door when another thought came to Vic and he turned back to Mendelbaum.

"One other thing, Mr. Mendelbaum."

Mendelbaum's eyes blinked at him from behind his glasses.

"When you were representing Mr. Varelli, did he ever say anything to you about a storage unit? Make any dispensation on how to handle one if he passed away?"

Mendelbaum tapped a knuckle on the top of the table, as if the sound might unlock a door in his memory. Vic was glad that he was at least making the effort to remember.

His gaze cleared. "Nothing I can recall. Although it was some time ago."

"Thanks, I was just wondering."

Vic turned and followed Liz down the hall.

Chapter Twenty-Four

Vic and Liz were silent all the way back to the car. Inside, Vic didn't turn the ignition.

Liz stared at the windshield. "Thuds Lombardo."

"Starts to explain why he was acting weird last night, but I still don't know what it's all about. And Mendelbaum as much as told us Bandini is the other signatory on the contract."

Liz turned to him. "We have something to ask Bandini, now. Wish we'd had it last night."

"And the other interesting question is why Bandini doesn't care about any of this. It's like Bandini doesn't think the document is in force anymore." Vic tapped the steering wheel, following his thought through. "If Bandini was worried about something he signed years ago, he would have called Mendelbaum himself. Kept the call under the umbrella of confidentiality. But he didn't. I'm thinking Bandini doesn't even know that Thuds called Mendelbaum. I'm wondering if Thuds is working a different angle."

"Different than Bandini?"

"He's done it before. Remember what happened with Mary Monahan? Bandini had a bunch of his businesses in his daughter's name when she was a minor. It was some kind of tax dodge. The document gave her control of the businesses when she turned twenty-one, but the lawyer was supposed to dissolve the agreement before that and move them under a new trust. Thuds knew the lawyer had forgotten to do that, told Mary about it, and on her twenty-first birthday, she sued for control of the businesses. In the end, she retained ownership but gave the cash flow back to her father, on the condition he give better benefits to the people working for him. Thuds could have stopped that happening, but he didn't."

"Bandini let Thuds go behind his back?"

"I don't think Bandini ever found out. Ask Levon, he knows about it. At the time Mary sued for control of the businesses, she was smart enough to drop out of sight. Bandini hired Levon to find her. That's how Levon and Bandini met. But when Levon found her, she told him why she was hiding. He ended up brokering the deal between Mary and her father."

Liz let out a slow breath. "So Thuds is going rogue again?"

"Maybe. Or Bandini knows something Thuds doesn't. Or both." Vic started the car and checked before pulling into traffic. "And we don't even know what the document says. Or who else signed it."

"Has to be Bandini." Liz fished her phone out of her jacket pocket. "Bandini said he was left in charge when Zielinski went to jail."

"That's my thinking as well," Vic said.

Liz fell silent, staring at her phone. After a long minute, she said, "Screw this. I'm getting tired of it."

Vic glanced at her as he pulled onto the freeway. "What?"

"Damn Newsburgh has another story about us."

Vic went cold, thinking about his unlocked desk drawer. "What does it say?"

Liz read the story out loud as he drove. Again, the focus was on the lack of progress solving the case, and ended with an attack on Hana Richards, complaining about her inexperience and youth. It also suggested she should go back to being a public defender. "Hana has to respond," Liz said when she finished reading.

"Lee and Hana think it's Gabe Chilton talking to Newsburgh. Lee said they discussed it, and they're waiting for Chilton to say something he shouldn't, so they can jump on him with both feet."

"Threaten his pension, or something?"

"I would think." Vic squeezed the steering wheel. "Here's the other thing."

Liz turned to him, waiting.

"You know how I keep a binder with hard copies of all the case notes and reports?"

"Yeah. Mr. Old School."

"I locked it in my desk drawer last night when I went home. When I came in this morning, the drawer was unlocked. I checked, and it turns out Gabe Chilton was in the office last night to pick up his stuff. Dave Norbert brought him in as a guest."

"Jerk."

"Chilton might still have a desk key. He could have looked through the binder. And today there's another Newsburgh story. Luckily, I hadn't added notes on our meeting with Bandini and Lombardo. That wouldn't look good and if it got in the paper, Bandini would never meet with us again."

"You need to quit using the binder."

"Or take it with me wherever I go."

"Better to stick to department policy."

Vic knew she was right, but didn't like the idea of changing his work habits. "I need to ask Chilton if he has a desk key."

"Great. Two old white guys slugging it out. You're on your own on that one."

Vic suppressed a smile as he pulled into the parking lot. A few minutes later, as they walked onto the floor, Karen called to them. "Commander wants to see you guys in his office."

"Thanks, Karen," Vic said quickly, so she'd know he remembered her name.

He and Liz shed their jackets at their desks and walked to Lee's office. Vic knocked on the doorframe. Carter was on the phone but waved them in.

They both sat. Unlike Crush, their last commander, Carter ended the call as quickly as he could. Crush liked to make people wait before he talked to them.

"Just a quick update," Carter said, hanging up the phone. "You know we tried that weekly meeting and it took two hours?"

Vic nodded.

"Format is wrong. We can't take two hours a week to update. I'm dividing the detectives into four teams. A, B, C, and D. I'll meet with each team once a week to stay up to date. We can probably get through each meeting in fifteen or twenty minutes. Then every couple of weeks we'll all meet with the prosecutor's office and only update them on cases relevant to them. Does that work?"

"Beats a two-hour meeting," Liz said, after a quick glance at Vic.

"Works for me," Vic agreed.

"Good. You guys are team C. You can come up with your own name, if you want. Just the two of you right now. I've got two empty positions to fill and they'll both be for your team. Hopefully, in a month or two, you guys will be up to four to match the other teams. Okay?"

They both nodded, and Vic said carefully, "You saw there's another article in Newsburgh?"

"I did." Carter waved a hand, his brown eyes intent. "Chilton is digging his own grave."

"Is Hana going to respond?" Liz asked.

"Not yet. We'll get there. Let us handle that." Carter's phone rang and he glanced at the caller ID. "I have to take this, that's it."

Carter lifted the phone and listened as Vic and Liz rose, but cupped his hand over the phone's mouthpiece and said quickly, "Wait."

They sat down. Carter asked a couple of questions and wrote down an address. He hung up and looked at them. "You guys said you visited those two old-time gangsters last night, right? What were their names again?"

"Dom Bandini and Vince Lombardo," Vic told him.

"Yeah. You better get out to this address." He pushed the note he'd written across his desk. "Somebody just found the Lombardo guy shot."

"Thuds is dead?" Liz's voice was a combination of anger and shock.

Carter blinked, staring at her. "Two bullets in your chest will do that."

Chapter Twenty-Five

V ic and Liz didn't speak until they were halfway to the address.

"Do you know if this is his house or somewhere else?" Liz's voice sounded distant, as if it was filling a gap left when her anger evaporated.

"No idea." Vic was still trying to gather himself. He kept seeing Thuds as he'd seen him the night before, quietly testy about Bandini's answers. The way Thuds gazed at him as if he wanted Vic to make a connection, or miss one.

"I guess we'd better figure out time of death." Liz's voice was stronger, the shock wearing off.

Vic brought his mind to bear. He knew what she meant. They weren't the last ones to see him alive. Mary Monahan, Bandini, Aaron Holt, and Mike Turcelli fit that description. But they might be close, and the closer the more likely they might be pulled from the case. Without even discussing it, Vic knew that was behind Liz's question. Like him, she wanted to be lead investigator.

"Must be his house," Vic said, more to himself, as they turned onto the street listed in the address. They were in Shadyside, a wealthy residential neighborhood east of downtown Pittsburgh. Vic pulled up behind a pair of city police cars.

Once they got out, Liz eyed the patrol cars. "Let's hope they were careful with the scene."

Vic stared at the house. It was a rectangular, two-story brick colonial perfect for somewhere like Georgetown or Charlestown. He was surprised.

He'd expected something less conventional from Thuds, but he second-guessed himself, wondering why he thought that way.

They showed their IDs to the young, uniformed officer at the front door.

"I'm not supposed to let anyone inside." He sounded nervous.

"I haven't seen you before." Liz hooked her thumbs on her belt. "I worked with the city police until last week."

"Yes ma'am. I graduated from the Academy this spring. I've only been working a few weeks."

Vic felt a little sorry for him. He remembered his first year on the force, and how intimidating the detectives were. "Where are the other officers, then? They aren't inside, are they?"

The officer pointed down the block. "Preliminary canvass of the neighbors. Our Sarge told them to get on it."

"Okay. Do you mind if we walk around the house? Take a look at the outside?

"That's fine, sir."

Vic started across the grass, his eyes down, and Liz took up a position several feet to his right, her gaze also downward. Together, they swung around the side of the house, working as a team, looking for anything out of the ordinary. When they reached the back of the house they stopped.

Vic stared. "I would not have expected this."

"That boy Thuds, there was a lot going on with him."

Vic followed the contours of the two-story extension that ran the entire rear of the house. It was ultra-modern in design, with endless floor-to-ceiling windows. Architecturally, it was the exact opposite of the traditional front of the house. The brick was flat grey and the window frames black. He and Liz circled onto the back lawn, staring inside the house. Most of the back wall of the original house had been knocked out during the renovation, opening the rooms into one another. What remained was naked brick. The kitchen was sleek, with grey cabinets, stainless-steel appliances, and concrete countertops. The couches and armchairs were low, modern, and upholstered in light grey textured fabrics. Offsetting the muted colors was a large abstract painting in bright colors, directly facing the family room and kitchen.

"There he is," Liz said quietly. "Next to the armchair."

Thuds was sprawled chest down on the floor between a glass coffee table and one of the armchairs. He lay on his right cheek, face turned to the windows. Vic shifted position to get a better look, his gaze never leaving Thuds' face. A roil of anger churned inside him.

He looked away, to the high walls around the garden and the screen of trees. "Do you know who called this in?" His voice sounded distant. From the look of the back yard, he doubted anyone nearby would have heard the shots.

"I know as much as you." Liz sidled to her left. "He had to know the person. Only way it explains him being in that room. He didn't open the front door and take a bullet."

Vic took in Thuds' surroundings. "Yeah. But there's only one glass on the table."

They fell silent as someone appeared at the end of the hall, swathed in a white Tyvek bunny suit, their face mostly hidden by a mask and goggles. Because of their clothing, Vic couldn't tell the person's gender. They carried what looked like a large tackle box in one hand. The person stepped into the room and spotted the body. A moment later, a second person in identical dress appeared and stopped next to the first person. They started to confer.

Vic turned for the side yard. "Let's get inside."

When he and Liz emerged at the front of the house the navy-blue forensics van was parked in front of a neighbor's house. Fifteen minutes later, they stepped into the front hall of Thuds' residence, outfitted in disposable white bunny suits, masks, gloves, and booties.

Vic took a few steps down the hall, lifted his mask, and sniffed. Nothing unexpected. He led Liz down the hall into the addition.

One of the techs was snapping photographs of a small revolver, a .38, sitting on the kitchen counter. Vic turned to the body. Now that he was inside, he saw a stain of blood on the back of the armchair at about chest height.

"He was shot while he was sitting in the chair," Liz said quietly.

"And tried to get up but collapsed," finished Vic.

Liz nodded. Vic stared at Thuds' remains. He couldn't sort out his feelings. Thuds was a killer, he knew it. But he'd always been straight with Vic. Tough, but never one to try and trick him. He realized slowly he had a grudging respect for the man. Somehow, this seemed like the wrong end for him, even if it was the most likely.

"Never expected this." It was as if Liz was reading his thoughts. "I never thought someone would get the drop on him. He didn't seem the type."

"Agreed. And we need to remember that." Vic took another step toward Thuds' body. There was only one glass on the coffee table, but he could see a ring from a glass directly across from it, in front of the couch that faced the armchair.

"I know," someone said.

Vic turned to the sound of the voice. Standing behind the armchair was the crime scene tech they'd seen first enter the room. Now that he was closer, Vic saw that behind the goggles was a young face and square glasses that he thought were familiar.

"It's me, Detective Lenoski. Craig Luntz." He pointed at the couch and the glass. "That's likely where the shooter was sitting. There's another glass in the sink. It's been washed. I'll go over them both really carefully."

"Good to see you again, Craig." Vic meant it. But Craig was completely out of context. Before Vic's retirement, Craig was a technical specialist who handled computer and cell phone processing for the city police. His father had trained Vic when he first joined the force. "Craig, you were in tech. How the heck did you end up here?"

"Thought I'd try it. Took a bunch of classes and got a certification." He shrugged. "They hired me. I started about a year ago."

"Good." Vic gestured at the glass. "Make sure you figure out what was in it. I've never seen Thuds drink liquor. Only water. And follow your instincts. You've got good ones."

Craig nodded. "Thanks. About the not drinking alcohol." Despite his goggles and glasses, he looked embarrassed. He bent down behind the armchair.

Liz stepped closer to Vic. "Sorry, I meant to tell you and I never got the chance. Craig went to night school for two years to get his certification."

Vic nodded absently, his gaze sliding back to Thuds' body. His anger surged back. First Geno, and now this. He had no doubt about it now. Something was going to happen, and he felt no closer to understanding what it was. He turned to Liz. "Let's look upstairs."

As the afternoon swam by Vic gradually determined that Thuds only wore blue, grey or black clothes, kept his belongings neat, and overall led an orderly life. He found no photos of family or friends. He did find a wall safe in the back of the master bedroom's walk-in closet, and tagged it to be drilled open. But he knew it would be the last thing the CSI unit did.

Liz came in from another room. "You're still here? Thought you'd be on your way to get Lettie by now."

Vic tightened and glanced at his phone. He'd been so focused he'd forgotten he needed to pick her up from daycare. He raised his phone to call Anne, and stopped. She had to work late tonight, something about hosting a dinner for long-time season ticket holders.

He looked at Liz. "I may have to go."

She shrugged, watching him.

Vic hesitated a moment longer. "I'll make some calls." He left the bedroom and walked downstairs. At the front door, he stripped off his gloves, booties, and coverall and dumped them in a box placed there by the CSI team. He walked to his car, thinking.

He wanted to keep working the scene, which meant he needed a babysitter. He leaned against his car. There was only one person he could call. He didn't like it, but it was worth a try. Slowly, he scrolled his phone's call list and pressed a number.

Barb answered on the second ring. "Detective Lenoski?" she asked.

"Hi Barb." Vic leaned his elbows on the roof of the car. He made a mental note that the medical examiner had arrived. "I wanted to let you know, I did look into that address where the boy lives?"

"Yes!" She seemed to realize she was too excited. "I mean, thanks for taking the time."

"No problem. As it turns out, we haven't responded to any calls from that house. I'm at a bit of a dead-end on that one."

"Oh." Somehow, Barb made the word sound like air escaping from a tire.

"We'll just have to keep an eye on the house and see what turns up." He hadn't forgotten the exchange with the boy's father, but he didn't want to mention it to Barb and deepen her suspicions. "And I do have another question."

"Yes?"

"I was wondering if you know any babysitters? Is there anyone the mothers from the park feel good about? I've run into a problem tonight. We've had a shooting and I have to work late investigating the scene. My wife has an appointment, and that means I need someone to take care of Lettie." He scrunched his eyes shut, hoping she might take the bait.

"Oh. Let me. We know some babysitters but you won't find anyone tonight, not on short notice. Lettie and my Josh get along great. Lettie can just stay with us until you're free."

"That would be fantastic," Vic said, trying to remember the last time he ever said that word. "Should I drop her off?"

"Where is she now?"

Vic heard a get-down-to-business tone in Barb's voice. "At daycare."

Barb cut him off. "Text the address and I'll pick her up. I have to go out to the supermarket anyway. Let the daycare know I'm coming."

Vic felt the urge to argue but decided to enjoy the lucky break. "That's very helpful, Barb. I really appreciate it." He cringed as he spoke. He knew Barb would consider this free license to ask him about his job and push him about the boy from the playground, but he had little choice.

After he'd arranged when he would stop by her house for Lettie, he called Anne and explained what he had done.

"You trust this Barb?" she asked so quickly Vic had to mentally backtrack to give her an answer.

"I do. I've been seeing her at the playground for two years now. She has a son just a little older than Lettie. Josh. I've talked to her quite a few times. And she knows I'm a cop."

CHAPTER TWENTY-FIVE

Anne took a long breath. "Well, I guess we can try it."

"And I'll pick her up from Barb's. I should be done by about eight."

"Okay. But if she's going to babysit again I want to meet her."

"I'll tell her."

After he hung up he called Carter Lee, gave him an update, and said he would be at the scene until about seven-thirty. As he turned from his car he saw Liz come out of the house. He met her halfway. "All set. I'll be here until we're done. Or close to it."

She nodded and tilted her head to look down the street. "Is that who I think it is?"

Vic followed her gaze and spotted a black Cadillac Escalade parked halfway down the block. It hadn't been there when he left the house to make his calls.

"Let's go find out," he said. As they walked, Vic called Lettie's day care and told the person who answered the phone that Barb was allowed to pick up Lettie. He found her annoyingly unconcerned about it.

Chapter Twenty-Six

As Vic and Liz approached the Cadillac, Mike Turcelli slid from the driver's seat and stood by the back door, his arms crossed over his chest. Vic called out to him. "Hi, Mike."

Mike flexed his biceps as if that was how he started every conversation. "Mr. Bandini wants a word."

"We need a word with him."

Turcelli unclamped an arm and knocked on the window of the back door. It slid down. Mike stepped back and Vic looked inside the SUV.

Bandini sat leaning back against the headrest, his face pale, exhaustion in his eyes.

"Mr. Bandini," Vic said.

It took Bandini some effort to respond. "It's Vince?" His voice was hoarse.

"It is. No question. I'm sorry."

"Christ." He looked at the opposite door and took a deep breath.

Vic wondered how long Bandini and Lombardo had worked together, what secrets they held. "I'm sorry, Mr. Bandini, but I need to ask you some questions."

Bandini straightened and turned back to him. "Yeah?"

"When did you see Vince last?"

"Last night. After you guys left, we did too."

"Together?"

Bandini blinked. "No. Mike here took me home. Vince drove himself."

Sensing Bandini was too distracted to argue, Vic took him through a string of questions to pin down when Mike dropped Bandini off at home, and what he did for the rest of the night. Bandini answered in monosyllables. Finally, Vic said slowly, "Do you have anything going on right now that might explain this?"

Bandini sighed. "No. We've been in maintenance mode for the last few years. I'm looking at buying a couple new franchises, but that's it."

"No idea why someone would shoot him?"

Bandini shook his head slowly, as if it was suddenly three times heavier than normal.

Liz stepped next to Vic. "Does Vince have a wife? Girlfriend?"

Bandini glanced at Liz. "Nah. Dated a lot, but he liked living on his own."

Vic thought that sounded right, based on what he'd seen inside the house. "Thanks, Mr. Bandini. We're just getting started on this and we'll need to talk to you again."

"I want the body," Bandini said quickly. "I'll bury him. You make sure that happens."

Vic nodded and tapped the windowsill with his hand. "I will." He stepped back from the SUV and the window slid up.

Vic turned to Mike Turcelli. "How about you?"

Mike frowned in confusion. "What about me?"

"After you dropped your boss off last night, where did you go?"

Mike scratched his nose with his left hand and Vic caught the glint of a wedding band on a beefy finger. "Home."

"Anybody confirm that?"

"My wife. Kids."

Vic stared at him. This surprised him, somehow. He couldn't remember if Mike wore a wedding band the first time they met, but that was easily five years ago. He'd never paid close attention to him, beyond investigating his criminal record and assigning him to the role of hired muscle.

"How many kids?" Vic asked, genuinely interested.

"Two. Daughters."

"Did you read to them last night?" Liz asked, sarcasm lingering in the shadows of her sentence.

Mike turned to her and Vic was certain he saw a redness on his cheeks.

"Nah. My wife does that."

But Vic saw a flicker in Mike's eyes. Something evaluating Liz, considering her. A split second of clear-eyed intelligence, gone as fast as it appeared. Vic found himself on guard.

"Mike, what's going on?"

The voice was from behind Mike, and he turned to the sound of it. Vic looked around Mike to see Aaron Holt. Aaron was taller and more broad-shouldered than Vic had noticed the night before, with a tethered energy that radiated from him.

"You're here too?" Mike asked, sounding perplexed.

"Yeah. Thuds called me this morning. Asked me to stop by..." he glanced at a heavy watch on his wrist, "right about now. He wanted to talk about one of the businesses."

Vic stepped away from Mike and in front of Aaron. "I'm Detective Lenoski, we met last night?" He gestured at Liz. "And you'll remember my partner, Liz Timmons."

"Sure." He didn't hold out his hand, instead his gaze strayed to Thuds' house. He frowned. "What's happened?"

Instead of answering his question, Liz asked one herself. "You said Vince Lombardo called you this morning. What time was that?"

Holt took a few seconds to turn his face from Thuds' house and the activity around it. He looked at Liz evenly. "About nine this morning. Said he wanted to talk to me about now."

"Someone killed Mr. Lombardo," Mike Turcelli said, as if he was just catching up to Aaron's earlier question.

Aaron stared at Mike for a few seconds, his jaw clamped shut. "In his house?" He finally said.

"Yeah." Mike waved a meaty hand at Vic and Liz. "They're checking it out."

Aaron nodded, and Vic thought he caught just a split second of Aaron bemused by how slow Mike seemed to be.

Aaron looked at Vic. "What happened?"

"What he said." Vic pointed at Mike. He didn't like how Aaron had twice made the point he was supposed to stop by at this particular time, and twice asked what happened. It could be nervousness, but Aaron's eyes had that odd, calm look Vic had spotted the night before.

Aaron stared at him for a few seconds, and Vic sensed he was being sized up. Aaron's gaze slid to Mike. "Sorry to hear it." He pointed at Bandini's Escalade. "Could I talk to Mr. Bandini?"

Mike stepped to the back window and tapped. The window slid halfway down and Mike asked a question so quietly Vic couldn't hear it. Mike stepped away and gestured Aaron forward. The window dropped the rest of the way. Aaron spoke louder than Mike and Vic heard him tell Bandini he was sorry about Vincent. Aaron asked what seemed to be a work-related question, and Vic couldn't hear Bandini's response. When Aaron stepped away from the Escalade he told Mike he was leaving.

Aaron didn't say anything to Vic and Liz, just turned to go. Vic asked quickly. "What kind of work do you do for Mr. Bandini, exactly?"

Aaron stopped and took a second before turning around. "I manage some of his restaurants. Tonight, I'm going to Pesto's first."

"Do you have a card so we can reach you?" Liz's question was gruff, and Vic knew she'd picked up on the way Aaron ignored them.

Aaron dug out his wallet, extracted a card, and walked it over to Liz. "You can reach me on my cell. I work late so afternoons and evenings are better for me."

Vic was about to make a sarcastic comment about being glad to work around his schedule, but bit it off. No point angering someone they needed to interview later. Vic said goodbye to Mike Turcelli, who slid into the SUV, started the engine, and executed a neat three-point turn. Aaron disappeared into his own car. Vic and Liz turned back to the house. As they walked, Vic thought about that one moment of lucidity in Mike Turcelli's eyes. He didn't know what to do with it. He also thought about the beating Thuds had given Mike all those years ago. He wondered about that, as he walked. Did Mike carry a grudge about that beating? And just like regrets, aren't grudges another kind of secret everyone carries?

The kind that might demand to be put right?

Chapter Twenty-Seven

The Fifth Day

As he drove he thought of sitting in Thuds' house, the glasses of orange juice in front of each of them on the coffee table, and that single moment of clarity. The house delivered it to him. It was those floor-to-ceiling windows. How the soaring space above his head merged with the light of the sky, the firmament.

Thuds asking him why he'd entered the storage unit. How he knew it existed.

And in that single second when Thuds finished the question, he sensed all the birds in the air, the fish in the sea. He was part of it. They were part of him.

He'd felt no anger. No fear. In that moment he was joined to the entire world, felt it unfolded inside him. A feeling of being fruitful. Multiplying. Thuds' question was nothing, in the face of that enormity. And he'd told Thuds the truth. He was the son of Paul Zielinski. That unit belonged to him. Everything in it belonged to him. Everything Thuds and Bandini owned, belonged to him.

The revolver in his fist. His mother's gun, the one she carried for all those years, kept on her bedside table when she slept, held in her hand when someone knocked on their front door.

The squeeze of the trigger. Twice. He hadn't hesitated, as he knew he wouldn't. Paul Hammer Zielinski was his father. That true blood throbbed in his veins. Thuds started to stand when he saw the gun, but the chair was too low for quick movement, the time between the gun appearing in his hand and the trigger pulls too short. He remembered the buck of the gun in his hand, Thuds sinking back into his chair, staring at the holes in his chest. The leak of blood down the front of his grey shirt.

Thuds knew. He knew. One shot was probably enough. Two was just insurance. It was done. He watched Thuds struggle upright, some instinct powering him, and collapse chest down on the floor, his face turned toward him. Whatever was in his eyes dwindled to nothing, until they simply reflected the outside sky.

He'd stood, then, the revolver in his hand. Spoken to the body. "Look at you," he remembered saying. "Alone in this house. This is what you stole. Stole from my mother and I. My father. Nothing of it is yours. This is just emptiness." He recalled looking around the broad room, staring at the high ceiling. "And you built this temple to that emptiness. To die in."

He took his glass to the sink. Placed the gun on the counter and carefully washed the glass. Rinsed it thoroughly and dried it with folded paper towels, careful not to touch it directly again. Used the same towels to wipe down the butt of the gun, before pocketing them. His mother's gun. He didn't need it anymore. He wanted to leave it. A message, if anyone had the intelligence to understand. For years, his mother lived in fear of Thuds and Bandini, scared they would find her and end it. Tie off the last remaining witness to their theft of his father's businesses. Now Thuds was finished. Bandini was next, but he required a different plan. A gun was too simple and swift for him.

He thought about Bandini as he drove, his eyes flicking to the rear-view mirror sometimes. But his mind shifted. He frowned, his view of the road suddenly sharper, the hum of the tires on the road a vibration in his hands. Thuds knew he went to the storage locker. How was that? Surely the security cameras weren't working. Surely Thuds didn't monitor the feeds.

Something else.

A shadow slanted through him. Some kind of notification system on the unit door? He hadn't checked the door frame. He thought of the cameras along the roofline. Hard-wired or wireless? Video or stills? He hadn't checked that, either.

Another thought.

An alarm linked to the operation to the door meant a notification would be sent the next time he opened it. But who would receive it? Nobody. He smiled at that. Thuds certainly couldn't. He tapped his hand on the top of the steering wheel. He had Thuds' phone, so he'd tied off that loose end as well.

And he did need to go into the unit at least one more time.

The gun he'd used to shoot Geno Varelli was there.

Chapter Twenty-Eight

Vic was still upset about Thuds when he parked in front of Barb's house. She lived in a two-story red-brick home similar to the others on the street, all of them neatly aligned behind a small lawn and fronted by a porch that ran the width of the building. Lights blazed from the windows on both sides of the front door. He climbed the four steps from the walk to the porch and pressed the bell.

As he waited, he listened to music coming from inside the house. A female singer. It reminded him of Craig, swathed in his white Tyvek bunny suit. Before Vic's retirement, every time he visited Craig in the tech department music was blasting from his computer. Vic was sure Craig would have recognized the singer.

Barb answered the door, dressed in the activewear she wore to the park. Her face was flushed and her eyes bright.

"Vic, come on in. Lettie's been running around everywhere. It's so much fun."

She closed the door behind him and led him through an archway into the living room. Vic smelled pizza, and the toys and cushions scattered across the floor reminded him of his own house. His stomach tightened. The lived-in look of the room contrasted sharply with the neutral colors and relentless neatness of Thuds' house, and it disjointed him in a way that forced him to concentrate as he followed Barb through to the dining room. Lettie and Barb's son sat on booster seats at a broad table, drawing on large pieces of paper with crayons. Both were hunched over, completely focused. A large stack of similarly-sized paper sat at the far end of the table.

"Well done, Barb," Vic said quietly, using the scene to refocus himself. "Lettie doesn't usually concentrate so hard on things."

Barb smiled, the flush returning to her face. "Oh," she waved a hand in dismissal. "That's not me. That's Josh." She pointed at her son. "When it comes to drawing, it's like he's in another world."

"Hard to get him to stop," said a voice, and Vic turned to find a medium height, slender man in the doorway to the kitchen, a glass of water in his hand. He had a full head of hair for his age, and the same brown eyes as Josh, although they were behind rimless spectacles. They shook hands, Vic surprised at the firmness of the man's grip. "I'm Ned, Josh's dad."

Vic stepped back so he could look at Ned and Barb at the same time. "I want to thank you both for taking care of Lettie on such short notice. I just started a new job, and my wife and I just weren't ready for this. We'll get ourselves sorted out for next time."

"Oh, we're glad to do it." Barb bounced on her toes.

"Lettie's been great, no problem at all," Ned added. "And she likes to draw, which is about Josh's favorite thing to do." He crossed to the stack of paper at the end of the table, held up a sheet, and flipped it over. The backside was a paper placemat for a restaurant. He grinned. "I work for a restaurant supply company. We always have overruns when we print these things. He'd be drawing on the walls if we didn't have enough paper." He replaced the sheet. "I understand you're a detective?"

Barb flashed Ned a glance that said, "I asked you not to bring that up."

"I am." Vic crossed to Lettie and touched her on the shoulder. She looked up at him with a big grin and Vic softened. He turned back to Ned. "Allegheny County Detective. I used to be Pittsburgh Bureau of Police, but I retired early a few years ago. I was offered a job when the new DA came in."

"Oh, Hana Richards. I voted for her." Barb pumped her fist in what Vic took to be comradery or an expression of solidarity with Hana, or perhaps women in general. Barb glanced around the room. "Lettie has a jacket around here somewhere." She disappeared into the living room.

Vic bent down and told Lettie they had to leave. She nodded and held up her drawing. It showed a house and two stick people, holding hands with a smaller stick person. Vic wondered if that was Lettie, and he and Anne were the figures holding her hands. He hoped so. He helped Lettie off the booster seat. Josh looked up and blinked at him, as if he had to readjust his vision or concentration.

"Thanks for being friends with Lettie," Vic said to him. Josh nodded and went back to his picture. Vic glanced at it. It showed the archway leading into the living room, and on the other side of the arch, the back of the couch and other furniture. He'd shaded the picture in places to represent shadows and the perspective looked accurate. Vic was surprised. It was art he would expect a twelve or thirteen-year-old to produce. He knew Josh was older than Lettie, but it wasn't by more than a year.

Vic turned to Ned and nodded at Josh's picture. "That's something. Has he been to classes or anything?"

Ned shrugged. "Nope. He seems to figure it out on his own. We got some book out of the library that's like the best hundred paintings of all time, that's about it."

Barb returned, holding Lettie's jacket. She held it open so Lettie could shrug into it. It took Lettie a moment to realize she couldn't slide her arm into the sleeve without first taking the picture out of her hand, but she worked her way through the problem.

"Did you get a chance to write down some babysitter numbers?" Vic asked her.

Barb waved her hand. "I did, I put it in Lettie's jacket pocket. But don't worry about calling me. This worked out great." She smiled at him.

"Glad to help," echoed Ned.

"Thanks again." Vic led Lettie out of the house, all of them calling goodbyes as they left. He strapped Lettie into her car seat and slid behind the wheel. He started the car but didn't pull out right away. It was the whiplash. Thuds dead on the floor, shot by someone who didn't hesitate to pull the trigger. And Barb and Ned, kind, helpful, and willing to go out of their way to help someone they barely knew. He closed and opened his eyes, clearing his head. But the feeling in his stomach wouldn't go away. It took him a moment to recognize it. Frustration. He hadn't felt it since he was chasing his daughter's kidnapper. The stark counterpoint of the two houses and their inhabitants had brought it back. He wanted to get moving, to do something.

"Are you okay," he called back to Lettie.

"Yep," she called back, the single word sounding like a note in a song.

"Well, I'm not so sure about your grandad," he said under his breath. And then louder, "Let's get home and see how Nana's doing, okay?"

Chapter Twenty-Nine

The next morning Vic and Liz updated Carter Lee on what they'd found at Thuds' house before heading to their car. They'd talked the evening before, and Vic had convinced Liz they should at least take a look at the storage facility. The tattoo on Geno's arm felt like a loose end to him. Liz was skeptical it was worth the time, pointing out that even if Geno once rented a unit, they didn't know which one. Vic understood her logic, but still wanted to go. He couldn't shake the feeling he was playing catch-up on the case, and he wanted to run down every lead. Even obscure ones.

They drove north of the city, Liz watching the map on her phone and calling out directions. They found the storage facility just off a two-lane road that ran at right angles away from one of the interstates. Vic pulled in and stopped by what appeared to be the office for the storage facility. A quick glance through the large window told Vic the room was empty. Liz studied a sign in the window and punched the numbers into her phone. Vic heard the muffled voice of someone answering and Liz asked them to come to the facility.

"Caretaker. He said he lives ten minutes away," she said, sliding her phone into her jacket pocket.

"Then we have time to look around." Vic pulled the car to one side and parked. The facility sat on a slight rise above the nearby two-lane road. A light wind blew from the direction of the interstate, bringing with it the sound of rushing cars. Together, they circled around the rows of storage units until they covered the entire facility. They were alone.

As they walked back to the office Vic pointed at the cameras along the roofline. "Do you think any of those work?"

Liz gave a short laugh. "I doubt it. Where would they keep all the data? And I don't see motion detector eyes, which would be the easiest way to do it."

Vic peered through the glass window of the office, cupping his hands around his face to block the sunlight. Inside was a metal desk and chair and a single four-drawer filing cabinet. A bar was slotted into brackets at the top and bottom of the cabinet, and ran vertically through the drawer handles. A padlock connected it to the top bracket. But what attracted his attention was a small black box with short rabbit ears sitting on top of the cabinet.

"I think they have Wi-Fi," he said, slowly.

Liz copied him and peered inside. "Why the hell would they need that?"

"I wonder if they're using Wi-Fi to operate the cameras, somehow." He tracked along the wall and saw an electrical outlet with a white plastic box plugged into it. The box also had two stubby rabbit ears. He didn't know what it was.

Liz backed off the window. "Doesn't make sense, motion detectors would be easier."

"Must be a computer in there we can't see."

"Same deal. There must be an easier way to do it."

Hearing the crunch of tires on gravel Vic turned to see a beat-up pick-up truck slow to a stop.

A tall, lanky man in his sixties with snow-white hair lowered himself from the cab. As he crossed to Vic and Liz he sized them up with bright brown eyes. He stopped in front of them. "Allegheny County Detectives, huh?"

"I'm the one who called." Liz introduced them both and showed the man her ID.

He held out his hand to Liz. "I'm Roofus Peterman. Don't mess this up for me. I retired a few years ago and this job is great. Real part-time and it's near where I live." He shouted a laugh and offered Vic his hand.

As they shook, Vic said, "We just have a few questions for you."

Roofus pointed at the office. Let's go in there."

148

They crossed to the office and Roofus produced a set of keys, unlocked the door, and swung it open. Once he was inside he turned back to them and waggled his eyebrows. "Now I'm on the clock." Vic and Liz followed him inside. Roofus pointed at a small black box on the wall next to the door and showed them an even smaller black component on the door, just across from it. "When the door opens it breaks the seal between these two, and sends a text notification the door was opened."

"And that proves you're here," Liz said.

"Exactly. Since I drove down here, might as well get paid." He gave a quieter version of his shouted laugh and closed the door. "Now, what can I do for you?"

"The address of this storage facility came up in an investigation," Liz said. "We just had some questions about it."

"Sure. Any specific unit?"

Liz shifted her weight. "We can't say at this time."

"Okay." Roofus pushed his hands into his jean pockets. "Can you tell me the name of the renter?"

She returned his gaze. "We don't know that either."

Roofus eyed her. "Don't mean to sound like a jerk, but what *do* you know? Right now I don't understand why I'm here."

Vic saw the corners of Liz's mouth tighten, more in frustration than anything else. He knew she wasn't upset at Roofus or him, but rather the situation.

"As I said, the address of this storage facility came up during an investigation." She hesitated. "Let's do it this way." Her voice gained confidence, as if she'd found her way out of a maze. "Tell us the steps involved in renting a unit, how many units are being used, that kind of thing."

Roofus didn't react for a moment, as if he couldn't possibly see what good that information would do. Vic knew differently. It wasn't the content; it was the method. Liz wanted Roofus talking, to see if anything fell out that might help them or provide a line of questioning.

"As I said," Roofus started, "I only started here a few years ago, so everything I can tell you is from while I was here."

"That's fine," Vic said quickly, to keep him talking.

"People want to rent a unit, they call the number like you did. I'm on call, nine to six. I come out here, tell them what units are available, they take a look, then I try to get 'em to sign a contract. We ask for one year minimum, but some people are just parking stuff for a couple of months while they move houses, that kind of thing, so we do shorter periods if we have to."

"And how many units are available right now?" Liz asked the question just as Roofus took a breath. Vic knew she was finding her rhythm.

"Four. We have a couple of different sizes, so there's differences. I take them out, if they like one, they sign on the dotted line."

"And do they pay you?" Liz's question was timed to the end of his statement.

"Yeah. If they want a unit on the spot, they write me a check and I have them sign the contract. If they don't have a padlock or combination lock I sell them one." He crossed to the desk, opened a drawer, and placed a couple of locks on the desktop, still sheathed in blister packs.

Liz came right back with a follow-up. "You said you try and get them to sign up for a year. What's the average length of time someone rents a unit?"

Roofus frowned. "Beats me. Like I said, some are for a few months and we know that. There's others that rent way longer."

"Wait." Liz said it so loudly Vic blinked. She shuffle-stepped toward Roofus. "Which unit has been rented the longest?"

Vic understood immediately what Liz was getting at. Inwardly, he kicked himself for not thinking of it sooner. If the address on Geno's arm indicated the address and number of a storage unit, it dated to the opening of the business.

Roofus thought for a few moments. "There were four or five that were already being rented when I started." He crossed to the filing cabinet and produced his keys again, singled one out, and undid the padlock. It took him a few moments to work the metal bar out from behind the drawer handles and it was touch-and-go that he didn't scrape the ceiling, but it was flexible enough to avoid leaving a mark. He opened the second drawer down.

He tried reading the files' headers, gave up, and dug a pair of readers out of his pants' pocket. He perched them on his nose and adjusted his stance. After a few moments of shuffling through the files, he pulled one out, checked inside, and placed it on the desk. He went back to checking the files in the drawer. When he finished, five files sat on the desktop. Roofus straightened and pointed at them.

"Okay, those five are the oldest." He fanned them out on the desktop, checked each one, and read them the date each unit was rented.

"None of those work," Vic said when he was finished. "The oldest is seven years ago."

"We're looking for a unit that goes back to when this place was opened," Liz added

Roofus looked from Liz to Vic, his eyes apologetic behind his readers. "That's all I have. No one has rented that long. Usually, around five years people stop paying and we chase them, and if they don't pay we clean out the unit and rent it to someone else."

"What do you do with the stuff left behind?" Vic was genuinely interested. He knew this must be a common problem for storage facilities.

"There's a company that comes and takes it away. They sell it, and we get a cut of whatever they sell it for." Roofus frowned, following his own chain of logic. "Although we go through the unit first. If there's anything we think is valuable..." his eyes lit up and he punched his palm with his other fist. "Wait. Anything valuable we put in a unit the business owns until we figure out what to do with it. That unit's been around since the place opened." He shouted his laugh. "Ha. And guess what. I have a key for that unit because I move stuff in and out. But the business owns a second unit. I don't have a key for that."

Liz smiled. "And that unit's been around since this place opened?"

"Both of them have."

"Can you show us?" Vic asked.

"Sure. Give me a second. I can't leave the office with these out." He replaced the files, maneuvered the bar back into place behind the drawer handles, and snapped the padlock shut. He slid his readers from his nose and pushed them into his pocket. "This way."

Vic and Liz followed him out of the office and across the facility. He turned into the drive between the next to last and last rows and led them to the end unit. "That's the one I have a key for." He pointed to a larger one next to it. "And that's the other one."

Vic stared at both of them and turned to Roofus. "That one." He pointed at the one Roofus didn't have a key for. "The combination lock looks new. Was it always like that?"

Roofus frowned and studied the lock. He looked at Vic. "It's new. The lock that's usually there is rusted and faded. I guess someone changed it." He sounded doubtful.

"And there it is," Liz said softly.

Vic felt a surge of excitement. They were still guessing, but that unit had been there long enough, ever since Thuds built the storage facility. "Have you ever seen anyone go in or out of this one?"

"No, but I'm only here maybe once a day when someone calls or I have to clean something out. It's more likely I wouldn't see anyone."

Liz took a picture of the locker with her phone. She stepped closer and snapped others of the unit number and the combination lock. She flipped the lock upside down and took a picture of the serial number on the back.

Vic looked at Roofus. "Do you have master keys or something? I mean if the business owns this unit, you could open it for us, right?"

Roofus shifted from foot to foot. "No. I have a bolt cutter that takes care of the units we have to open. But I'm not opening that, not without my boss' permission."

"And who is that?" Liz's question was a bit sharp, but Vic liked it. They already knew the business was owned by a holding company controlled by Thuds, so her question was really designed to see who Roofus believed was his boss.

Roofus shrugged. "Only guy I ever met was when I got hired. He talked to me over the phone, and when he hired me I met him here. He showed me what to do and I signed the paperwork."

"What is that person's name?" Liz asked.

Roofus frowned. "I just met the guy once. Here." He pulled out his phone and swiped through several screens. "He gave me his phone number. Yeah. Mike Turcelli. Big guy. Looked like he lifts. Too much bulk, you know what I mean?" He looked at Vic.

"What's his number?" Vic asked. "We might want to call him."

"Better yet," Liz said quickly. "Why don't you call him and ask if we can look inside these two units."

Roofus hesitated, clearly unhappy about making the call.

"Look, Roofus." Vic straightened. "We know Mike Turcelli. We talked to him yesterday. Call him, tell him Vic Lenoski and Liz Timmons are asking to look inside the units."

Roofus hesitated, but pressed the name in his phone's address book. He turned away, although Vic heard the phone ringing and someone answering. The wind lifted and fell. Vic realized he missed being outside, that he'd got used to his frequent trips with Lettie to the playground. He remembered sitting on the bench, the newspaper shivering as he read it, the distant shouts of the Watch Mother's children as they ran about.

Roofus turned back to them. He kept his gaze to the ground, silently, until he lifted his eyes to Liz. "He says show him a warrant, and no problem. He'll drive out here himself and open them for you."

"And that answers that." Liz pointed in the direction of the office. "We might as well go back."

They returned to the office in silence. Vic had the impression Roofus wanted to open the units for them, but wouldn't disobey Mike. When they neared the office, Vic glanced through the glass door and noticed the white box plugged into the wall outlet. He pointed at it. "What's that?"

Roofus gazed along the track of Vic's pointed finger. "Oh. That's the system that sends the notification of me entering the office."

"Or anyone entering the office," Liz added.

"Yeah, I guess so. Basically, it's just the door opening, so it's a notification that the door was opened."

How does it work?" Vic was interested.

"That's why we have Wi-Fi. When the door is opened it sends a signal to that white box via Wi-Fi, and the box uses Wi-Fi to connect to the internet and send a notification to an app."

"You pay for Wi-Fi just so Mike is notified when the office door opens?" Vic couldn't keep the skepticism out of his voice.

Rob turned to him. "The Wi-Fi covers the whole complex. When someone rents a unit, they can choose to get a notification whenever the door to their unit is opened. It's a few extra bucks a month. There's maybe only a couple of people using it." He smiled and lowered his voice. "I figured out it's usually people getting divorced. They're worried about a wife or husband stealing their stuff."

"Or they're hiding things from their spouse." Disgust soaked Liz's words. "And the cameras? How do they work?"

"They're just there to scare people. Unless you pay for the notification system. Then they take still photos of whoever opened the door and send them along with the notification."

"Wait." Vic concentrated. "If you use the notification system and someone goes into your unit, you get a text the door opened and photos of whoever went inside?"

Roofus nodded. "If it works right."

"Are the two units you own set up that way?" Liz asked.

"The one I have a key to isn't. I don't know about the other."

Liz and Vic glanced at one another. Vic stuck out his hand to shake. "Thanks, Roofus, you've been really helpful."

"Well, sorry about not being able to open the units."

"Don't even think about it," Liz told him as she shook his hand.

Inside the car, Vic started the engine and looked at Liz. "Are you thinking what I'm thinking?"

Liz nodded. "Like why we didn't find Thuds' phone in his house?"

Vic put the car in Drive. "Because maybe Thuds got a notification and a photo of who went into the unit."

"And that person didn't want anyone to know they'd been in the unit."

"Maybe enough to shoot Thuds to keep it secret." Vic steered the car onto the two-lane road. "We need to get onto the phone carrier and see what texts Thuds got."

Chapter Thirty

Vic and Liz ate lunch at their desks, writing up their notes from the investigation over the last two days. Vic updated his binder while Liz focused on the online system. A little after two o'clock Vic's cell phone rang, the caller's number blocked.

Vic answered guardedly.

"Vic Lenoski?" a reedy voice asked. "This is Evan Gelhorn, at Allegheny Cemetery?"

"Yes. Mr. Gelhorn. What can I do for you?"

"Thought you might want to know, since your partner asked when that Geno Varelli guy was going to be buried?"

"Right, tomorrow."

"Nah. Today. In about an hour."

Vic hunched over his phone. "How did that happen?"

"Beats me. Something about the body being released. I got a call asking if they could do it today and I moved some stuff around. Guy said some family thing had come up and he needed to get home. And he's a minister. Thought you might want to know."

"Thanks, I appreciate that, Evan. Um, this was a Mr. Jefferson who called?"

"Yeah, that's the guy."

"Did he say where home was?"

"Didn't mention it." Evan sounded annoyed. "Look, it's pain enough I have to move crap around.

"Thanks, Mr. Gelhorn. Could you text me the plot number?"

"Sure," came the distant reply, as if Evan was already lowering the phone from his ear.

Vic ended the call and looked at Liz. She was watching him, her hands poised over her keyboard.

"Gelhorn. I guess they released Geno's body and that John Jefferson guy arranged to have the funeral today. In an hour. I'm going. If he shows up I'll talk to him. Interested?"

"Do you think he'll show?"

"No idea, but he spent good money to put Geno in the ground. And he bought two plots, next to each other. I'd want to see what my dollars bought."

"I'd like to hear what he knows." Liz lowered her hands and stretched her back. "But Levon is back today, flying in around dinner time. Can you handle it?"

"Sure thing. Anne's turn to pick up Lettie today. I'm free and clear. But I didn't know Levon was out of the country. When I called him to set up the meeting with Bandini, he didn't mention it. He did all that from overseas?"

Liz waved a hand at him. "Yep. They have these things called cell phones now."

Vic cleared his desk and locked his drawer, but slid his binder into a briefcase he'd brought that morning to carry it.

In the cemetery office, a heavyset, elderly woman with smoker's wrinkles marked Geno's plot on a cemetery map and gave it to him. Evan was nowhere to be seen. When Vic reached the site, all he found was a coffin sitting on brass rails above a hole in the ground. The only person nearby was a maintenance man using a motorized trimmer around nearby headstones.

Vic passed the plot, drove another fifteen yards, and turned the car around so he could see the coffin. He stared at it for a few moments and reversed another ten yards, following the road down from the hilltop. That placed headstones and the natural rise of the ground between him and the coffin, which he hoped would make the car less obvious. He cracked a window, turned off the ignition, and settled down to wait.

Three o'clock came and went, and by three-fifteen, only a battered ATV had arrived, driven by a workman who stopped long enough to pick up the man with the weed trimmer. They parked ten yards from the grave site and cut the engine, the wind snatching away the motor's sound as if it was an annoyance. Vic caught a whiff of gasoline and cut grass as the men made themselves comfortable in the ATV seats.

Ten more minutes passed, and a silver taxi cab appeared at the crest of the hill and stopped. For a few moments, nothing happened, until a tall black man with gray hair unwound from the back seat. His movements were slow and stiff, but as he neared the grave site his stride lengthened. Vic studied him. Even at that distance, the man carried himself well, his posture stern, his hair so white it was almost a cloud in the blue sky. He wore a black suit, dark tie, and white shirt, and carried a small black duffel. When he reached the coffin, he placed the duffel on the ground and bent his head, his hands clasped in front of him. A prayer. It lasted almost a minute, until he placed his right palm flat on the coffin lid for a full fifteen seconds. Finally, he straightened, searched the sky for a few moments, and looked around, taking in the hilltop, the graves nearby, and quite possibly, Vic thought, the air itself.

The taxi slid away.

The man unzipped the duffel and removed something. Opened it. A Bible, Vic realized. A large palm flat against the pages to anchor them against the wind, the man's mouth began to move.

The service had started.

Vic slid from his car and slotted the door closed behind him, careful not to slam it. He hiked along the road, past the two men in the ATV, and turned onto the grass. A few more strides and he neared the end of the coffin. He stopped, keeping a respectful distance. The man was reading a passage, his voice resonant, taking his time, as if instead of reading he was releasing words one at a time into the wind, for each to find a nesting place.

Vic didn't recognize the passage. He just waited, giving himself to the warmth of the sun on his head and shoulders, the lull of the man's voice. The velvety softness of his accent. Vic's mind drifted until a sudden silence brought him back. The man's head was bent. Vic watched him raise it, lay his right palm flat on the coffin lid one more time, and turn to face him.

Their eyes met. Vic felt something click in his mind, something about the

157

accent and the man's posture. His regal bearing, even in old age, despite the deep lines of his face..

"You're Priest," Vic said evenly.

The man stared at him for what had to be thirty seconds. Finally, in a deep voice, he said, "A priest, yes. And you're a lawman."

Vic glanced at the sky. He couldn't remember anyone using that word to describe him, ever. "I bet I have that look. And I bet you're Priest."

"A priest," he repeated. "I have my own parish in Mississippi." He waved a hand at the casket. "This is what I do. I see people off this earth. I baptize them into it. I join them in marriage. Counsel them when times are hard."

"And I take care of the ones who don't take to your teaching."

The man didn't answer, but Vic saw a flicker of humor in the man's eyes. "I'm Detective Vic Lenoski. I'm looking into Geno Varelli's case. I want to find who shot him."

"And I'm looking into what's good for his soul." The man returned the Bible to the duffel, zipped up, and moved a few steps from the casket. Vic mirrored his steps, maintaining eye contact, understanding the man didn't want to talk directly in front of Geno's body.

"You paid for Mr. Varelli's funeral," Vic said, modulating his voice. "Even moved it up a day, which I'm guessing cost even more. Came up here from Mississippi to speak over the casket. You're John Jefferson. And maybe you are a priest. It's been hard to find out anything about you."

The man didn't answer.

Vic felt the same frustration he'd felt after finding Thuds. It rose inside him like the first tendril of smoke from kindling. "Do you have a few minutes to talk?"

"I have to get to the airport. I have a flight."

Vic nodded in the direction of his car. "I'll drive you. Cabs are expensive and yours left you."

Priest didn't follow the direction of Vic's nod with his eyes, which told Vic he'd spotted the car and guessed who he was, perhaps even before he started the service. Vic held his palms up. "Just a ride to the airport. Nothing more. We can talk. I need to understand who Geno worked with in the months before he was arrested. What happened back then. See if anyone might still have a grudge. Maybe something from those days is playing out now."

The man lowered his duffel to the ground with the slow, thoughtful movements of a patient man. Vic remembered how Bandini had characterized Priest as disciplined. Vic saw it in those movements. Priest turned to Vic and waited, his eyes calm and deep.

"And anyway," Vic added. "All those robberies Geno and Priest pulled off, back in the day, the statute of limitations is long gone. I don't care about them. Not at all. I just want to find the person who killed your friend." He had the fleeting wish that Liz was with him. Sometimes, seeing a black police officer helped convince people to talk, but he also knew that sometimes it backfired. That some considered black police officers a sell-out and shunned them.

The man stepped closer and held out his hand. "John Jefferson."

They shook. His hand was warm, the grip enveloping without being a show of force. A handshake you could trust.

"Like I said, my name's Vic Lenoski. Why don't we walk to my car?"

John picked up his duffel, made a 'lead the way motion' with his hand, and together they followed the road over the crest of the hill and down to his car.

As Vic turned the ignition, John slid the passenger seat back and unwound his long legs as best he could.

Vic drove the twisting road down the hill, wondering how to start the conversation. He automatically took a right at the next intersection and immediately wished he hadn't. This particular road took them past Dannie's grave, and as they neared it, he couldn't help but glance at the headstone. A small bouquet of wildflowers sat at the base. He wondered who put them there. They looked too fresh for Anne to have done it.

"I thought you'd be asking me questions by now," John said.

Vic concentrated. "I was thinking about something." He glanced at John. "Just to make sure I have the right guy. You *were* called Priest, back in the day, and you were Geno's partner?"

"I didn't call myself that, everyone else did." He shifted his legs. "What they didn't know was that I'd felt the calling by then. I knew my place was with the church."

"And you made that happen."

"With God's grace."

"Where is your parish?"

"I told you. In Mississippi."

"But which town?"

Priest stayed quiet. They reached the front gate of the cemetery and Vic took the exit road that branched to the right.

"If this is going to work," Priest said slowly. "We need boundaries. Don't misunderstand me, I'd like to help you find whoever killed Geno. He was my friend. A lot of what I have was because of him. But that doesn't require you to know every single thing about me."

Vic heard a firmness in his voice that wasn't going to bend.

"Okay. That's fair." Vic negotiated the turn onto Butler Street and gradually accelerated. "But I'll still call you Priest. So. Tell me how you guys met."

"The Army. Korea. He was in the motor pool and I worked in the kitchens. I used to run a regular craps game and he started showing up. Turned out he ran a poker game twice a week. We got to be friends."

"He was a mechanic?"

"Yes. Geno could figure out anything mechanical. And he liked working with tools."

Vic stopped at a red light. "What did you bring to the table, when you partnered up?"

Priest didn't say anything until the light turned green. "We had each other's addresses when we left the Army. He wrote and told me he was thinking about getting some kind of after-hours casino going. He wanted me to run the craps table, be the stick man, and he'd run the poker and blackjack tables. But when I got here, he told me he wasn't allowed to do it. I guess some crime boss ran all the city's gaming and didn't want the competition. We were both flat broke. He said we should hit some jewelry stores, that kind of thing. I talked him out of it."

Vic glanced at Priest, and his look of disbelief must have been obvious.

Priest shook his head slowly. "You're like a kid who reads a line out of the Bible and thinks they know God and His intent. You don't. You have to get past the words. Understand the context, why the line is in Matthew and not Corinthians, how it connects to other biblical stories."

"Okay."

"I talked him out of it because we'd get caught. I told him I'd only agree if we did smart jobs. And after three years, tops, we get out."

Vic liked this conversation. "You gave him a plan."

"I gave us both a plan." He held up a large hand and raised one finger at a time as he spoke. "Fewer jobs, smarter jobs, bigger paydays. That's the trinity. And we needed a plan for the money. Big cars, fancy houses, and girlfriends don't get you anywhere but broke, and it's waving a flag that says arrest me. You need a way to use the money that nobody notices. Maybe does some good."

"Like building a church."

Priest nodded, more to himself than anything else. "Like building a church. A brick one, with classrooms to teach kids. Enough to pay good teachers, give kids meals."

"And Geno went along with it."

"Everyone had Geno wrong. They thought he just liked a good time. But deep inside? He knew that wouldn't get him anywhere. When I gave him my terms, he jumped at it. We were both gamblers, and I think he also liked the idea of a three-year hot streak."

Vic wanted to ask what happened at the bank when Geno was arrested, but decided to wait. "What did you guys do first?"

Priest didn't say anything and Vic was preoccupied for a few moments as he negotiated the on-ramp to the parkway leading to the airport. As they drove through the Fort Pitt tunnel he glanced at Priest. "As I said, none of this matters now. Statute of limitations has passed."

Priest glanced at him. "Do you think I would put a foot in Pennsylvania without checking that first?"

"You'd be surprised what some people do."

161

"Do I seem to be someone who wouldn't bother to check?" He shifted his long legs. "I haven't thought about all this in a long time. Give me a minute."

Vic wondered if he was playing out the ride to the airport to say as little as possible by the time they arrived.

"Do you remember those days?" Priest asked slowly.

"I talked to a reporter about the eighties, and I heard a lot of stories when I started on the force. I have a pretty good sense of it."

"Then you'd know if we were going to hit some big paydays, we needed protection from one of the bosses."

"I hadn't thought of it that way."

Priest looked out of the side window. Vic eased off the accelerator subtly, staying at the speed limit. He could time their arrival at the airport as well.

"We had two problems," Priest said to the window. "We needed protection, and we needed a way to wash whatever money we got."

"Makes sense."

Priest turned back to the windshield. "But we also wanted our choice of protection. Geno came up with a plan. He always had ideas. Some of them were good, his problem was staying disciplined and seeing them through. But he knew that about himself and tried to account for it. I thought his idea was crazy, but it worked."

Vic remembered what Justin Day had told him. "You stole from the gang bosses."

Priest turned and gave him an appraising look. "Right. Geno's theory was that the cops wouldn't come after us for that, and it would piss off the bosses enough that they would team up with us to stop the robberies."

"Or put a bullet in your head."

Priest smiled for the first time and it warmed his entire face. "That was a possibility. Sometimes I look back and I want to talk to myself back then. Tell myself I'm a fool. But we played it out. After we hit a few places, we put the word out we knew who was doing it. And we were careful to sell what we stole out of state, so we couldn't be connected to it. When the bosses came calling, we said we weren't going to rat out the people stealing from them, but we could make them stop. Take care of it for them. And we asked every boss that if we did that, would they be willing to work with us?"

"They actually believed that?"

He smiled again. "I doubt it. But around then Geno hit a bank. It was a big payday. We let slip it was us. Told the bosses we had money to invest with them. That meant their choices were shoot us to stop us robbing them, or join us, and make money *and* stop the robberies. Those guys go for the money every time."

Vic found himself grinning at the sheer audacity of it. "Is that how you hooked up with Zielinski?"

"Yes. He was the only one willing to make us partners. We bring in the money, he invests it in legitimate businesses. But I was out by then."

Vic glanced at him. "How were you out?"

"I told you. I'd felt the calling, and couldn't deny it. Plus, our three years was about up. I wanted to start a church. Repent my ways."

"Geno was okay with that?"

"We'd agreed on three years and he had enough money to do what he wanted. We had a couple of drinks together, and I took my share and left. Didn't come back."

Vic drove for a few seconds, thinking. "What do you know of the deal Geno made with Zielinski?"

"Not much. It was an official partnership, I know that. The more cash Geno put in, the bigger his partnership share. And he put in quite a bit. When I left, Zielinski had used Geno's money to buy three or four restaurants."

"Do you remember their names?"

Priest shook his head. "Too long ago. And I wasn't paying that much attention at the time. By those last few months, I was worried about getting out clean. It was all I could think about." He chuckled, a murmur from deep in his throat. "I was praying a lot."

They drove in silence, Vic reviewing the conversation. Finally, he couldn't help himself. "The one thing I don't get is why Geno got caught. I read the arrest report. He spent way too long in the bank. It just doesn't fit with the other robberies."

Priest nodded slowly. "I've thought about that myself. Geno knew better.

163

He never hit a bank when it was open, that was the first time. He always went in on the weekend." Priest glanced at Vic. "Or so I've heard."

"Then why?"

"Only thing I can figure is that he was desperate. I mean Geno was impulsive, no question about that. But to make that kind of mistake was not how he worked. He must have needed the money so badly he broke all the rules."

"And you were gone by then?"

"I think by a year."

Vic was feeling comfortable with Priest now, and he had the sense that Priest felt the same way. The off-ramp to the airport loomed ahead. "Look over your shoulder much after that?" He said it in a kidding way, wondering how Priest would react.

Priest settled back into the seat. "I do give a fine sermon about repenting your sins. It's my best one."

Vic had a smile on his face as they pulled up to the airport drop-off. A last thought came to him. "Before you get out," he said quickly, as Priest reached for the door lever. "How did Zielinski and Geno get along?" He thought of Geno's missing file. "Any bad blood between them?"

Priest dropped his hand and frowned. "I don't know much about what happened after I left. But before that." He hesitated and studied the sky through the windshield. "When we decided on doing three years, Geno pretty much stopped going out with women. But towards the end, he was seeing someone. He kept real quiet about it. I only saw them together once or twice, and I knew right away they were good for each other. It felt real between them, and Geno was happy when she was around. They were in love. I remember thinking she was the one Geno would settle down with."

"How does that connect with Zielinski?"

"Because she was Zielinski's girlfriend. It's why they had to keep it quiet. Sneak around. If Zielinski found out his girlfriend was dating Geno behind his back, it would be over for both of them."

"Did he find out?"

"I don't know. But Zielinski married her, not long before Geno went to jail."

Vic remembered Bandini and Thuds saying much the same thing. "We've heard about her. Do you know her name, where she is?"

Priest blinked at the sky. "I just remember the first name because of the Bible. Mary. Her first name was Mary. And I heard that she disappeared. She didn't stay married to Zielinski." Again Priest reached for the door lever.

"Two things," Vic said quickly.

This time Priest kept his hand on the door. "Be quick."

"I'd like a way to reach you. I may have more questions."

Priest turned to him. "Why do I think that's a bad idea for me?"

"However you want to arrange it. Maybe the phone number of someone who can reach you."

For several seconds he was absolutely still. His eyes searched Vic's face. Finally, he asked, "Are you married, Mr. Lenoski?"

"I am. I live with my wife and granddaughter."

"Your granddaughter. And your children?"

Vic fought down a lump rising from his stomach. "Not anymore. On the way out of the cemetery, we drove past my daughter's grave."

Priest nodded slowly, his eyes sad. He sat for a moment in silence, and then recited a number. Vic took out his phone, entered it into his notes, and read it back to be sure it was right.

When he looked up Priest's gaze bored into him. "That's my daughter's number. I'll tell her you might call. She's on the staff of a Congressman in Washington DC. All three of my children went to college. First ones in my family to do so. I gave you that number so you know, if you decide to come after me, that all the pain you felt at your daughter's death will move to my children. You'll break all three of their hearts, and the heart of their mother. And it will extend to my congregation. All any of them know is that I'm a minister, that I run a church. I was never *that* Priest to them. The pain you suffered upon the death of your daughter, I'm trusting you don't want to pass it on to my family, to my parish, and you'll only call for help about Geno."

"You can count on it," Vic said, meaning it.

"And what was the second question?"

Vic smiled. "That armored truck robbery, the one where you and Geno walked into the depot and said you were FBI agents? Left with a carload of cash? That was something. People on the force still talk about it. The sheer balls of it."

Priest blinked, and Vic again thought he saw a flicker of humor in Priest's eyes. "You should know that my second-best sermon is about believing in yourself. Because when you believe in yourself, you feel God's grace inside you." The hint of a smile tugged at the corners of his mouth. "Goodbye, Mr. Lenoski."

Priest pulled the door lever and shifted his long legs out of the car. Vic watched his broad, straight back rise away from the seat.

"Thanks for talking to me," Vic called after him, and a moment later the door thumped shut and he was alone. But Priest stopped, turned and came back to the car. He knocked on the glass and Vic lowered the window.

"I do have a favor to ask in return," Priest said carefully.

"What?"

"As you conduct your investigation, I would find it helpful if you could tell me Mary's last name. If you find her, I would like to know where she is, so I can speak to her."

"Why would you want to do that.?"

A far-away look came into Priest's eyes. "I was impulsive. I bought two plots. It crossed my mind that Mary might like to take her final rest beside Geno."

Vic wasn't sure what to say at first. Then he managed to eke out, "If we find her, I'll call your daughter."

"Thank you." Priest gave him a warm smile and rose from the window.

Vic closed the window, pushed the transmission into drive and pulled away from the curb. As he pointed the car toward Pittsburgh he said out loud, "I bet he is one hell of a minister."

Chapter Thirty-One

Frustration jarred Vic awake the next morning just after dawn. As Anne helped Lettie dress, Vic put out breakfast, and they ate together quickly. Vic responded in monosyllables to everything Anne asked him, and he had to force himself to acknowledge Lettie each time she needed attention. As Anne was about to leave, her arms freighted with Lettie and two bags, she presented a cheek for Vic to kiss. After he did she looked at him, a wry smile on her face.

"Someone is back in work mode."

Vic caught himself. "Sorry. I had an interview at the end of the day yesterday and I think I blew it. I asked the wrong questions."

"Call the person back."

"Not easy to do. That was my only shot at it, most likely."

Anne shifted Lettie in her arm and hefted the bags dangling from her other arm. "You'll get back in the rhythm, Vic."

He smiled at her. "Let's hope."

She looked down at Lettie. "Like riding a bicycle." She threw him a bittersweet glance and turned for the door. Vic stepped in front of her, opened the door, and propped it open for her.

"Good luck today," she said, sweeping past him.

Liz wasn't at work when he arrived, and Vic was in the process of printing out the preliminary autopsy results on Thuds' shooting before she appeared. She swung her bag onto her chair and went through the process of moving some of the contents into the pockets of her short leather jacket. The daily ritual meant she didn't need to carry a purse on duty, keeping her hands free.

"Levon make it back okay?" Vic called.

"Some bruises. I'm thinking a cracked rib."

Vic sat back and looked at her. She jammed something else into her jacket pocket and hung up the jacket, her movements quick and angry.

"You're acting like I feel."

Liz sat down. "I don't know what that man gets up to. And he was in a good mood. Just said things went well. Meanwhile, he looks like he jumped out of a moving truck."

Vic had trouble keeping a straight face. Levon was about the only man he knew who might actually have done that. "Maybe he did." He studied Liz. It was a new situation to see her frustrated by a man. "Anyway, autopsy prelim for Thuds is here. Nothing unexpected. One shot to the chest, bullet severed an artery. He didn't have a chance."

"And with that, he stood up?"

"Did you ever think Thuds would roll over?"

Liz took a long, cleansing breath. "No." She looked at him. "What are you pissed off about?"

He shook his head. "More frustrated. Interview with Priest. It was actually him. Pretty sure I blew it."

She arched an eyebrow at him.

"I asked him about how he and Geno met, what they did, what happened at the end. All that. But he's the guy who knew Geno best. I should have asked more about what Geno was like. Who he was as a person. I was too worried about finding the shooter, I forgot that understanding the victim gets you to the shooter."

"Walk me through it." She settled herself into her desk chair.

Vic described the drive to the airport and his conversation with Priest, and how cagey Priest was about revealing himself.

"But he didn't deny he was Priest?"

Vic shook his head. "No. But he was careful never to say he was, either."

"He took his money and started a church." She closed her eyes for a moment, a small smile on her lips. "Do you believe him?"

"He's definitely a minister. I heard him read the service over Geno's body. He almost didn't need the Bible he knew it so well. And the way he said the words, it was practiced. It sounded good. It was someone who'd done it before and believed what he was saying."

She slowly shook her head. "He took the money and started a church. You know, the older I get the more I believe you can never tell how shit will work out. I mean look at that. All those robberies, and then he uses the money for a church. A school."

"Agree with that. Anyway, in terms of who Geno was, I did confirm a few things." He squeezed the bridge of his nose between his fingers. "He liked to party, but cleaned it up when Priest put them on a plan. Justin Day told us that as well. Priest also said Geno was creative and good with his hands. But here's the big one." Vic took a second to let the tension build. "Geno had a serious girlfriend. And, get this, she was Zielinski's girlfriend. The one Zielinski married, so it has to be Mary. And Priest thought it was so serious they made sure Zielinski never found out."

"We don't know for a fact that he didn't find out."

"We don't."

Carter Lee's voice interrupted Vic's thoughts. Carter was walking down the aisle toward them, holding a worn manila file up in the air. "Here's something that might help you guys." He handed the file to Vic. "Geno's criminal and incarceration files. They showed up, finally. It was buried in the DA's archives."

Vic weighed the file in his hand. "Did you read it?"

Carter peered at him. "That's what you guys are here to do. But yeah. I skimmed it. He was a CI. And guess who he ratted out?"

"Paul Zielinski." Both Vic and Liz said the name, Liz a hair faster.

"You got it. Let me know what you think." He pivoted away from them but continued around until he was looking at them again. "And did you guys see Newsburgh today?"

Vic shook his head. He didn't need to check the news site. He could guess what was coming.

"They went after Hana again. Another murder, where does it all stop?

Why is our DA so incompetent? That kind of crap." Carter's dark eyes flashed.

Vic was silent for a moment. "That can't be Chilton. He doesn't know anything about Thuds' shooting."

"Yeah, there was a change with that. It's no longer a 'well-placed source in the Allegheny County Detectives,' but 'multiple sources.'"

"That makes it sound worse," Liz said quietly.

Carter nodded, his lips pursed. "Exactly. It's less explicit and sounds way worse. You guys need to get on it." This time when he turned, he headed back to his office.

Liz and Vic glanced at each other and turned to their computers to check the Newsburgh site. Vic skimmed the story and came away shaking his head.

"They've got nothing but the fact of Thuds' being shot."

"Even that's too much. I mean, we haven't had a press conference about it yet. How do they know he was shot?"

"Good question. I really need to talk to Chilton."

Liz lifted her head from her computer screen. "Like I said earlier, you're on your own on that one."

Vic lifted the file folder Carter had just given him. "Let me go over this, you can too, then we need a plan of action."

"Works for me."

Vic took his time reading through Geno's file, and when he was finished gave it to Liz. As she read, he went to the Newsburgh site and found all the stories written about the reorganization of the DA's office and Allegheny County Police, and the murders of Geno and Thuds. He read them in chronological order, oldest to newest. Carter was right. The way they named the source in the last article had changed, and the ending had a new twist.

Newsburgh said they reached out to the DA's office for comment and had received none. It was subtle, but Vic could see a gradual escalation of the attack on Hana. In the first articles, it had more to do with tone and a gradual increase in how strident the complaints about the DA's office

170

became, ending with this latest article that suggested multiple sources were now complaining about Hana, and she wasn't willing to go on record to defend herself. It felt orchestrated to him, as if someone was tightening a noose.

He wondered if Justin Day might have an opinion about the articles, given his years of working for newspapers. He weighed calling him, but decided against it. He didn't want to give Day the impression he was worried about Hana's press coverage. That would be blood in the water for him.

"So Geno rats out his partner Zielinski, and doesn't get a reduced sentence."

Vic turned to Liz. She was sitting straight-backed in her chair.

"Right, and the reason he doesn't get a reduced sentence?"

"I had to read between the lines on that one." She held up a piece of paper. "He rats out Zielinski, and a few months later a guy on the inside jumps Geno in jail. I'd guess after Zielinski was arrested he sent a guy on the inside after Geno in revenge."

"Snitches get stitches."

Liz pursed her lips. "But Geno sees it coming, and when the guy attacks, Geno kills him with a shiv."

"And there goes his early release. When that happens, Geno is no longer your model prisoner. Then he gets into more scrapes, and the prison board keeps tacking additional years onto his sentence. But did you notice the one interesting thing?"

Liz returned the sheet to the file. "What?"

"As a CI, who else did he rat out?"

Liz's eyes lit up as she understood what Vic was saying. "No one. It was only Zielinski."

"Exactly. But my question is this. Did he turn CI just to get Zielinski, or, when his sentence wasn't shortened, did he get pissed off and refuse to rat anyone else out?"

"No way to know."

Vic smiled at her. "But there's one thing we can do that might help. Priest kind of gave me the idea."

Liz waited, her arms crossed.

"Run down everything we can on Zielinski's wife, this Mary person. Geno was sleeping with her and Mary didn't marry Zielinski until Geno was already in jail. I'm wondering if that has something to do with it. Maybe Geno was so pissed about Zielinski and Mary getting married he ratted out the new husband."

Liz smiled. "Sounds like men. If I can't have her, you can't either."

"Exactly."

"But that doesn't get us anywhere near who shot Geno. Or Thuds."

"Killjoy." Vic stood up, crossed to Liz's desk, and retrieved the file. He sat down, placed it on his desk, and looked at her. "We go back to Thuds. Start interviewing. See what we can shake out."

"Who do you have in mind?"

"Start at the bottom and work our way up. First this Aaron Holt guy, then Mike Turcelli, then Bandini."

She stared at him, her arms tight on her chest. "Doing it in that order means you think Bandini shot two people. You want your ducks in a row before you talk to him."

Vic nodded. "Only thing that makes sense. If Bandini, Zielinski, and Geno had some business deal, and Geno and Zielinski go to jail, guess what, Bandini is running the show. Everything is great for thirty-some years, until Geno shows up. Maybe Geno wants his investment and businesses back. So Bandini gets rid of Geno, but that means he has to take out Thuds, because Thuds knows the history. That would explain the weird interaction between Bandini and Thuds when we saw them a couple of nights ago, and Thuds calling that lawyer, Mendelbaum."

"Bandini will lawyer up. I just don't know if Bandini is cold enough to shoot Thuds. Those guys go back forty years."

"It's easier if you just order the shooting. That's another reason to interview this Aaron guy and Mike first. Those two guys are competing to take over the businesses. Bandini could be playing one off the other, and one of them might be willing to do Bandini that favor. Plus, we'll only get one chance at Bandini, and it will last exactly as long as it takes him to figure out we consider him a suspect. We need to be ready for that interview."

Liz cocked her head. "It's one way to go. And I can look into this Mary person. Maybe she's still alive."

"We could use some luck on this case."

Liz creaked her chair toward her monitor. "Then let's go make some."

"And I say we track down Aaron this afternoon as a starter."

Liz nodded, but she was already absorbed in work. Vic turned back to his own desk. He actually hadn't thought through any of what he'd just said. He'd made the decisions and patched the idea together as he was speaking. But he didn't mind. It was just a theory, after all, and theories never put anyone in jail. But they did give investigations purpose.

His phone rang, and without thinking, he answered.

"Detective Lenoski," asked a slightly nervous voice.

"Speaking."

"This is Craig Luntz. From Crime Instigations?"

"Oh sure. Craig, how are you?"

"I'm good. I, um, think I might have something for you. It isn't in the preliminary report I sent over. I just found out."

"Okay."

"It's the gun at the crime scene. We got lucky. I guess the store where the gun was bought closed a bunch of years ago, and they sent their ledger with the serial numbers of the guns they sold to the ATF. Our trace on the serial number came back way faster than normal."

Vic cocked his head. "You're talking about the gun found at Thuds Lombardo's house?"

"Yes. It was bought in nineteen eighty-two. And I thought this would be important. The guy the gun is registered to, it's the same person you're already investigating. Geno Varelli."

Vic squeezed the handset of his phone. "You're saying the gun used to kill Thuds belonged to Geno Varelli?"

But what he thought was, how the hell does that make sense?

Chapter Thirty-Two

Liz tracked down Aaron Holt and Mike Turcelli and arranged meetings with each separately, one after another. After lunch at their desks, Vic and Liz headed to one of Bandini's restaurants to find Aaron.

"I do like the idea," Liz said, as Vic negotiated the downtown traffic.

"What?"

"Geno comes back from the dead and shoots Thuds."

"It would make more sense if Geno shot Bandini. This just complicates things."

They drove in silence for a few blocks, until Liz turned to him. "If Thuds and Geno had talked before they were both shot, it does fit your Bandini theory. But I don't know how we prove that. And it would be motive for Bandini. He might think they'd started working together. But I have no idea how Geno's gun got into the mix."

"It's just a theory. I literally made it up while we were talking."

"Still, it's the best one we have. It connects the dots."

Vic thought about that. "But, like you said the first time, would Bandini throw away forty years of partnership just like that? The same holds true for Thuds. Would he? Seems hard to believe. Thuds would need a really good reason."

"Or, maybe Thuds took out Geno on Bandini's orders, and then Bandini took care of Thuds so there wasn't a loose end?"

Vic turned that scenario in his mind. "That's more logical, but if Bandini asked Thuds to kill Geno—and we still don't know why—it was because he trusted Thuds to do it. Then he wouldn't need to kill him afterwards. Anyway, anything more on Aaron?"

"Still waiting on phone records. He said Thuds called him yesterday morning, I want to see if they texted."

"Did you ask for records far enough back so we can see where he was when Geno died?"

Liz cocked an eyebrow at him. "You telling me how to do my job?"

"Just wondering."

"Of course I did."

"Okay, then." Vic spotted the restaurant and eased the car into the half-empty parking lot next to it. Given the time of day, he wasn't surprised at the open spaces. Inside the restaurant, the breadth and height of the ceiling assailed him. With only two tables occupied by small groups lingering over late lunches, the space asserted itself, trivializing the dingy mural of rolling hills of vineyards that filled the entire right wall. On the opposite wall, a shelf holding antique pasta-making machines and clusters of squat, straw-wrapped wine bottles needed a dusting, as did the wrought iron lamps hanging from the ceiling.

Vic couldn't see how anyone would find the place friendly.

A waitress directed them toward the bar, and the bartender pointed them down a nearby hallway that led to the bathrooms, the kitchen, and an unmarked door. Vic knocked.

"Come in," a voice called.

They entered to find Aaron Holt in a small, disheveled, and badly-lit office. He was hunched over a large black ledger, handwritten, the kind of accounting tool Vic didn't think anyone used anymore. Aaron looked at them, took a moment to unwind his back, and straightened up.

"Thanks for taking the time," Liz said.

He rose and waved his hand. "Not a problem." He circled around the desk and moved a small stack of files and a box from two chairs facing the desk. He placed them on the floor, and gestured at the chairs.

Seeing Aaron away from the jumble of activity outside Thuds' house allowed Vic to commit his features to memory. Aaron's face was square, his skin tight with good health and exercise. His brown eyes were deep and, Vic thought, a little hard to read. His dark hair showed no sign of receding. Vic placed him in his late thirties, although he looked so healthy he might be older than he appeared. He was, Vic thought, almost handsome. Someone women would find attractive.

"How can I help you?" Aaron asked.

Liz took the lead. "Just walk us through how you came to be at Thuds', sorry, Vincent Lombardo's house yesterday? When we ran into you?"

Aaron nodded as if he expected the question. He took a moment to compose himself, and repeated what he told them the day before. He explained Thuds' call to his cell phone and the request to stop by. Vic noticed he was specific about the time of the call and when he was supposed to show up, which Vic took to mean that Aaron might be precise by nature, or knew that he and Liz needed specifics as they tried to reconstruct Thuds' day. He doubted he was doing it to buy himself an alibi. His statements were too easy to check against the log of his phone calls.

"And did he say what the meeting was about?"

Aaron shook his head. "Not really. I knew he was worried about this restaurant. Numbers have been off lately. I guessed it had to do with that." He waved a hand at the large black ledger. "I thought I'd better get at it. If Mr. Lombardo was worried I'm sure Mr. Bandini will be."

"Do you manage this restaurant?" Vic asked.

Aaron stared at him, and again Vic had the odd sense that he couldn't read the man. He almost seemed too calm. "Not directly. Mr. Bandini owns twelve restaurants. Each has its own manager, but they report to me and I'm in charge of their profitability. There's an executive chef responsible for the menus and kitchen staff. I work with him quite a bit. My job is to make sure all the restaurants run smoothly and make money."

Liz leaned forward. "I didn't know it was that many restaurants."

"We're regional. We have restaurants in Youngstown, Greensburg, and Uniontown, even two in West Virginia."

"Not counting the strip clubs." Liz's response was so quick Vic knew she was trying to rattle him.

"Even the strip clubs." Unshaken, Aaron spread his hands.

"Who manages those?" Vic asked. "You as well?"

"No. Mike Turcelli." A small, smug smile crossed Aaron's features. "Those require different management skills than balancing the books and staying ahead of the competition and trends."

Vic remembered Roofus calling Mike when they visited the storage facility. "How about the other businesses? Storage facilities, that kind of thing?"

Aaron shrugged. "Could be Mike, I don't know. I only discuss the restaurants with Mr. Lombardo and Mr. Bandini. That was my training. And the restaurants generate the most money."

"How do you get into a job like this?" Vic was genuinely interested.

"I always had food service jobs when I was in high school. Part-time, that kind of thing. I went to Pitt for a couple of years, and then switched to Pitt Bradford. They give a degree in Hospitality Management. When I was at Pitt's main campus I got a job at one of Mr. Bandini's restaurants. With the degree, Mr. Lombardo made me manager, then switched me around to manage a couple of the other restaurants. In the end he moved me into this job."

"Nice run." Liz's comment sounded genuine.

Aaron started to say something more, but caught himself. He waited, his dark eyes switching from Vic to Liz and back again. Vic had the sense that at some point in Aaron's life, he'd learned to only answer the questions he was asked, and not volunteer information. But he was proud of his career, and his ego made him want to talk.

Vic couldn't come up with anything directly relevant to the case, so he asked, "You're from Pittsburgh originally?"

Aaron shook his head. "I grew up in Florida. Came here to go to Pitt."

Vic was about to follow up and ask why he chose Pitt, but Liz took over. "Anything we should know about the restaurants Mr. Bandini owns? Are they in trouble? Doing well?"

Aaron frowned. "What does that have to do with Mr. Lombardo's death?"

Liz smiled. "Just interested. I was wondering what you might have heard."

"I don't know what I would have heard. I manage the restaurants. I know

177

what the situation is, I don't have to *hear* anything. And under me they make money."

"Except this one," Liz shot back.

Again, Aaron seemed to catch himself before he said anything. When he responded his voice was thoughtful and measured. "This one is profitable. Just not as profitable as last year."

Vic thought of suggesting they dust the shelves and wrought iron and repaint the main dining room, but let it go. Instead, he came back with, "When you talked to Mr. Lombardo yesterday, what exactly did he say? About wanting you to stop by?"

Aaron turned to him, pointedly not looking at Liz. "As I said before. Nothing specific. He told me he had a question and asked me to stop at his house before work."

"Nothing else?" Vic pressed.

"Just that he wanted to warn me about something."

Out of the corner of his eye, Vic saw Liz cock her head. "Warn you about what?"

"I don't know. That's all he said. That's why I guessed it might have to do with this restaurant. I thought he wanted to warn me that Mr. Bandini was thinking of closing it. I mean if I couldn't turn it around."

"Did he ask you out to his house a lot?" Vic shifted in his seat. "I mean was this an unusual request?"

"It happened sometimes, not a lot. Sometimes he'd just show up at the restaurant."

They fell silent for a few moments, until Liz asked, "Can you turn it around?" Vic knew she was asking more to see how he responded than his actual answer.

Aaron gave the small, almost smug smile again. "I've done it before. No reason to think I can't do it here. The question is whether there's money to invest. For not a lot of money, I can fix the biggest problems."

"What are the biggest problems?" Vic had his own opinion, but he wanted to hear what Aaron said.

"Just one, really. The size of the restaurant floor. Ceiling is too high.

It's fine when we have a crowd, but smaller groups don't like it. They feel like they're sitting in a warehouse. A drop ceiling and some dividers with grouped tables would do it. But that takes money. We'll see."

Vic was surprised Aaron had landed on exactly the same thing he'd spotted. He'd expected something more subtle, or revealing about how the industry ran.

Liz was watching Aaron, just the smallest of frowns on her face. "Tell me something," she asked slowly. "How involved is Mr. Bandini in the business? Compared to Mr. Lombardo."

Aaron seemed put out by the question and took a moment to answer. "Well, as I said before, I don't see what that has to do with anything, but Mr. Bandini is the owner and Mr. Lombardo was like the Chief Operating Officer. Mr. Lombardo ran day-to-day operations. I reported to him. Take fixing this restaurant. Probably by next week I would have gone to Mr. Lombardo and made my recommendations. He would then talk to Mr. Bandini about it. You have to think about it from their point of view. For them, the question isn't whether they can afford eighty or a hundred thousand dollars to fix the space, they have to decide if they can live with the lost cash flow while the work is being done, how they get customers back afterwards, what's the right timing for the renovation given how the other restaurants are performing, that kind of thing. Once all that was decided, then Mr. Lombardo would call me and tell me if the money was available."

Vic suddenly remembered how the businesses had transferred to Mary Monahan in the confusion over the trust. He remembered Mary saying she'd retained ownership of the businesses and only handed the cash flow back to her father. "But is Mr. Bandini actually the owner?"

Something flickered in Aaron's eyes, the first real spark Vic had seen. "What do you mean, is he the owner? Of course, he is."

Vic waved his hand. "Ah, I might be misremembering things. Anyway." Vic glanced at Liz, who nodded slightly. Vic rose. "Thanks for your time."

Aaron and Liz rose as one. Aaron's eyes were hooded and he seemed distracted. They shook hands all around and Vic told Aaron they would find their own way out. The restaurant floor was empty of diners now, and

Vic was struck again with the restaurant's shabbiness.

Back in the car, they sat for a moment, Liz writing something in her notebook.

"Smug little guy," she said, without looking up. "That's the problem with guys who know they're good-looking."

"Yeah. He has an ego, but his career kind of justifies it. He's done pretty well. Interesting how the only thing that got under his skin was the idea that Bandini might not own the businesses."

Liz looked up. "I saw that. Not sure what to do with it, but I saw it."

"We have Mike Turcelli next, right?"

Liz nodded.

"Let's mention the same thing to big Mike. See how he reacts. Maybe there's something going on with that."

Chapter Thirty-Three

When Mike Turcelli finally realized he couldn't avoid being interviewed, he'd asked to meet at Bare Essentials, one of Bandini's strip clubs. It wasn't the first time Vic and Liz had run into this kind of passive-aggressive reaction to an interview request. Mike wanted to stay in his comfort zone and make them feel awkward. As they drove to the club, Vic suggested a five-dollar bet that Mike would skip meeting in an office in favor of planting them by the stage while a show was underway.

Liz refused the bet.

She missed out on five dollars. When they arrived at Bare Essentials, Mike was sitting at the edge of the stage, watching a blond woman wearing a G-string and stiletto heels gyrate to Heart's song Barracuda. Her movements were aggressive, her arms and legs working like pistons every time she threw herself into a new pose. Her perfectly enhanced breasts looked like armor. Vic couldn't see the attraction in it. The bouncer who'd escorted them from the front door tapped Mike on the shoulder, who rose and clapped his hands. The music stopped and the woman stopped dancing.

"I need to talk to these people," Mike said to her. "Take a break. We can finish up when they leave."

The dancer skated a bored gaze from Vic to Liz and lowered herself to the stage floor. With her legs pretzeled in front of her, the music and emphatic dance moves gone, she looked younger and almost vulnerable. She slid off one of her stilettos and massaged her toes, a look of relief filling her eyes.

Mike gestured to Vic and Liz and led them to the back. Liz caught Vic's eye with a look that said, "Okay, I'm surprised."

The office was at the end of a long cinder-block hallway. It was small, windowless, and smelled of talcum powder and sweat. Mike lowered himself behind the desk and pointed at a lumpy fake leather couch.

Liz considered the cushions and said, "I'll stand."

Vic decided she was right.

Mike shrugged. "What did you think of the girl out there? She's out'ta New Jersey. We're gonna headline her and move her through our clubs. Couple of weeks in each one." He shifted his gaze to Vic. "Nice bod, huh?"

Vic stared back. Somehow, away from Bandini, Mike no longer had the confused look on his forehead. He seemed more at home. "I'm not the right guy to ask." He held up his left hand and pointed to his wedding band.

"Never too old to look." Mike licked his lips. "I'm married, too, but I get to do this. My wife says look but don't touch. She says those girls can pump up my tires all they want, but only she gets to ride the bicycle." His eyes flashed with humor.

Liz looked pointedly at the couch and back at Mike, to make clear she knew what happened on the couch. But what surprised Vic was that Mike found humor in a joke more sophisticated than crude. He wondered if perhaps he'd underestimated him.

Not seeing a reaction to his wife's joke from either of them, Mike looked from one to the other. "Okay. Let's get on with it. What do you guys want?"

"Let's start with where you were yesterday morning." Liz's statement, instead of a question, was a quick way to take control of the conversation.

"I told you yesterday. I was with Mr. Bandini. All day until we met you guys."

"And how about the day Geno Varelli died?" Liz rattled off the date of the shooting. "That morning."

Mike frowned and pulled out his phone, which looked like a credit card in his large hands. He swiped a few times and squinted at the screen. "Out of town." He looked up. "I was in West Virginia."

"Can anyone confirm that?"

"Sure. I can find people."

Liz barely let him finish his sentence. "Do they all work for you?"

Mike blinked. "Yeah. Pretty much. Why?"

Vic had the immediate sensation he was stalling for time. The logic of Liz's question was so simple anyone could understand it.

Liz cocked her head. "Big guy like you, you think your employees would say anything you don't want them to say?"

Mike gave them a crooked smile. "Hadn't thought of that."

Vic didn't buy it for a second and the frustration he'd felt that morning resurfaced. He was sure of Mike, now. "Okay, Mike. It's time we had a serious conversation. You've been playing the dumb goon with us, you always have. But Thuds put you in charge of a bunch of businesses, and when we asked your permission to open the storage container, guess what, you didn't need to check with anyone before asking for a warrant. So let's start there. Have you been in that storage unit lately?"

Mike shifted, and Vic saw something flicker on his face. It might have been the way the overhead fluorescent light played off the planes of his cheeks as he moved, but Vic didn't think so.

"Nah. No reason to." Mike's eyes hardened. "You just here to bust my balls about that?"

"No. My point here is that we have to trust you, and you're making that hard. You play dumb, but I'm starting to think that's an act. I mean, Thuds put you in charge of a bunch of businesses. Thuds is smart. He wouldn't do that if you're really that stupid."

"Maybe I'm just lucky?"

Liz crossed her arms. "You know the problem with luck? It runs out. You're an ex-con with two assault charges. You look like a big, mean son-of-a-bitch, and any jury will see exactly that. Your only alibi for Geno Varelli's murder is from people who work for you, so that doesn't count, and your alibi for Thuds' murder is someone who might have motive to kill Thuds. It starts to look like you and Bandini are covering for each other. And my partner and I here will testify that you don't cooperate. Does any of that sound lucky?"

Mike blinked and for a moment looked oblivious, like the boulder someone could never quite push all the way to the top of the hill. He leaned forward and his eyes flashed. "Mr. Bandini had motive to kill Mr. Lombardo? How stupid are you guys?"

"Why do you think that?" Vic said quickly, ignoring how Mike threw back his insult.

"I'll give you two reasons." Mike sat back. "Thuds ran everything. He's forgotten more about Mr. Bandini's businesses than Mr. Bandini ever knew. And guess what, Mr. Bandini knows that. And second. Those guys fit like bullets in a gun. One doesn't work without the other. You should have seen Mr. Bandini when he heard about Thuds. He was gut punched. Still is. He hasn't said ten words since. Most he was able to talk was to you. And here's a free reason. Those two guys. All they've been through together? The years watching each other's backs? Mr. Bandini would never order Thuds dead. If it came to something like that he would have died for him. Not even a question."

"See that?" Vic said gently. "You're smarter than you act. Quit bullshitting us."

Mike stretched his chin into the air, the thick corded muscles of his neck flexing. "People look at me, they think big dumb-ass ox. I let 'em think that way. No law against that."

Vic smiled, finally feeling like he was getting somewhere. "Actually, it's smart. You let people underestimate you."

Mike shrugged. "Whatever. Now what do you guys want?"

"An alibi for the morning Geno Varelli was shot, corroborated by someone who doesn't work for you," Liz said.

Mike shook his head in disgust. "Yeah. By then I was probably driving home. I had to pick up Mr. Bandini at nine-fifteen and take him to the funeral. I went home, showered and changed, went to get him. I can give you some names."

Liz finished writing down his answer. "Okay, and for Thuds?"

"I told you. I picked up Mr. Bandini about nine-fifteen. After the funeral he had a meeting at his bank. I took him there. Then he met some guy he's recruiting to invest in a restaurant he wants to open. That was a couple of hours. After that, he got a call from a reporter. He calls Mr. Bandini sometimes. He was the one told him about Thuds."

Vic felt a frown crowd his forehead. "Which reporter. Do you remember?"

"Yeah. Some Day guy."

"Justin Day?"

Mike pointed a finger the thickness of Kielbasa at him. "Yeah. Most of the time Mr. Bandini ignores the guy, but he took the call this time."

The frown on Vic's forehead migrated to Liz. "Do you know why?"

"Beats me. He took the call. He does shit like that. Unexpected."

"Back up," Vic said. "Can anyone at the meetings confirm you were with Mr. Bandini?"

"Sure. Guy at the bank. I was in the meeting. Mr. Bandini was arranging to move some money around to pay off a credit line. Then he had a meeting about his own portfolio, I waited in the lobby for that. Bunch of people saw me. I sat in on the meeting with the investor."

Liz asked the details about the investor and who they talked to at the bank. Vic watched the exchange. Now that Mike had shed the dumb goon act he seemed relaxed, more natural. He wondered how long Mike had play-acted it. Another thought crossed his mind, the one about who was in line to take over from Thuds. Was it Aaron or Mike? But it was Mike who sat in on the meetings with Bandini, not Aaron. If Aaron was likely to take Thuds' place, surely he would have met the investor. After all, they were discussing a restaurant, one that Aaron might manage. He wondered if that had anything to do with Mike dropping his act. Perhaps Mike saw a time coming when he wouldn't need it anymore.

Liz fell silent and glanced at Vic. From the front of the strip club, Warrant's song Cherry Pie started up.

"Tell me something, Mike," Vic said slowly. "You run that storage facility with the unit we wanted to look into. Do you get text notifications from it when someone enters a unit?"

Mike shook his head. "I have no idea what you're talking about."

"You might want to ask Roofus," Liz said placidly. "He's got a handle on it."

"And one other thing," Vic added. "We're just trying to get our heads

185

around something. Who actually owns all of Bandini's businesses? I mean I heard it isn't him."

Mike cocked his basketball-sized head. Confusion flickered in his eyes, but this time it wasn't the calculated confusion of Mike playing the goon. "What are you talking about? Mr. Bandini owns them."

"Yeah, does he?" Vic smiled at him and glanced at Liz. The look on her face said she knew Vic had just dropped chum in the water, and it would be best to let Mike feed. Vic settled his gaze on Mike. "Okay, Mike. We appreciate you helping us. We can find our own way out."

Liz turned and ducked through the door. Vic followed her. He glanced back at Mike as he turned into the hall. Mike was still behind the desk, head still cocked, staring at him. The confusion was gone from his eyes, replaced by a thoughtful, considering look. The inward gaze of someone reorienting their thoughts, changing the way they looked at things.

On the stage, a redhead with black roots shimmied against a pole. Two young men sat center front of the stage with large glasses of draft beer. Even from that distance, Vic thought the beer looked flat. In the same instant, Vic was seized with a memory of the burned-out hulk of the trailers where Dannie died in North Dakota. He wanted to get outside. He wanted out. Dannie hadn't worked in a strip club, but she'd been on offer just like the blond and the redhead. He shot through the door into the parking lot ahead of Liz. He slowed, letting Liz catch up, the sun hot on the top of his head. He didn't want her to notice how worked up he was. To ask what was going on. He just didn't want to talk about it.

He breathed and took his time getting into the car, to level himself out.

"Justin Day," Liz said, as she strung on her seat belt.

Vic concentrated so his voice was steady. "Did not expect that."

Liz turned her head to him. "Mike had no idea Bandini doesn't own the businesses."

"Right, and he's already working out what it means. Our boy Mike has a plan."

Liz studied him for a moment, and Vic knew she sensed something about him. After a moment she said, "Sounds like he wants to be the one who takes

CHAPTER THIRTY-THREE

Thuds' place. And that is motive."

Vic started the car. "I was thinking the exact same thing. But I don't know how that gets us any closer to Geno's killer."

Actually, he'd been too worked up about Dannie to think that, but he knew Liz was right. Carefully, he put the car in gear and headed out of the parking lot.

Chapter Thirty-Four

The Sixth Day

So Bandini is naked, he thought. He doesn't even own his businesses. He felt some surprise, but more a need to laugh. In one way, of course, Bandini never owned the businesses. He stole them from his father, and so from him. But the profits still accrued to Bandini. He was sure of that, and little else mattered. That settled the laugh in his throat.

He shook his head. Of course Bandini doesn't own them. Create man, and they will bite the apple. They will enslave the needy to be king; find wars and lions to make martyrs of the faithful. And most of all, protect their riches behind walls and arcane secrets.

The ownership, he was sure, was a parlor trick. Sleight of hand by a black-clad magician with run-down heels and empty patter. A confection of legal constructs and underslinging.

It didn't change his plans, he knew. As before, he would approach Bandini. But instead of simply forcing him to sign over the businesses, he would first ferret out the facts of ownership. An additional, minor step.

He'd been surprised at how Thuds' death overwhelmed Bandini. He'd become vulnerable; he stank of rot and failure. A man bereaved was a man disarmed. The time had come to begin.

And he saw an advantage. He already knew no board or investment group owned the businesses, so ownership rested with a person or legal entity. If it was a person, there might be leverage. A way to force Bandini's signature and cooperation. And if there wasn't, Bandini would never survive their encounter. That was fine. His death would reveal the contents of his will, and he would launch a legal claim on the businesses, using that radioactive contract from the storage unit.

Perhaps it would take years to resolve, but he was patient. His mother had taught him that. Through the years of moving from place to place, her mantra was the same. "Be patient. He will come for us. Your father will come for us." She'd never mentioned he was in jail, but her faith had stayed unshaken. Every evening she pulled the front room curtains or lowered the blinds and checked the street, searching for anyone waiting, for his father returning. She always answered the door with her revolver pressed into the small of her back.

Having no memory of his father, he'd often asked who he was. Her response was always the same. A finger to her lips, a silent plea not to ask. And then, "It will be a surprise. And we'll be a family again."

Secrets.

He'd grown up with that patience and the unsaid. It had taught him to live within his own head. He had decided when he was ten or eleven, after another nighttime move to a new city, that his mother's refusal to say his father's name was a way to keep him from letting it slip at school. To protect him and his father. That idea filled him with fantasies. His father was a spy. A military man passing from secret mission to secret mission. A man of such importance that he must remain anonymous, or the country, no, the world, would falter.

Until his mother's cough began. The doctor trips. The treatments and hair loss. He'd watched her—starting when he was seventeen—shrink before his eyes. And when he'd asked her, with growing fear, if she would recover, she'd only smiled weakly and said, "Be patient. This will pass. Everything passes. Just wait, and your father will come for you."

But the sickness didn't pass, she did, just weeks after his eighteenth birthday. In a mixture of inevitability and shock, he was alone. She'd prepared his school, warned them, shifted her money and car title to him. His college counselor helped him navigate budgeting monthly rent, food shopping. And later, when he found his birth certificate and the name of his father, and his father's will—dated just five months after his birth—he'd written to the lawyer who prepared it. Received back a letter saying his father had died in jail just six months before the death of his mother. And received, enclosed with that formal letter, a sealed envelope addressed to him in his father's handwriting.

Finally, his father had come for him.

He'd sat at the small kitchen table in his apartment, studying the handwriting. Opened the envelope and read the letter inside. Committed the sharp upright lines and pinched vowels of his father's hand to memory. He'd smelled the paper, wondering if the tinge that came to his nose belonged once to his father. And he'd learned of Geno Varelli, the tattoos on Geno's arm and the arm of his father. His legacy, and how to collect it.

Secrets.

With death, they always tumbled out. And that Lenoski detective, he wasn't capable of grasping them, even now as he walked among their shadows. Lenoski didn't have it in him, he was sure of it. All he needed to do was learn the ownership structure of the businesses. Then he would retake them, the contract from the storage unit his atomic bomb, its radiation his salve for the cancers that shaped his youth.

He would earn his birthright.

Chapter Thirty-Five

After Vic and Liz returned from their interview with Mike Turcelli, Liz finished entering her notes into the online system and turned to Vic. "I told Levon I would go with him to his first physical therapy session. I can help him with the exercises if I know what he's supposed to do."

"I thought it was a cracked rib or something?"

"And something with his shoulder."

Vic shook his head thoughtfully. "How badly was he beaten up?"

Liz's eyes flashed. "How would I know? He doesn't tell me anything. He goes on these trips and who knows what happens. I feel like smacking him myself."

Vic grinned at her. "Just not on the bad shoulder."

Liz stood up and shrugged into her leather jacket. "If I hit him he'll need a damn hospital. But that man is trying me. He is trying me. I will tell you that."

Vic watched her start down the aisle toward the front door, but after a few steps, she turned back to him. "I know you said Mary Monahan owns Bandini's businesses, but we need to check that."

"I'll call her. I wanted to talk to her about Thuds. They were close."

"Right. Which got me thinking. If we have this right, Zielinski owned the businesses, and Bandini works for him. Varelli funded the new business, but then he goes to jail because of some weird screwed-up bank robbery. Right? In jail, Varelli rats out Zielinski. Zielinski knows he's going to jail, so he and Bandini sign some kind of agreement for Bandini to run the businesses for him. But Bandini doesn't own them, he just oversees them, or has power of attorney over them, or some damn thing. And then, as Bandini told us, those businesses went bankrupt. Right so far?"

"Right."

"So how did Bandini end up building new businesses? I mean the ones he owned himself, the ones that went to Mary? Geno was the money-maker and he was in jail. No money there. It makes me wonder if the businesses really went bankrupt. But say he did liquidate the businesses, isn't there money left over from that? Maybe enough to start new businesses? And wouldn't that money belong to Zielinski?"

Vic sat back, Liz's logic sinking in. He remembered the look on Thuds' face when Bandini said the businesses went bankrupt. He hadn't been sure how to interpret it. Perhaps this was the point Thuds wanted Vic to see, or not see. "We need to know that," Vic said slowly.

"I'll look into it," Liz said. "I can start tonight when we're done with physical therapy."

"Just don't hurt him in PT."

"He keeps trying me like this, that man will have earned it." Liz turned for the doors. Vic watched her go. He knew she wouldn't actually hurt Levon, but what surprised him was the strength of the emotion driving her words. He knew it came from her concern for him, a primitive need to protect him. She'd fallen hard for Levon, Vic realized, perhaps more than she even understood herself.

He turned to his desk and checked through his phone for Mary Monahan's number. Dialed.

It took almost a minute to work his way past the receptionist and Mary's secretary. Even then he was on hold another forty seconds before Mary came on the phone.

"Vic," she said. "It's good of you to call. I suppose I should have expected it after what happened."

Her voice was flat and hollowed out, and he steadied his own voice, not so much to match hers, but to respect her feelings. "I called to see how you are. I know you and Thuds were close."

She sighed. "Well, I wouldn't say close. I'm not sure anyone was close to him. But we understood one another. And I always thought he was on my side. Like you, he was someone I thought I could call if I needed to."

"You know you can always do that. And it looks like Liz and I also got the short straw on investigating Thuds' death. We'll do the best we can. I liked Thuds as well. I knew I could talk to him and get an honest answer, as much as he could give me one."

"I'm glad it's you and Liz. That will be more than enough, Vic. I know it will."

"Do you mind if I ask a question, then?"

Mary gave a soft laugh into the phone and Vic caught the unmistakable breathy tone of resignation. "Of course. I wouldn't expect anything less."

"You told me a story, some years ago, of your father's lawyer forgetting to update a trust, and because of that, your father's businesses came to you. You own them now, is that correct?"

"Well, not all of them. My father has opened at least two more restaurants in the last few years, and he owns those. He's also been pushing to let me sell some that aren't doing so well."

"But you own most of them."

Mary was silent for a few seconds. "I own the largest portion of his portfolio, yes. Why do you ask? Does this have something to do with why Thuds was shot?"

Vic sat back, the handset jammed against his ear. "It might. And maybe why Geno Varelli was shot." He was telling her more than he should, but he knew Mary wouldn't talk about it to anyone, and he wanted to keep her engaged. "Which led Liz and I to a question. Do you know how your father came to own the businesses originally?"

Another pause. "I'm sorry, Vic, I don't." Her voice was quicker, now. She was interested. "I was too small and my parents were getting divorced. Growing up I just knew that he owned businesses."

"And Thuds never said anything about it?"

"Not about that, no. Vic, is this why Thuds was killed? Do you want me to ask my father?"

Vic thought about that. He wasn't ready to approach Bandini yet, he needed to be sure of his facts before he did. "No need," he said lightly, hoping that she wouldn't pick up on his suspicion that Bandini might be a suspect. "It's just something we're thinking through, along with about five other things." He winced at his lie.

"Uh-huh." Again, Mary was silent for a few seconds. Vic knew this was why she was such a good businesswoman. She could spot a lie before anyone fully got it out. "I guess my father might be a suspect in all this."

Vic knew there was no way to soften it. "We always look at the people closest to the victim. We have to."

"And my dad is the common link between Geno Varelli and Thuds."

"He is."

"Well, twenty years ago I might have thought it was a possibility, but today?" She took a slow breath. "He's well into his seventies, Vic. He's got high blood pressure, glaucoma, and there's a list of fifteen things he shouldn't eat. He needs to lose thirty pounds and I can't get him to take a one-mile walk. Does that sound like someone who would shoot two people? To protect some businesses he doesn't technically own?"

Vic tried to formulate a response, but another thought rose in his mind. He'd dangled the idea that Bandini didn't own his businesses in front of Mike and Aaron. That would lead both of them to ask the next logical question: *who or what did own them?* A cold stab of fear shot between his ribs. If ownership of the businesses truly was behind the murders, and two people were dead because of it, he'd put Mary in danger.

Mary said slowly, "Well, I suppose that's not a question you can answer right now."

Vic realized she'd misunderstood his silence. She'd thought he simply couldn't answer her point about her father. Or wouldn't.

"Mary, it's too soon. We just don't know enough yet." He hesitated. "I'd like you to do something for me, if you could."

"Such as?"

"When you're at home, keep your security system on. Keep your eyes open when you're out."

194

The silence between them turned stony. "Do you think I'm in danger?" Her voice was a rasp with just the hint of a tremble.

Vic remembered the night six years ago when a man attacked Mary with a homemade knife. If it wasn't for Vic's intervention, and Levon's quick shot through a glass window, she would have been injured, or worse. He'd never asked himself how she might have internalized that attack, if it still scared her. She always came across as so self-possessed he'd never thought it bothered her. But attacks like that always did. It was impossible to forget them.

"Not immediately," Vic said slowly. "In interviews, we've mentioned to a couple of people that your father doesn't own the businesses. We haven't said who does. But someone might decide to find out. I'm guessing it's public record."

"Not really." She sounded distracted, and Vic knew she was doing her own analysis, weighing the pros and cons. "I moved them under a holding company. But the name of my lawyers is on the paperwork. It wouldn't take much to figure it out."

"I don't really think it's a problem," Vic said slowly, fighting between wanting to soft-sell the problem to reassure her, and be hard-headed about the risk. "Just stay alert. And if Liz or I spot something we'll let you know. We can always assign someone to guard you."

"Oh, I can't be bothered with that. Not over this. Killing me won't give the person the businesses. If I die they go into a trust." Her voice was quick and confident again, almost joking. Vic knew she'd finished her analysis, and given herself good odds.

"Well, I'll let you know if anything surfaces."

"And Vic?"

"Yes?"

"Keep me updated on your investigation into Thuds." Her voice caught on his name. "I want to know who would do that to him. I don't know why, I just need to know who did it. I want them caught."

"This is what we do, Mary. We'll get the person."

Vic hung up, feeling foolish. He hadn't thought through the ramifications of telling people Bandini didn't own his businesses, and he'd handled it badly with Mary. He shook his head, chastising himself. Right now, he and Liz had an advantage. Only Aaron and Mike knew, and if he and Liz contained the information just to them, one of them might act on it. He didn't know how, but it might be revealing. It might be the break they needed. But that only worked if the information was kept just to those two. He sat back in his chair, following his reasoning. The problem was almost everything they investigated ended up in a story on Newsburgh. If that happened, the whole city would know. Their advantage would be lost.

He couldn't wait any longer. He needed a conversation with Gabe Chilton. If Gabe was tracking their investigation, it needed to stop. There couldn't be any more leaks.

Chapter Thirty-Six

Vic found Gabe Chilton's address in an internal directory. The Allegheny County Police were as bad at updating their systems and records as the city police, he realized. It wasn't his day to pick up Lettie, it was Anne's, and he saw no point in waiting. Tomorrow he did have to pick up Lettie and that meant he wouldn't have time after work to drive into the northern suburbs and find Gabe's house.

Crossing from the south to the north of Pittsburgh took him almost forty minutes, thanks to the rush-hour bottlenecks of the tunnel and bridges. As he inched along, he looked up Craig Luntz's number with the forensics team.

Craig answered his office phone on the second ring.

"Craig, this is Vic Lenoski."

"Sure, Detective Lenoski." Craig' tone turned formal as he finished the sentence.

"Just call me Vic. Couple of questions. I read the preliminary on Lombardo's death, and you called me about the revolver you found. Has anything come in since?"

"Not really. We're still waiting on the tox screens, but the ME didn't see anything unusual."

"I mean the gun that was on the counter. You found the owner, but was that definitely the gun that shot Lombardo?"

"It was. We did forensics on the weapon and bullets. The bullet in the corpse matched one we fired from the revolver. It will hold up."

"We didn't get lucky with fingerprints on any of the unused cartridges?"

"No. Either the person wore gloves when they loaded the gun, or wiped

197

down each shell."

"Yeah." Vic glanced to his right at merging traffic and goosed the accelerator to move into a widening space in the next lane over. "We couldn't be that lucky. And I have one other question."

"Sure."

"Do you still do anything related to tech, or do you know someone over there? Do we even have a tech department?"

Vic swore he heard a muffled chuckle, but Craig was deadpan when he started talking. "We do, but like the Pittsburgh department, it's understaffed and swamped. Why?"

Vic wondered if that might be the reason why Craig left the city police. "Well, you know we didn't find Lombardo's phone, and I know he had one. I've seen it. There also wasn't any mention of a computer in the inventory list."

"Right, but we should have the phone details in a few days, we sent a warrant to the phone carrier. I can't do anything about a computer. You'll have to ask someone who knows him if he even had one."

Vic came to a dead stop behind a blue van. That was something else he hadn't thought to do. He should have asked Bandini, Aaron, or Mike. He'd noticed a computer wasn't on the inventory list of household items, and never thought to ask if he needed to look for one. "Okay, but here's what I'm really after. I'd like to know if Lombardo got a text notification within a few days of his murder, maybe with a photograph attached."

Craig was silent for a few seconds. "What kind of notification?"

Vic explained the system used by the storage facility, and that possibly Thuds was notified of someone entering a storage unit. And that he might have received a photo of the person.

Craig gave a slow whistle. "You're thinking the person entering the storage unit might be the killer?"

"Maybe. But right now, I'd just like to confirm he was the one getting the texts."

"The carrier can give us the text notifications, but photographs are unlikely. Carriers rarely keep the photographs a user sends, and never the ones they receive. I can call the carrier and ask. I still remember the guy who handles that for the company, I used to talk to him when I was in Tech."

"That would be a huge help, Craig. Oh, and one other thing. That safe in Lombardo's house. The one in the walk-in closet upstairs. Did you guys open it?"

"Tomorrow. Took a couple of days to line up a guy who could do it."

Vic spotted a break in the traffic and accelerated. "Thanks. And how's your dad doing?"

Craig chuckled. "Still fishing. You should hear his lies about what he caught."

Vic remembered Craig' father warmly. He'd been Vic's commander when he first entered the force, and taught him how to stay safe on the street. "Nice, Craig. Throw your dad under the bus."

"Like I said, you should hear the lies."

Vic was smiling when he hung up. The traffic was thinning out, but they were on one of the main highways. He knew once he exited it would cluster again.

It took another twenty minutes for Vic to negotiate the curving roads of a modern suburban plan before he passed through to a street of older houses, all of them two-story red brick with white trim in a size and style commonly built in the 1950s. Most had driveways that dropped below grade to a single garage door at the house's basement level.

Vic found the house number he wanted, parked, and walked past a newer model Ford SUV on his way to the front door. The mulch of the planting beds at the front of the house was faded and dotted with weeds. He couldn't see a single shrub or flower. He rang the bell and waited.

The man who answered the door was perhaps five-foot-eight, a pot belly pushing against his navy-blue t-shirt, with the pale face and washed-out eyes of someone just woken from a night of drinking. His faded blue jeans looked a size or two too big. The man waited, the glass storm door closed between them.

"Gabe Chilton?" Vic asked through the glass.

"Who wants to know?"

"I'm Vic Lenoski. I'm the guy sitting at your desk now." Vic hoped Gabe would be interested in why his replacement drove all the way to his house. It could go the other way and he'd be angered by Vic's appearance, but detectives were usually inquisitive, and he was hoping that would win out.

"Good for you." Gabe stared back at him through the glass.

"Do you have a few minutes to talk?"

"About what?"

"Bandini. Thuds Lombardo. Geno Varelli."

He blinked. "You got that case?"

"I did." Vic was starting to get annoyed. "Thought I might run some things by you."

Gabe blinked again, but Vic knew he was hooked. If Gabe was passing information to Newsburgh it would be tough for him to resist. "Why not." Gabe unlocked the storm door and pushed it open far enough for Vic to take the edge and open it the rest of the way, wondering the whole time why Gabe would bother to keep his storm door locked.

Gabe led him past a narrow stairway toward the kitchen at the back of the house, his new white sneakers almost gleaming in the gloomy light. Vic glimpsed a living room furnished only with a reclining leather armchair, a side table, and large-screen television. In the surprisingly neat and orderly kitchen, Gabe pointed to a small table and two chairs pushed against the wall. He turned and made a show of looking at a yellow wall clock, its face a plastic sunflower. The twelve, three, six, and nine were different colored butterflies.

"It's that time of day. You want a beer?"

Vic had already seen a beer can sitting in the sink, and he could smell beer on Gabe's breath. He nodded. "If you're having one."

"Yeah, I'm due."

As Vic sat at the table Gabe opened the refrigerator and returned to the table with two sixteen-ounce beer cans.

Gabe sat across from him, popped the tab on the top of the can, and said, "So you're the new guy."

"One of them."

"I heard about you." He took a long swig. "Thought you retired or something. Went out to North Dakota. Came back and quit."

"That's pretty much it."

"Looking for your daughter, right? Dave Norbert told me. How the hell he survived the shake-up I do not understand."

Vic sipped his beer, thinking of the best way to move the conversation where he wanted it. But what rushed to mind was the report of Geno Varelli's arrest record. There was a connection he hadn't made until this very moment. "Um, I was getting up to speed on Geno Varelli. I read his arrest record. You were one of the uniforms that found him walking down the street with a bag of cash."

Gabe sat back. "Yeah." He smiled. "I'd been working maybe six months. I was doing training with this other officer, Schieneman, I think it was. He was the one spotted it. I was so green I never thought that if we're searching for a guy just robbed a bank, then I should look for a guy carrying something big enough to hold a load of cash."

"How did Geno react?"

He shrugged. "He had his back to us. We pulled up behind him and lit him up. He pretty much jumped out of his skin. Didn't run or anything. Real cooperative. Next thing we have him in the back of the prowler. That's when we figured out who he was. I almost threw up. For a long time, I thought he might be the biggest collar of my career, and if it wasn't for Shieneman I would have missed it."

"Still a good collar. But I keep wondering why he spent so much time in the bank. That's what got him caught. Did he say anything about that?"

"No. Once I knew who he was I kept sneaking looks at him as we drove back to the station. He was just staring out the window. Looked like a kid who got his candy stolen. After hearing from people how good he was, and how tough, I couldn't get over it. I mean I'm pretty sure he was crying at one point."

"Huh." Vic sipped his beer. Gabe's hand was curled around his beer can and Vic noticed that the nails were perfectly trimmed. Maybe varnished lightly. Absolutely professionally done. He thought back to the drawer compartment full of nail clippings and had to take another sip of beer to kill the queasy feeling in his stomach. He thought about Gabe's story of arresting Geno. Gabe had sounded honest; he hadn't acted as if he'd made the collar himself. Even admitted he almost missed the arrest. Despite the fingernails, Vic felt his opinion shift. Given that honesty, he didn't want to be directly confrontational about Newsburgh.

"I wanted to ask you something," Vic said slowly.

Gabe cocked an eyebrow. "Didn't think you were here for the beer."

Vic tapped the top of his beer can with one finger. "Do you read the online rag Newsburgh?"

A small smile tugged at the corner of Gabe's lips. "Oh yeah. Been interesting lately."

"Well, we can't afford anything more to come out. It might put someone in danger."

"So why you telling me?"

"Just covering the bases."

Gabe took a swallow of beer, clunked the can on the table, and stared at him. "You think I'm leaking shit to Newsburgh? I mean it's obvious someone is. And you think it's me?"

"I don't know." That was a lie, he was sure Gabe was the leak, but he wanted to avoid a direct argument. "I'm just saying. Where the investigation is now, another story might get someone hurt. You already heard about Thuds, right? I don't want that happening to someone else."

Gabe studied him for a full ten seconds, then nodded at the sunflower clock. "You see that clock? My wife bought it. I always hated it. I thought it was the stupidest thing I'd ever seen. It looks cheap, it doesn't even keep time right. Butterflies, for Christ's sake. Then, about six years ago, my wife gives me divorce papers and moves out. Takes most everything with her. But she left the clock. You know why? Because she knew I hated it. She was spitting in my eye. So yeah, I was pissed when I was told to take retirement. Mainly because, when my wife walked out, part of the deal was she gets half my pension. And guess what? I can't afford to live here on half my pension. Losing my job means I have to sell the house, give her half the damn money, and move into some shithole apartment. The only reason I was working was to make enough to live in this house after I retired. So yeah. I was pissed when they told me to step out. Damn right. And that night I got shitfaced. I mean all-of-a-bottle-of-Jack shitfaced. And you know what I realized when I was halfway into that bottle?"

Vic shook his head, unsure where Gabe was going.

"I love that clock. I love that it's the damn ugliest clock ever. I love that my wife left it here to piss me off. Because I'm better than that. Screw my wife thinking she can knife me one last time. Screw her laughing about how mad she thinks I got when she left it behind. Nope, that clock is going to hang right there, where she can see it the few times she stops by. Understand. That clock is me saying I'm not going to play your bullshit, I'm better than that. And the same thing is true about my old job. I'm not some asshole who'll squeal to the papers or ream the DA. I'm better than that. Because right now, in the shit of where my life is, I need to know I'm better than something. And for me that something is not screwing with the people who fucked me. I'm better than that. Which makes me better than them."

Gabe glared at Vic for a few seconds and swigged his beer. Vic did the same.

"Forget I brought it up," Vic said when their beer cans were back on the table. "Anything you can tell me about Bandini or Thuds? Geno?"

Gabe tapped two of his beautifully manicured fingers against his can. "You talk to Justin Day? The newspaper guy?"

"My partner and I did. I guess he's writing a book about Pittsburgh crime in the eighties."

"You ever talk to him before?"

"Not really. But he seems connected. I called him because I found his number on your computer monitor. I was guessing you left it there."

"Yeah." Gabe swilled more beer and rotated the can, gauging how much was left. "And did he ask you for an exclusive when you break the case?"

"He did."

"Figures, but here's what you need to know. He always holds something back. It's how he stays in touch. He'll call to remind you he has the exclusive, then drop something more. That way he keeps you on the string, keeps you taking his calls. You might want to get ahead of that. Call him and ask if he remembers anything more about Bandini and Geno. There's always something. And he likes to keep the juicy stuff off the table until late, when you need it the most. Then you'll feel you owe him, which is what he wants. You might get some help from that."

"Thanks."

Gabe drained his beer. Vic drank a bit more to be polite and placed his can on the table. He couldn't decide if Gabe was lying to him about Newsburgh, but he sounded honest enough. And Gabe hadn't fished for information he could send to Newsburgh. He decided to drop it.

"Thanks for the beer. Let's hope whoever is leaking to Newsburgh quits. I don't need another victim. And I appreciate the tip about Day." Vic stood up.

Gabe rose as well and followed Vic to the front door. Vic opened it and turned in the doorway. "Any other thoughts about the case?"

Gabe looked up at him. "Yeah. No question Thuds popped those Columbians in the warehouse all those years ago. He got away with it. He's had it coming for a long time."

"I guess Geno had it coming, too." Vic let himself outside. But somehow he didn't believe his last statement about Geno. He belted himself into his car and hesitated before turning the ignition. At first, he'd assumed someone had a grudge against Geno and had carried it for all those years he was in jail. Unlikely, but possible. Then he'd thought it had something to do with the tattoos, and most likely it did. And possibly, he thought for the first time, maybe it was just a damn mistake. Somebody got something wrong.

He started the car, another thought coming to him. He and Liz had been so busy they never checked Zielinski's incarceration record. Whether he had a tattoo on his arm when he went into jail. A following idea came to him. The ME's report said Thuds had no distinctive tattoos or markings on his body. But if Zielinski had a tattoo, one that lined up with Geno's, then someone must have told each of them what to put on their arms. Someone they both trusted.

CHAPTER THIRTY-SIX

And for a crook, Thuds was the most trustworthy person he knew.
And now he was dead.

Chapter Thirty-Seven

That evening, after reading to Lettie and putting her to bed, Vic settled up to the dining room table with his laptop. For a moment he listened to the television mumbling in the living room, knowing that Anne was nodding off in front of it. He hadn't said anything when he came downstairs to avoid kidding her about it. He was just glad Lettie was his responsibility tomorrow, and that Anne would have a day off from the added errands of transporting Lettie to and from daycare.

Vic wanted to read Zielinski's incarceration file, but it was from so long ago that it wasn't accessible through the online county systems. It was locked in Liz's desk drawer at work. Instead, he did a public records search. It took some churning of the databases, but three wedding certificates appeared for a Paul Zielinski in the time frame of the late 1970s through the early 1980s. Only one listed a bride named Mary. Vic wrote down the maiden name Mary Twail. He returned to the other two certificates, stared at them and did a search on divorce certificates using the same name and time identifiers. Two appeared. Vic wrote down the dates, and the sequence of marriages and divorces showed that Zielinski had married and divorced twice before tying the knot with Mary Twail. His wedding to Mary was exactly a week after his second divorce was finalized. It was all interesting, but nothing suggested itself to him.

Next, he did a birth certificate search, and found one for David Zielinski, born to Paul and Mary Zielinski on May 18, 1984. Their only child. Paul Zielinski's only child. It was the first time in their investigation David's name had appeared.

He sat back. Canned laughter drifted from the television in the living room. Barely audible, he heard the engine-hum and swish of tires as a car passed in front of their house. The voices, that movement, somehow it all felt suspended and waiting, as if he'd reached a precipice. An idea slowly formed.

He'd accepted that the killings might be about stealing Bandini's businesses, but only because he needed a hypothesis to test evidence against. But he hadn't taken the theory seriously because he'd always thought greed alone wasn't enough. Not to murder two people in cold blood. Murdering two people required someone who felt wronged, or entitled. Or both. Who would fit that description? He thought through the names he knew of the people involved in the case. Only one seemed to fit. David Zielinski. The son. If David believed Bandini had stolen his father's businesses, he would feel wronged. And Geno had betrayed David's father by ratting him out. That was a monster-sized grudge.

He turned the name in his mind. David Zielinski. David might see murder as an acceptable way to get the businesses back, given the businesses were wrongly stolen from his father originally. He would feel entitled to them. Even if they didn't exist today. And Geno's death was revenge for a childhood of living without a father.

But who was David Zielinski? Where was he?

He searched public records for David Zielinski. Nothing. No wedding certificate, no death certificate. Out of desperation, he Googled the name. After another half-hour he didn't see how any of the people with that name could possibly be related to Paul and Mary Zielinski. They were all too old, too young. Too settled in their own lives.

He sat back. This was another question for Justin Day. But he liked the idea. Zielinski's son would harbor grudges against Geno and Bandini. He would feel entitled to take the businesses back. Yet, as Vic settled on the idea, he saw a flaw. Functionally, it didn't work. How would he legally take over the businesses? Did the murderer plan to kill at least two people and then run the businesses as if nothing happened? That made no sense.

Assuming the businesses actually *were* stolen by Bandini. Hopefully, Liz would have an answer for that in the morning.

He closed the laptop. He was tired and couldn't do more. He found Anne sleeping in her chair in the living room and gave her a gentle shake. She woke up, and after a quick kiss, staggered upstairs to bed. Vic turned off the television, sat, and stared at the black screen, organizing his thoughts. Tomorrow he would start a real search for David Zielinski, if for nothing more than to scratch him off the suspect list. And while he liked the motive of being wronged and feeling entitled, he had to consider the possibility that the two deaths were unrelated. That Geno's death was just a mistake. Something random.

Grudgingly, he swallowed the fact that if the murders *were* unrelated, he had no leads at all.

Chapter Thirty-Eight

The Seventh Day

I t was almost three in the morning and he was tired and needed to rest. He'd visited Terri after work and told her he would buy her a car if they chose it together. She'd responded as expected, and that had energized him for a time. But now his laptop screen glowed as if flush with the energy it had drained from him.

On the screen was a short profile from the city's business newspaper. He barely remembered the chain of web searches that brought him to this point. He'd started looking up specific businesses Bandini managed, which brought him to public filings that revealed the name of the holding company that registered the businesses. That gave him the name of the law firm that prepared the legal filings. A search on the law firm's website revealed a string of non-profits they supported, including photographs of fundraising events. And prominent at those events? Mary Monahan, Bandini's daughter. He would recognize her anywhere. A quick search on Mary produced the profile that currently sat on his screen. There, along with the names of the high-tech start-ups her company supported by her investment firm, was a list of other businesses she controlled. Several of them were restaurants. All of them supposedly owned by Bandini. One of them was actually Pesto's.

He sipped his whiskey. It roiled his stomach and left his mouth sour. His father's businesses should have passed to him, father to son, but instead, they passed to Bandini's daughter, father to daughter. That was what exhausted him, the layer upon layer of deceit and treachery.

He would make it right, and then he could rest.

He remembered his mother. Another Mary, and for the first time that night he smiled. The irony of it. That his mother and Bandini's daughter had the same name. One Mary who spent her life protecting him, another whose life was defined by what she stole from him.

He closed the laptop, the only light in his study a small desk lamp. The darkness settled around him, exactly as he remembered. The long night drives from one city to another in the rain. His mother singing to her Janis Joplin cassette, him pretending to be asleep, but staring through the car windows into the empty darkness.

Layer upon layer of irony. The gun he'd used to shoot Thuds and left on his counter. It was the same revolver his mother held against the small of her back when she answered their apartment door. His mother had warned him about Thuds all those years ago. Described him. How he dressed in grey and looked like a knife blade. Told him Thuds was the one to fear. He was the one Bandini would send. The only one with the courage to finish the job.

That was why he needed to shoot Thuds with that specific gun. It was the one that protected his mother from Thuds for all those years. After he pulled the trigger, he knew it had completed its task and banished his mother's fear. It was a totem, and so he left it on the counter. An offering to the past, one only he could understand. That idiot Lenoski didn't have the brains. He couldn't understand the subtlety of all this. The totems and the delicious irony. The true, long reach of the past and the clutch of its secrets as they strangled the present. The rage of it. The tragedy. The rightness of what he was doing.

His mother driving through the night, singing to that Janis Joplin cassette. Me and Bobby McGee. He knew the words by heart. How they echoed his mother's life.

He took a long slow breath, drawing in the darkness. He spread his arms and stretched out his fingers. Let out the breath. He *was* the past, he thought. The secret past. The only *true* past. And he had returned. He folded his arms in front of himself. And just as the song said, after this last day Bandini would be free.

Oh, the layers and layers of it all.

Chapter Thirty-Nine

Vic woke before dawn. He was sweating lightly but felt cold, as if he was fighting off a fever. He knew better. He hadn't had this feeling in years. It was a reaction to his brain failing to connect the disparate pieces of the case, to find a through-line connecting all the facts.

He rose without waking Anne and slid into a t-shirt and sweatpants. Carrying tube socks, he crept downstairs, through the kitchen, and into the basement. Only then did he turn on the lights.

He laced up his Title boxing shoes and shook out his boxing gloves. He started on his weight bag slowly, flexing his knees and loosening his shoulders with light punches until he felt ready to go. He drifted back from the bag, concentrating, flipped a switch in his mind, and darted forward. Hit the heavy bag with a three-punch combination and danced back. Surged forward again, four punches now. As he skipped back he felt his rhythm return. He charged forward and fell back, again and again, landing three or four punch combinations, timing his movements to the swing of the bag. He stuck to the rhythm, believed in his movement, even as his breath turned ragged and sweat rose to his face. His hands began to ache, his shoulders burn. Each punch was a coughed breath. His brain counted down. One minute fifty seconds. Could he go the full three minutes? Back and forth. Breathe. Body punch, body punch, left jab, right cross. Mix up the order. And then the imaginary bell in his mind rang and the round was over.

He walked the basement floor, his sweat speckling the concrete. When his breath settled into a regular rhythm he went back to the bag, took a deep breath, and started again, barely hearing the dull thuds of his fists on the bag or the shuffling sound of his feet on the concrete as he moved backwards and forward. His entire world was the rhythmic pounding of his fists, the arm jolt each time a punch landed and the creak of the metal hook as the vibrations of each strike traveled up the chain to the joist. When his brain told him three minutes was up he stopped, his breath ragged, his arms dead weights. The fever-like symptoms had left him. He shook his hands, liking the stiffness in his knuckles. He wiped the sweat from his forehead with the hem of his T-shirt.

As he walked about, catching his breath, his gaze strayed to the stack of cardboard storage boxes underneath the stairs to the kitchen. Some hadn't been opened in years. They were stacked there when he and Anne moved into the house, with the intention of sorting through them. Somehow, neither of them had found the time. He recognized one of the boxes on the bottom row. Without thinking, he tugged off his boxing gloves, placed them on top of the weight bag, and lifted away the boxes stacked on top of the bottom box. He ran his thumbnail down the center of the packing tape and pulled back the flaps. Everything inside was from a different time. His baseball glove, a collection of Sergeant Rock comics, baseball cards held together by a rubber band that broke as soon as he picked them up. He returned the cards to the box and spotted the cover of a small photo album. He lifted it out. The album was the size of a three-by-five index card, the photographs stored inside plastic sleeves. The whole album a throwback to the seventies, to the way photographs were returned to customers after they were developed in a drugstore. Vic leafed through them. The roll was taken during a family outing to Kennywood, Pittsburgh's amusement park. One was of him and his father climbing into a roller coaster car. Another, Vic standing with his mother.

He stared at the photograph.

His mother wore a white sundress with small blue flowers, her bronzed shoulders bare except for the spaghetti straps of her dress. Her brown hair was cut shoulder length. She was smiling. Vic stood just in front of her, his ten-year-old self squinting into the sunlight, his grin wider than a Pittsburgh bridge.

Thick emotion rushed up his throat. If he was ten, his mother would be dead within four years, beaten down by cancer. His father in less than twenty, fighting an oxygen tube for his last breaths. But in that photo, in that moment, they were smiling, happy. He imagined his father on the other side of the camera, snapping the photo, wanting to capture that one pure moment.

Vic started to turn the page and stopped. He went back to the photograph. Something shifted in his mind. It had something to do with how his mother was holding him. Her hands were on his shoulders. He realized it wasn't how she was holding him, it was what she was doing. Her arms were outstretched slightly, as if she was presenting him to the camera. No. To his father. That mattered, but he couldn't quite see how. It was as if his mother was saying to his father, look, see what we created? What you and I did?

He understood suddenly that what his mother was doing was instinctive, as ancient as the human race, and still potent. It was the silent communication of two people who had brought a child into the world. He blinked back the thought. He was overthinking it. He chastised himself. Something like that could not be so significant.

Vic closed the photo album carefully and placed it back in the box. He stared at it for a moment, regulating his breathing, then lifted some items to see what else he might find. Toward the bottom, he spotted the corner of what looked like an eight by twelve double-pane glass window. He knew immediately what it was. With a little shifting and maneuvering of items, he pulled it out.

Enclosed in the space between the two panes of glass were tiny iron filings. As he lifted the glass, he spotted a wooden frame with an upright leg at each corner and grasped that with his other hand. He carried both items to his workbench, placed the frame on top, and slotted the window-like glass into the upright legs of the frame, so the glass sat flat about six inches above the base of the frame. He returned to the cardboard box and dug around until he found a plastic bag holding several different-sized bar and horseshoe magnets. He carried those to the workbench.

He removed a horseshoe magnet and moved it carefully underneath the glass. The iron filings jumped and clustered, drawn by the force of the magnet.

Vic smiled. He'd been given this gift for his birthday when he was perhaps seven. Only later had he learned that his father had brought the iron filings home from the steel mill where he worked, and in the evenings after Vic went to bed, cut and bonded the two glass panes just far enough apart to let the filings inside move freely. He'd then constructed the wooden frame so Vic's seven-year-old hand could maneuver a magnet underneath the glass. He'd spent months fascinated by the way different movements of the magnet and type of magnet caused the filings to rearrange themselves from swirls to straight lines, from clusters to sweeping arcs. He moved his hand now. The filings shifted as he remembered, and so did something inside him, as if his insecurity about handling Geno's case was rearranging itself, changing form. He removed his hand from below the glass and stared at the magnet.

Maybe that's what childhood becomes, he thought, a kind of force that shapes the pattern of your life. For better or for worse. A little shift here or there and twenty years later your hands create loops instead of arcs. Clusters instead of a spread. It's a complete crapshoot. And yet it isn't.

He slid the magnet back in the bag with the others, watching it snap onto them. He collected the glass and its stand to take it upstairs and show Lettie. For some reason, he had never shown the toy to Dannie. He didn't know why. It had been under the stairs in that box the whole time she was growing up.

He knew that only six minutes on the heavy bag wasn't much of a workout, but he wanted to feel like himself, to banish the feeling he woke to and prepare himself for the day. He would do a longer workout that night. He put the toy on the dining room table, unlaced his boxing shoes, and placed them at the top of the stairs to the basement. He used a dish towel to wipe off the last of his sweat. As he started back upstairs he heard the morning alarm on Anne's phone go off.

After several days of being taken to daycare by Anne, Lettie was excited to be going with Vic, and she was cooperative and in a beaming mood all through breakfast. Anne looked rested as well, enough that Vic kidded her lightly about falling asleep in the living room the night before. She took it well enough that by the end of breakfast they were both laughing, with Lettie following suit, even though the conversation was beyond her.

When Vic reached daycare, Lettie was quick to get out of the car seat and was almost hopping when they entered the room. She barely gave Vic a hand squeeze and abbreviated 'bye!' before she was sitting among friends on the floor.

Vic's reaction to that, when he was seated in his car, was to think it was a good thing that she was settling in. He was also mildly annoyed over it. Somehow it shouldn't have been that easy. He shook his head at himself and put the car in gear.

Liz was already at her desk when he arrived at work. Vic slid off his jacket and after checking his emails, told her about his searches on Zielinski and his theory that David Zielinski was the person they needed to find.

"Makes sense." Liz gestured at her computer screen. "And I'm almost there figuring out if your friend Bandini stole those businesses. Something is definitely hinky, I just haven't got it nailed down yet."

"Okay, you keep working on that, I'm going to call Justin Day. See if he knows anything about Mary Twail and David Zielinski. What happened to them."

Liz nodded and pivoted in her chair to face her screen. Vic found Justin's number, but checked the Newsburgh news site before he dialed. A quick scan showed no new stories on their investigation, only a long, unsigned editorial pointing out Hana Richards's failures as the new DA. Vic and Liz's cases were listed with some others that remained to be solved. But the focus was on her lack of a plan to address racism within the Bureau of Police. Vic shook his head, annoyed. It was a cheap shot. No DA would have presented a plan about something so complicated this early into their tenure, and from what Vic had seen, with the hiring of Carter Lee, Liz, and some others, Hana *was* making changes. No fancy strategic plan was going to fix the problem. The changes had to start with new hires, supported by management practices. There was no simple, short-term cure. But the topic was a convenient way for someone to win political points. He was sure of it, now. Someone was out to get Hanna in the next election.

As he dialed Justin Day, Vic wondered if the editorial had anything to do with his visit to Gabe Chilton. It didn't seem that way. Vic hadn't given Gabe any information, but the shift of focus suggested Gabe might have been honest when he said he wasn't the leak. That complicated things. Then again, Gabe might just be laying low.

Day answered on the second ring, his voice rough from cigarettes. "Day. Talk to me."

"It's Lenoski. County detectives?"

"Yeah." Day stretched out the word. "I was wondering when you'd call. Was about to call you myself. Where are you on the Varelli case? Tell me it isn't connected to Thuds."

Vic smiled at the backhand way Day tried to confirm the deaths were linked without actually asking the question. "I just had a question, do you mind?"

"Sure, sure."

"When my partner and I visited you, we talked about Paul Zielinski, right?"

"Sure."

"So we're running down leads, making sure we talk to everyone related to this. That got us wondering about Zielinski's wife, Mary? And I guess their son, David Zielinski. Do you have a line on them in any way?"

"Huh. Let me think."

Vic heard a clinking sound, and guessed Day was stirring coffee in a mug. "Give me a second."

The phone clunked as if Day had put it down. A few seconds later came thumping noises that sounded like cardboard boxes being moved around.

"Yeah, got it," Day said suddenly into the phone. "I kept a file on Zielinski. Let's see what we got." Vic heard paper shuffling. "Yeah. Mary was his third marriage. You look at the divorce certificates and you'll see the first one was four years, the second two years, and Mary's right after that." He fell silent for a moment. "Yeah. I got a note here says he wanted kids. I interviewed him one time and he said family was important, everyone needs kids, all that crap. I figured that's why three marriages. Took him three to get the kids part right."

"And do you know anything about them? Mary and David?"

"Let's see." More paper shuffling. "Yeah, here, I talked to the wife after Zielinski went to jail. I thought he was on bail, called the house to interview him, got her."

"Anything interesting?" Vic felt like he was dredging information out of him.

"Nah. She didn't want to talk to me."

Vic almost rolled his eyes. So much for Gabe's statement that Day had a habit of dropping key information late in the conversation to keep detectives on the string. "Okay. Well, thanks."

"We still have a deal, right? I get first look when you catch Geno's killer? And I know the Geno shooting is related to Thuds getting shot. Has to be."

Vic steered past Day's statement that he 'knew' the murders were related. "Thanks. I'll keep looking. See if I can find them."

"Well, that'll be tough, given Mary and her kid were on the run after they left Pittsburgh."

Vic froze, his phone a few inches from his ear. He pressed it back to his head. "They were on the run?"

"Oh yeah."

Vic waited, but it was clear Day was going to make him ask. He closed his eyes, hating that he had to take the bait. "How do you know they were on the run? And why?"

"Well," Day strung the word out. "I still get the first call when you make the arrest, right?"

"That's what I said."

"Just lucky. You remember Art Rizolli, Ragman Rizolli?"

"The guy who was buried the day Geno died. Geno was there for the funeral."

"Right. Few months back, he's dying, and I snuck some red wine into the nursing facility where he was, figured I might learn something. We talked about the old days, a bunch of crap I'd already heard, and he told me one of his guys was in Florida maybe twenty years ago, family vacation or something."

"Right?"

"Anyway, his guy has trouble with his rental car and takes it back to a local outlet for the rental company. Not the airport. Walks in, who's behind the desk but Mary Zielinski. He goes hey Mary, and she turns red and says her name is Rose. Points at her name tag. But he knows it's her, he was at her damn wedding, for crap's sake. But he plays it cool, apologizes, and she gets him a new car and out of there so fast he got windburn. But he worries about it. He knows she left Pittsburgh maybe two or three months after Zielinski went to jail. He goes back the next day to talk to her. And guess what. They tell him she quit at the end of her shift the day before. Hadn't been back."

Vic felt warm. Day was right, that was the behavior of someone who didn't want to be found. Plus, she was working under a different name. "But why would she be on the run?"

Day chuckled, but it devolved into a hoarse cough. When he recovered he managed to eke out, "I asked Ragman that as well. Turns out, when Zielinski was picked up by the cops, the question going around was who ratted him out. Some people thought Mary might be the one."

Vic stayed silent. He and Liz had assumed Geno had informed on Zielinski, with the CI file and attempt on Geno's life in jail as proof. "Why would she turn over her husband and the father of her child? She can't testify against him anyway."

"Right question. Turns out Zielinski was handsy with the ladies. His talk about family was all bullshit. I knew that. He slept around, and check his first wife's divorce complaint. She said he beat her."

"So he stepped out on Mary and she ratted him out to get back at him?"

"That's what people were thinking back then."

"Does anyone have proof?"

Day sighed. "No."

Vic turned over the information in his head. "That's helpful."

"Figured it might be. If I think of anything else, I'll call."

Vic smiled at how neatly Day had set the hook. No question that next time Day called he would take the phone. He'd be a fool not to. Gabe was absolutely right. Day was very good at what he did.

"Thanks," Vic said, "I appreciate it."

"Here to help," Day said, and hung up.

Vic sat back, thinking about Day's story, how it didn't quite fit with the information in Geno's CI file.

Liz looked up from her computer screen, her eyes bright. She had an off-kilter smile Vic hadn't seen in a long time. "Got it. Or at least a good scenario."

"How Bandini ended up owning the Zielinski's business?"

She rapped her computer screen with the knuckle of her index finger. "Yeah. And he was pretty damn tricky. It was clever."

Vic opened his palms in a 'well?' movement.

"Okay, so Zielinski goes to jail. At the time he has three restaurants, right? All owned legit by a holding company under Zielinski's name. Public information. When I found that I was able to identify the names of the restaurants, where they were located, all of that. But guess what? Within eighteen months all three restaurants file for chapter eleven, one after another. They're all bankrupt. And they close."

Vic shook his head. "I don't get it."

"I didn't either. So I searched the restaurant addresses, and I noticed all three rented space in old buildings. I thought that was interesting. They weren't free-standing places. Next step, check who owned the buildings. Guess what, within six weeks of Zielinski going to jail, one of them changes ownership, a few months later the second one does, and the third a little while after that."

"Coincidence." Vic said it to get a rise out of her. It wasn't coincidental at all.

"Right. And all three were bought by the same holding company, but that holding company doesn't list the owner. Only the lawyer who set it up."

"And who is that?" Vic could guess.

"Our friend Andrew Mendelbaum Esquire in Squirrel Hill. I'm thinking we go back and have a discussion with him about this. That holding company doesn't exist anymore, but I bet they just shifted the ownership a couple of layers deeper behind false companies to hide the real owner."

"But how does that change the ownership of the restaurants from Zielinski to Bandini?"

"It doesn't, but it creates a way to do it. Think about it. The restaurant rents the space, but the building owner sets the rental cost."

Vic stared at her. "You mean Bandini bought the buildings then raised the rents high enough to drive the restaurants into bankruptcy?"

"That's my guess. I can't prove it yet, but restaurants operate on a tight profit margin. Double or triple the rent and all three go from money-maker to loser in a month. As long as the ownership of the buildings is a secret, Bandini just raises the rental cost and tells Zielinski it's out of his hands. Bandini was fine unless Zielinski found out Bandini owned the buildings. So Bandini closes down the restaurants, and reopens them a week later under a new name. I found the records for that as well. And when he does, Bandini legitimately owns the new restaurants, but no one knows that because his ownership is buried under two or three layers of holding companies."

Vic saw the cleverness of the plan. "And he keeps the same staff, maybe even the same menu. Just the name of the restaurant and the owner change."

"Right. And as part of the bankruptcy, the liquor license goes on sale and he snatches it up. He's good to go. Maybe he even uses the extra money he charged Zielinski's restaurants in rent to pay for the license. Sweet little deal for himself."

"Unless Zielinski gets out of jail and finds out."

"That's the risk. But that never happens."

Vic turned the concept in his mind. "But where did Bandini get the money to buy the buildings?"

Liz shrugged. "I can guess. Buying real estate is pretty easy. You don't need a ton of cash upfront to get a mortgage. And then you write off the mortgage payment each month to the new restaurant as a business expense. As long as he had enough for the down payment, he was good to go."

Vic sat back. "And another piece is what Day just told me about Mary Twail, Zielinski's wife. He said the scuttlebutt was that she turned in Zielinski before she went on the run. Maybe she actually gave Geno the information that Geno used with the DA. She does that and Zielinski goes to jail, Geno is free a lot sooner and she and Geno end up together."

"All's fair in love and war."

"But something went wrong. Maybe Zielinski found out and Mary had to run."

Liz nodded. "Not sure we'll ever find that out."

"Unless we find Mary or her son."

"Right."

Liz was silent for a few moments. "And how does this help us find who shot Geno?"

Vic's thrill at piecing together what happened all those years before sagged. Liz was right. But as quickly another thought came to him. "Well, if that's how Bandini stole the restaurants, it puts him back in the spotlight. What if Geno found out what Bandini did to get hold of the restaurants? Zielinski's restaurants were opened with Geno's money. Geno would have a beef with Bandini, he would want his money back. And Thuds is in the middle of all this. I bet Thuds knew what Bandini did. Maybe Geno and Thuds talked in the last few weeks and Thuds told Geno what happened. Then Bandini found out. It gives Bandini motive for killing both of them."

"But why go to all that trouble? Wouldn't you try and pay Geno off first? Much easier."

Vic frowned. "And Thuds was shot with Geno's gun. That feels like a message."

They both fell silent, and a moment later the ringer on Vic's cell phone filled the quiet. He answered, still preoccupied with what Liz had discovered.

"Vic? It's Mary Monahan."

Vic pulled himself back to the present. "Mary, what can I do for you?"

"It's my father. He was supposed to go to a doctor's appointment but he never showed. The doctor's office called me."

"Just call him, he probably got busy."

"No, that's my point." Her voice notched higher, and Vic caught a trace of panic. "I can't find him. I called his phone, his house. My stepmother said he was planning to go to a doctor's appointment, but he isn't there or at his office."

"Call Mike Turcelli. He'll be driving him."

"I did, but Mike isn't answering his phone either."

Chapter Forty

Vic put his hand over his phone and called to Liz, his muscles tingling. "Do we have a list of all of Bandini's businesses?"

She frowned and nodded.

Vic dropped his hand. "Mary?"

"Yes?"

"We'll call around your Dad's places and see if we can find him. Is he driving the Escalade?"

"Always."

"And you're sure he can't be anywhere else?"

"I've been calling him on and off for an hour."

"Okay. I'll see if we can track down his vehicle. Stay by the phone."

"Thanks, Vic."

Vic ended the call and turned to Liz again. "Look up Bandini's Escalade plate. I'll see if we can get an APB out on it. Call it a welfare check."

"If Turcelli isn't answering his phone he might be involved."

Vic was already standing. "Right. Approach with caution. Give me a second." He strode to Carter Lee's office and knocked on the door frame. Lee looked up from a file he was reading and waved Vic inside.

Vic gave him a sketch of the problem, an overview of Turcelli, and how Bandini might be in danger.

"What do you want to do?" Carter asked quickly.

"APB on the Escalade, call it a welfare check but approach with caution."

"Is this Turcelli guy likely to be armed?"

"Guaranteed. He's Bandini's bodyguard. He'll be armed. Plus he might be involved with the murders, we don't know yet."

Carter let out a quick breath. "History of violence?"

"Oh yeah. Assault and battery. Did time for it."

Carter picked up his phone and relayed his instructions on the APB to Karen, adding 'approach with extreme caution.'

When he hung up, Vic said quickly, "we have a list of Bandini's businesses. Liz and I will start calling them, see if we can find him. If we get a lead we'll head out."

"Keep me updated. At least we have something moving on this case."

As Vic turned, he called over his shoulder, "Right, but we just don't know what." He headed back to his desk.

Liz was walking back from talking to Karen. "APB is out," she called. She was holding her phone in her hand and it lit up. She gave Vic a 'hold it a second' gesture and answered. She said a few words and ended the call. "That was Levon. I asked him to call Bandini, I thought he might have a different number. Levon's call went to voicemail as well."

"Okay. Let's start calling the businesses."

They stood at Liz's desk while she printed out a list of sixteen businesses. They agreed Vic would work up from the bottom, Liz down from the top, and they would make whoever answered the phone search the business. Vic looked up the phone number for the strip club at the bottom of the list, called them, and almost lost his temper at the disinterested man who answered the call. Vic finally got through to him who he was, and after making him search the premises, finally believed the man was alone.

So it went with the next seven businesses, Vic all the while watching the morning slip away. He looked across the aisle at Liz when he hung up from the last call. She was sitting with her arms crossed, watching him, slowly shaking her head.

"I got nothing," she said.

"Same here. Are you sure these are all the businesses?"

"No. That's just what I got to when I was making the list."

"Dammit." Vic looked around. The few detectives on their floor had their heads cocked toward their computers or were on the telephone. He didn't know why he thought they might help.

His phone rang. He snatched it up, half expecting it to be Mary, or Bandini complaining about he and Liz calling his businesses.

"Detective Lenoski, It's Craig Luntz."

It took Vic a moment to focus. "Craig, sorry, I was expecting someone else."

"No problem, hey, remember you called me yesterday and wanted me to check with the carrier about Thuds' phone? You were asking about photos that might have been sent to it? From some storage unit?"

"Right, yes." Vic gathered himself.

"Hate to tell you, but they don't keep the photos long. They do a refresh every night and delete them. Like I thought, they only keep the ones their customers send. But Mr. Lombardo did get a text from the storage facility system the day before he died. We identified that line of code."

"Damn. Well, the fact he got one is important."

"But get this. Even though we don't have the phone, I told him to keep the number live because it's an active murder investigation. And guess what, the carrier guy just called me. A photo came in to the number from the storage unit again. He kind of bent the rules and sent it to me. I can send it to you."

Vic sat upright. "Send it. What's in it?"

"Looks like it's important, but I can't tell. Plus the angle of the camera is a pain. You should have it."

Vic brought his computer out of sleep mode and saw Craig' email. He opened it and clicked on the photo attachment. Stared at the image. He pressed his phone against his chest and looked at Liz. "We found Bandini." He lifted the phone to his ear. "Craig, you're a genius, we've been looking for one of the guys in the photo. He went missing this morning."

"Glad to help." Craig's voice sounded bright.

"You helped all right. Thanks, and I have to go."

Liz materialized next to him and bent over to look at the photo on Vic's screen. It showed Bandini, closest to the camera, his arms bound behind him, held upright by someone on the far side of him, clutching a handful of Bandini's sports coat. The photograph was black and white, but Bandini's head lolled toward the camera and a dark streak that might be blood ran from the ridge of his eye over his cheek.

"Is that Turcelli?" Liz asked.

"I can't tell. Craig was right, the angle is wrong to compare proportions. It distorts the body size."

"Plus, he's kind of hiding behind Bandini." Liz clucked her tongue. "And we told Turcelli about the cameras and how they worked. He could be hiding from it."

"Which is why his head is turned away. And maybe why the car doesn't show." Vic sat upright. "We need to get to the storage locker. Do you still have that guy's phone number…Roofus, I think his name was?"

"I should." Liz headed for her desk. Vic forwarded the email to Carter Lee and stood up. "We need a warrant for that unit," he called to Liz, and headed for Carter's office.

When he got there, Carter had the photo open on his screen and was staring at it. "We need a warrant to search that unit," Vic said quickly. "Looks like Bandini is inside. Liz and I are headed up there."

Carter waved his hand. "Email me the details, I'll make sure you have it by the time you get there."

As they left the parking lot, lights flashing, Liz reached Roofus and told him to meet them at the unit.

"Tell him to bring bolt cutters," Vic called to her.

Liz repeated the request to Roofus and told him they had a warrant on the way. She then texted Carter Lee with the address and number of the storage unit. They made good time, cars pulling aside to let them pass all the way up the interstate.

When she finished her text, Liz turned to him. "Bandini was alive when he went in."

"Let's hope he stayed that way."

They said nothing else the rest of the way, until Liz's phone dinged. She checked it. "Got the warrant," she said, as if she was thinking out loud.

Roofus was waiting for them outside the unit, bolt cutters in hand. Vic and Liz hopped out of their car. As they approached him, Roofus called out,

"You got a warrant?"

"We do," Vic called.

Liz started to lift her hand to show him her phone but he waved the bolt cutters at her. "Just needed to hear you guys say it." He slid the bolt cutter blades into position and tugged the ends. The lock jumped with a snap. Wearing latex gloves, Vic grabbed the lock, and maneuvered it out of the clasp. Liz had a plastic bag waiting for him to drop it into.

"You didn't touch that, did you?" Vic asked Roofus, as he bent to the door handle and started to lift.

"Hell no."

Vic slid the door all the way up and light fell inside the unit. Bandini lay on his side beside a large black steamer trunk, his arms, and legs bound with duct tape. Liz stepped over to him, kneeled down, and felt the carotid artery of his throat. She looked at Vic. "Pulse. Need an ambulance."

Vic already had the number up on his phone. He pressed it, identified himself, and gave the dispatcher their address. As he talked, Liz used a small folding knife from her jacket pocket to slice the duct tape. She then eased Bandini onto his back, careful not to let his head smack the concrete floor. Bandini coughed once, harshly, but his breathing seemed to strengthen.

Vic walked around the unit, staring at the steamer trunk, the tools propped up in one corner, and finally the bag against the wall. It was unzipped and he pulled the sides apart using his pen so he didn't touch anything. Inside were well-worn tools, but nothing else. Vic came back around the trunk and stopped next to Liz.

"How's he look?"

Liz was still on her knees. "He got pistol-whipped, would be my guess. Knocked out."

"If he hasn't woken up by now, that could be a problem."

Liz carefully rose, her knees cracking. "Yes, it could." She looked at the door to the unit.

Vic followed her eye gaze. Roofus stood just outside the unit, his eyes wide, bolt cutters forgotten in hand. "Roofus," Vic called, "Can you do us a favor? Go out front and direct the ambulance back here."

Roofus nodded with a fast bob of his head and headed for the front of the facility.

Chapter Forty-One

Vic walked to the mouth of the storage unit and looked around. Closed storage unit doors stared back, the asphalt a black empty strip between them. He studied the camera placements at the corners and rechecked the photo Craig Luntz had emailed him. From the distance came the soft wail of a siren, just as a local township police officer pulled up at the end of the row of storage units. He climbed out of his prowler and lumbered toward him.

"You're the Allegheny County detectives?" the officer called, as he approached.

With two fingers, Vic pulled back his sports coat so the officer could see the badge on his belt. "I'm Vic Lenoski, partner Liz Timmons is inside. Thanks for coming."

"Officer Tom Leto," the officer said when he reached Vic. "I heard the call." He glanced inside the storage unit where Liz was kneeling beside Bandini. "So that's where people put their crazy uncles these days."

Vic gritted his teeth. "Just keep the way clear for the ambulance. And this is a crime scene now, I'll need someone to watch it until our crime scene folks get here."

Officer Leto nodded. "You got it." He pivoted and headed back to his prowler.

Vic telephoned Carter Lee, updated him, and asked for the crime scene unit. Then, with the distant siren much closer, he went back inside. "How's he doing?"

Liz had placed a grease-stained towel behind Bandini's head to keep it from the concrete floor. "Coming around. It's slow, though." She gestured at his sports coat. "His cell phone is gone."

Vic noticed that the lock to the steamer trunk was broken and lying on the floor. He flipped the trunk's latch and lifted the lid. Empty. He lowered it back in place. That didn't sit right with him. The missing phone he understood—someone didn't want Bandini calling for help. But an empty steamer trunk in a storage unit was unusual, and the broken lock meant someone had opened it recently. As he stepped to the front of the unit he wondered what it might have held.

He watched Leto direct the ambulance toward them, siren silent now. Vic waved and guided it in front of the unit. The driver slid out, a thickly bearded man with the name George Calper on a name tag below his paramedic patch. He checked Bandini's location, opened a small side compartment near the ambulance door and retrieved a box of equipment. Moments later he was kneeling beside Bandini. George's focus and speed made Vic feel better.

Liz joined Vic outside the unit. "You call Mary Monahan?"

"I want to find out which hospital they're taking him to." He pointed in the direction of the camera. "See that? The ambulance is blocking the camera's line of sight. How about an Escalade?"

"Isn't as tall."

"Right, but that means if it was Turcelli, he must have parked clear at the end of the aisle and carried Bandini here. You'd want to make the walk from the car as short as possible."

"Turcelli is big enough to do it."

"He is." Vic watched the second paramedic—a Phil Stemsede, according to his nametag—trundle a gurney into the unit. "I feel like we're missing something."

"Yeah. Turcelli. Where is he?"

"That's one question."

Vic took a call from the crime scene team and explained where they were. As he finished, George and Phil trundled Bandini out on the gurney. Vic and Liz walked around to the back of the ambulance to watch them load him in the back.

"Where are you taking him?" Vic asked.

"Passavant is closest," Phil answered, aligning the gurney with the back of the ambulance.

Bandini's forearm rose and he weakly waved Vic toward him. George, who was next to him, nodded to Vic. Vic stepped next to the gurney and looked into Bandini's blotted eyes. Bandini mouthed something Vic couldn't hear. He bent closer and Bandini hoarsely repeated himself. Vic nodded to George and Phil and they finished loading Bandini into the ambulance.

As the ambulance doors closed Liz turned to him. "What did he say?"

Vic shifted on his feet. "Hard to make out, but it sounded like 'get Turcelli.'"

"Then maybe we better."

Vic lifted his phone and called Mary Monahan's personal cell phone. It rang through to voice mail. Vic left a message about finding Bandini and told her where he was being taken. He then called her office and reached the receptionist. He asked to be put through.

"She's not here," Mary's secretary replied to Vic's request to talk to Mary.

"Can you reach her?"

"I don't know where she is. She said something came up and ran out of here. She didn't tell me anything."

Vic said his thanks and ended the call, his stomach tight. He looked at Liz. "Mary Monahan went someplace and isn't answering."

"Hinky," Liz said, frowning.

"Not good. That's for sure."

"Not much we can do about it right now." Vic kicked the asphalt with the toe of his shoe. He gestured at the storage unit, and they did another once-around the inside, studying its contents. Liz snapped photos as they went. Nothing jumped out at either of them, so they taped off the unit and asked the local officer to watch the scene until the CSI team arrived.

"Hey, that's what I do," Tom Leto answered. "Take store of the storage. Unit."

Vic thought Liz might punch him, but she turned on her heel and headed for their car. Vic thanked the officer and followed.

When they were on the thruway, Vic called Carter Lee and put the phone on speaker. He handed his phone to Liz so he could drive. They ran through an update, but Carter sounded distracted, as if he was reading something else at the same time. They were finishing the call when he told them to stay on the line.

A muffled conversation took place from Carter's end, and he came back on the call. "Your APB panned out. One of the city boys spotted the Escalade."

The tightness in Vic's stomach sharpened. "Did they pull it over?"

"No. It's parked, no one in it. He and his partner are down the street sitting on it."

"What street?"

Carter told him the street and block. Vic and Liz looked at one another.

"We're headed there," Vic said quickly.

"Suit yourself," Carter answered, "but I think the city guys have it under control."

"We'll call if we find anything."

Without waiting for Carter to respond Liz ended the call as Vic flicked on the car lights.

"Mary Monahan's apartment, right?" Liz asked.

"Exactly. And Mary left her office in a hurry. It's worse than hinky." He accelerated.

Chapter Forty-Two

The Last Day

He stared at Mary Monahan. She looked small, sitting on the large couch in her spacious living room. She was beautiful, even with the streaks of blood from her nose and the corner of her mouth. He'd seen her many times, of course, but usually, her confidence detracted from her beauty. He didn't like how she flaunted it, used it like a shiv to get what she wanted. He liked her better this way. Her arms tight in her lap, head bowed in front of him, legs drawn together.

Utterly submissive.

He glanced around. Of course, she lived in a place like this. A renovated warehouse in one of the trendiest sections of Pittsburgh, bare brick walls, exposed beams, conduit, the whole package of the industrial look. Track lighting and vibrant modern art. It was everything his own father would have given him, but instead, Bandini stole it all and gave it to her.

"Payback is a bitch," he said to her.

She flinched. Good, he thought. She's getting it. The document he wanted her to sign was on the table in front of her.

"Again," he said, enjoying how bored he sounded. He knew she would sign, this was just bookkeeping. "You don't sign, your father is dead. Look." He held up his phone so she could see the photo of Bandini lying on the storage unit floor.

She raised her head and glanced at the photo, eyes tear-streaked, and turned her face down quickly as if she'd been stung. Still, she made no move. He glanced at his watch. Fifteen minutes and she had yet to sign, this was taking too long. He had an appointment to make. Women, he thought. The world's answer to indecision.

"Maybe this will help," he said slowly. He glanced at his phone, opened the recording app, and played a file.

"Maria," Bandini's rough voice said. "Listen to him. Sign the document. Please."

Mary shuddered.

He'd been saving that recording for the coup de grace, and also because he wasn't sure why her father called her Maria. He'd worried it was a code, but dismissed the idea. There was no reason for them to have worked one out in advance.

"Tell me, why does he call you Maria?" He was actually interested, and thought some friendliness might help the moment. Maybe the switch in tactics would get her moving.

She stared at the document on the table, and he could see enough of her face to see her blinking back tears. "That was my name when I was born," she said in a rush. "I changed it to Mary later. He can't remember to call me Mary." She gulped the last word, as if fighting down tears.

Look at that, he thought. We have something in common. But you only changed your name once. How many times did I change mine? Fifteen? He'd lost count a long time ago. Names were just clothing.

To his surprise, she reached for the pen. Picked it up and drew the document to her.

"There you go," he said soothingly.

Her head lifted and she stared at him with her deep brown eyes. Her eyeliner was smudged but her eyes were dry, somehow, as if she'd come to a decision. "This does nothing." He was surprised at the anger and forcefulness in her voice. "I sign this and we come after you. It's signed under duress. We'll sue you into the ground."

He held her gaze. He'd been waiting for this moment, rehearsing it. He gave her a smile. "Do you actually think I want your businesses? Do you? I could give a shit about your businesses. I want my inheritance. What's due to me. I leave here and the businesses are mine. By five o'clock they'll belong to someone else, and I'll be rich. And the terms of the deal? A cashier's check for me."

"It'll never stand up. Your sale won't be whole. It'll get torn down around you. How stupid are you?"

He was impressed by her anger, how controlled it was. The way she goaded him with her last question, hoping to rattle him. And how comfortable she was on this legal turf. That was something. He'd read in her bio that she'd negotiated the purchase and sale of businesses. It showed. But in business deals, you had to hold one card back. And he had.

"Sue me," he said, and gave her his best smile. "I don't care. Go for it. Let's get into it. I don't think you have the balls." His turn to goad her. He removed from his jacket pocket the contract he'd found in the steamer trunk, opened it, smoothed the creases, and placed it on the coffee table. "See? Signed by your dear dad. His partnership with Paul Zielinski. *My* father. Because, like you, I go by a different name. My real name is David Zielinski."

Mary stared at the new document, motionless.

"So sue me. All you want. I will burn you to the ground."

Anger flushed Mary's face and with a violent movement, she scribbled her name on the document. She looked up. "We're going to bring down hell on you."

Are you? he thought, almost giggling out loud. "Well, I guess that's all the t's crossed and i's dotted?" He reached out and picked up the document with his left hand, folded and stuck it in his shirt pocket. Did the same for the steamer trunk document.

It wouldn't do to get blood on the document, he thought. Because that's my real last card. The one I held back. The one you weren't quick enough to figure out. If you're dead, and your father is dead, who the hell is going to sue me? Thuds certainly can't, I made sure of that. And by the time the bodies are found, I will be long gone. He had a flash memory of Thuds, a bullet in his chest, staggering out of his armchair. He thought, let's see how well you do getting off the couch. I don't think you have it in you.

CHAPTER FORTY-TWO

He started to shift his hand toward the pistol at his waist but froze as the apartment door crashed open.

Chapter Forty-Three

Vic spotted an open space a few doors down from the entrance to Mary's apartment. He pulled into it, ignoring it was a ramp leading to a garage door. He and Liz jumped out and ran through the lobby of the apartment building. Vic hammered on the elevator button.

"Stairs?" Liz asked.

The elevator doors opened as if appalled by Liz's suggestion. They piled in, Vic smacking the floor button and jabbing at the door-close button simultaneously. Out of the corner of his eye he saw Liz loosen her weapon in its holster. As the elevator started to move he did the same, wishing he'd spent more time at the range. Turcelli was a big man. It would take more than one shot to put him down.

As the doors opened they slid out of the elevator, hands on holstered weapons, each taking one side of the hall. The door to Mary's apartment was partially open and voices came from within. Vic crossed the hall and positioned himself next to the open door. Liz came up behind him. He saw splintered wood around the deadbolt and silently pointed it out to Liz. From inside the apartment, Turcelli yelled something. Vic unholstered his Glock, his heart hammering in his chest. He glanced at Liz. Her eyes were electric. She nodded. Vic lifted his Glock in front of him and spun around the doorframe and into the room.

"Police!" he shouted.

The three people in the room spun to him. Mary, sitting on the couch, had made herself so small she was almost in a ball. Turcelli and Aaron Holt stood on the other side of the coffee table. Turcelli held a pistol in his huge right hand. From Vic's angle, Holt was partially behind Turcelli, and Vic couldn't see if he was armed. Vic pointed his Glock at Turcelli. "Put the gun down. Now." He was conscious of Liz shifting to his right, opening another angle on the big man.

"You got it wrong," Turcelli said sharply. His eyes flashed.

"Gun down, on your knees," Vic shouted. He flicked his Glock barrel downward to get him moving.

Turcelli shook his head violently. "You got it wrong." His huge body was alive, not exactly shaking, more shimmering, somehow.

"Put the gun down," Vic repeated, trying to moderate his voice, calm the situation.

Turcelli shifted on his feet, but bent over and tossed his gun to the floor, his hands wavering from adrenaline. Vic suddenly knew that was wrong. It took him a second absorb the problem and remember. The shooting of Geno Varelli and his analysis of the shooter. The shooter's unusual calmness. How he unbuttoned a shirt cuff immediately after shooting Geno twice. Turcelli couldn't do it, not if stress got him worked up like that, especially with those broom-handle-sized fingers.

He started to turn his head to tell Liz and glimpsed Holt disappear behind Turcelli's bulk. As he flicked his gaze back to Holt, Turcelli reared back and thrust his chest toward Liz. A gun appeared, jammed into his throat. Holt had grabbed the back of Turcelli's shirt and turned him, using the man's bulk as a shield. Turcelli's eyes were wide.

"Nobody moves," Holt called, almost conversationally.

"You dumb asses," Turcelli said, looking down at Vic, thunder in his eyes.

Vic was aware of Liz shifting on her feet, trying to find a shot.

"Put your guns down," Holt said, as relaxed as if he was ordering fast food. His eyes appeared over Turcelli's shoulder. They didn't move, didn't blink. "You don't, I shoot Sasquatch here and then Mary. Or should I say Maria?" It sounded as if he was making a joke for his own enjoyment.

"You can't win this," Liz said sharply.

"You'd be surprised. Guns down."

Vic lowered his weapon but didn't let go of it, his mind whirring. Holt's eyes were placid and Vic held his gaze. With as little movement as possible, Vic used his free hand to slide his phone from his pants pocket.

"Bandini is in the storage unit," Turcelli said. "You gotta help him. Holt put him in there."

"Did I?" Holt said from behind him. "Or was that you?"

"How do you know he's there, Mike?" Liz asked, conversationally. Vic knew from her tone that she was following his lead, trying to calm the tension.

Turcelli shifted his gaze to her, not an easy thing to do, given his face was forced upward by the gun barrel. "*You're* the one told me about the app for the storage unit, remember?" His sarcasm was thick enough to make pancakes. "I talked to Roofus and he sent me a link. I got a photo on my phone when Holt put Bandini inside. I just didn't see it until a while ago."

"Shut up." Holt pressed the barrel into Turcelli's neck.

"What do you want to do, here, Aaron?" Vic asked slowly. Something shifted in his mind, as if he'd changed the angle of the magnet as he moved it under the iron filings. An entirely new pattern emerged. He remembered the photograph of his mother, her hands on his ten-year-old shoulders, how she was presenting him to his father.

"I'm leaving," Holt said, as calmly as if he was taking his dog out for a walk. "You guys let me. I still get what's mine. You can catch me later, if you can."

"He's got the contract." Mary's head was up, staring at Holt. She was the only one, Vic realized, with a clear view of Holt. "I had to sign it or he was going to kill my father. He said his name is David Zielinski."

On hearing the name, Vic clearly saw the curves and swirls of the new pattern of the iron filings. Understood it.

"And you can shut up as well," Holt said. Vic thought he heard a note of annoyance in Aaron's voice, the first he had heard.

"So how does this work?" Vic asked, keeping his tone moderate. "I mean mechanically. You walking out. What do we all do to make that happen?" Vic risked a glance at his phone. With his thumb, he opened the Photos app.

Holt's hand flexed around the gun. "I said. You two, guns on the floor, back up into the kitchen. Sasquatch here gets on his knees. I take Maria and leave. You come after me, she's dead. And that's on you."

"And then you get what's yours," Vic said.

"You got that right."

"Except it isn't yours," Vic said, forcing his voice to be conversational. "You have it wrong. Exactly wrong. Don't worry, we'll let you walk out of here. But I just want to show you something first. Won't take more than five seconds. Then out you go."

From his peripheral vision, Vic saw Liz turn to him, a frown on her face.

Holt shifted the gun against Turcelli's neck. "I do not have time for this," he said, from behind Turcelli's broad chest.

"I've got it right here. A photo of you and your mother. Mary Twail. I bet you've never seen it. Just look at it, and then you can go. No problem. But you need to know how wrong you are."

"I'm not wrong. I'm never wrong."

"Here. I'm going to hold up my phone. Take a look." Slowly, Vic raised his arm, his phone toward Aaron, a photograph on the screen. "Is that her? Your mother?"

Aaron's eyes, as still as pond lilies, focused on the photograph.

"Yeah. Where'd you get that?"

"Your Dad's apartment. Geno Varelli's apartment. He took the picture. Your mother was showing him his son. You. Paul Zielinski isn't your father."

The silence was thicker than marble. Mary's head was up, eyes wide, staring at him. Turcelli's mouth was open as if he'd lost the power to speak.

"Bullshit. I know what's on my birth certificate." Holt's voice softened.

"You need to do a DNA test, Aaron. Your mother lied when she wrote down the father's name on the certificate. She had to. The reason she took you and ran? She was getting away from Zielinski, planning to meet your father, Geno Varelli."

"Bullshit."

Vic didn't hear as much conviction in the word. "Hear me out," Vic said slowly, "and then you can go. No problem. We'll let you. You see, before you were born, your mother was dating Zielinski, but she was having an affair with Geno Varelli. And me? I think your mother and Geno were in love. Geno's best friend told me that. But your mother couldn't get away from Zielinski. He wouldn't let her. That would make a fool of him and he couldn't have that. No way his fiancée runs off with his partner. Even the ushers at the ballparks would laugh at him. But I think Zielinski found out about your mother and Varelli."

Vic shifted a step closer to Aaron. "So Geno made a plan. He figured he'd rob a bank and get the money he needed to run away with your mother. He told his lawyer it was his last robbery. But Zielinski heard about it and paid the wheelman to run out in the middle of the robbery. Then Geno spent too long in the bank, because he wanted as much money as he could get. Without a getaway car he had to escape on foot, and sure enough, he was caught. Geno goes to jail and your mother marries Zielinski, especially because, by then, she's pregnant. Of course, she had to use Zielinski's name on your birth certificate. But your mother and Varelli weren't done trying to be together. Your mother gave your dad information about Zielinski, enough to pin a murder on him. Geno turned informer to shorten his sentence. It might have worked, but Zielinski sent someone to kill Geno in jail and Varelli defended himself. Bang, Geno gets twenty more years tacked onto his sentence. And that's when your mother took you and ran. She was scared Zielinski would send someone after her. My advice is this. Take the DNA test. You're going to find out you got it completely, totally wrong. You're going to find out you shot your own father."

Silence crashed down on them. Vic noticed Turcelli staring at him, something in his eyes. A question. Vic shook his head just slightly. He couldn't have Turcelli try to take down Aaron. Vic slowly lowered his arm. Slid his phone into his pocket.

"No." Aaron sounded defiant. "Paul Zielinski got my mother pregnant."

"I doubt it," Vic said slowly. "Keep this in mind. Zielinski was married twice before he married your mother. Never had kids. He told a bunch of people he wanted a family, but his wives never got pregnant. He kept blaming them and divorcing them. I think the problem was with Zielinski. He was shooting blanks. I don't think he *could* get your mother pregnant."

"The tattoos," Aaron said quickly. "If my father, I mean Zielinski, set up

Geno, why did they share tattoos? Why leave the money and contract in the storage unit for when they got out of jail?"

Vic heard the tinge of desperation in Aaron's voice and knew he had him on the hook. Aaron was thinking about it. Trying to work it out. But Vic was impressed at how, even in this situation, for the most part Aaron remained calm. He wasn't yet sure how to stop him, but it would be easier if Aaron's confidence was shaky. "Easy. Zielinski didn't want to admit he set up Varelli in the bank. He had to act like everything was normal so Geno didn't rat him out. So they picked someone they trusted to hide the money and the contract, and got the tattoos. That way they had to be together to collect, and everything looked normal."

"You're speculating," Aaron said quickly, his confidence returning.

"Yes, it's hard to prove. And that's because you also shot the person they trusted with the tattoos. Thuds Lombardo. He could have confirmed all this. Thuds owned the storage unit, it was set up to warn him if anyone went inside. He got a photo on his phone of who went inside the day before he was shot. And look at that, he called you and wanted to talk. You told us that yourself. Now, why is that? I think he figured out who you really were. Only you could put the tattoos together and find the unit. I even think Thuds knew there was a copy of the contract waiting to be found. I know that because the day before Thuds called Bandini's lawyer and asked him about it. But you know what's worse? I bet Thuds would have helped you. With Zielinski and Varelli gone he would have figured you deserved whatever was inside that unit. Didn't matter who your father was. But you shot Thuds before he could help you."

"We're done," Aaron said sharply. "I'm getting out of here. Guns on the floor, you two cops into the kitchen."

"Okay, okay. Guns on the floor." Vic glanced at Liz. Knowing that Aaron couldn't see her, he mimicked slipping her gun under her belt against the small of her back. Vic laid his own Glock on the rug, where Aaron could see it. "Done," he said carefully, and he and Liz faded a few steps toward the kitchen.

Aaron popped his head around Turcelli's thick body far enough to spot

Vic's Glock on the rug. "Knees," he shouted at Turcelli.

Turcelli gave Vic a sharp look, but Vic nodded for him to follow Aaron's orders. Vic's mind was racing, trying to think of a way to separate Aaron and Mary. Aaron jerked Turcelli's shirt and Turcelli let himself be guided to his knees. And Vic saw it in Aaron's face. He'd got through to him. Aaron's brow was snarled in a frown, his face pale, eyes distracted. Aaron stepped around Turcelli as if by rote and distractedly waggled his gun at Mary to stand up. She did, shifting to her left and closer to Aaron as she did. In the split second while Aaron's gun arm was still extended across the front of her body she grabbed his gun wrist with her left hand, her right arm flashed up and down, crossed her left arm, and drove the pen she'd signed the contract with into the flesh of Aaron's forearm.

Aaron screamed, the gun dropping from his hand. Turcelli shot from his knees, his large hands grabbing Aaron by the back of the neck and his belt. He lifted Aaron like he was balsa wood and drove him head first down into the coffee table with a sickening thud. The table legs splintered and Aaron sank to the ground among the remains of the table. Turcelli raised a fist the size of a ham, but Vic shouted at him to stop.

Somehow, Turcelli actually did.

For a moment everyone froze, staring at Aaron. One of his legs slowly shifted.

"Cuffs if you can do it," Vic said quickly, and Liz moved. Vic picked up his gun and holstered it.

Mary was standing above Aaron, looking down at him. She reached down and slid a folded piece of paper from Aaron's shirt pocket, and then another. Tore them in half. Tossed the halves at his face.

"And that's how *I* dot my i's, asshole," she said to Aaron, as Liz kicked Aaron's gun away from him.

Chapter Forty-Four

Fifteen minutes later police and paramedics swarmed the apartment and Mary was on her way to Passavant hospital to see her father. She'd been tricked, she told Vic and Liz with some embarrassment, by a text sent from her father's phone asking to meet at her apartment. Aaron ambushed her from the stairwell when she got to her front door.

"You didn't think to call and tell us your father texted you?" Liz asked. "I was kneeling next to your Dad when that must have happened."

"I know, I'm sorry. I was just glad he'd shown up. I didn't think."

Once she was gone, Liz turned to Vic. "For a smart girl, she sure was dumb this time. And I ain't never signing a contract with her."

Vic smiled, distracted, watching the first responders sift through the apartment. He took a couple of deep breaths to finally calm himself and checked his watch. There were reports to write and he knew he would never get to daycare in time to pick up Lettie. He stepped into the hall and called Barb. She was so quick to agree to take Lettie, it was almost suspicious.

When he returned, he found Turcelli and asked how Bandini was abducted.

The huge man shrugged. "Bandini had a text from Aaron asking him to stop by one of the restaurants. I drove him over, parked in the back like always. Bandini went in and one of the waitresses came out and gave me a cup of coffee while I was waiting. Terri, or something. Whatever was in it knocked me out. I slept in the driver's seat for like four hours. I wake up, and when I get myself together, I check my phone and see the notification from the storage unit."

Vic showed him the photo Craig had emailed him earlier. "This one?"

"Yeah." Turcelli clearly wanted to know how Vic had a copy of the photograph, but didn't ask the question. "I knew it had to be Aaron, and I knew if he had Bandini, he'd go after Mary. Bandini had told me about the businesses being in her name. I drove here. I got to the door and I could hear them inside talking. I listened long enough to know what was up. Aaron always was a self-righteous prick. When Mary signed I figured I needed to get in here. The only way Aaron's plan works is if Mary and Bandini are dead."

It took Vic and Liz another hour to give a verbal report to Carter Lee. When they finally got to their desks, Vic figured he had at least two hours of report writing to get through everything. He didn't mind. He'd figured it out. Somehow, he'd pulled the pieces together and got to the right narrative. He felt like he was back. That he could do the job.

It was seven o'clock that evening when his cell phone rang. Vic saw it was Barb and answered.

"I'm sorry," Barb almost wailed into the phone.

Vic sat bolt upright. "About what? What happened? Is Lettie okay?"

"Yes. I just looked away for a few seconds." She blubbered over the last few words.

"Barb, walk me through it. Lettie is okay, right, you have her?"

She swallowed several deep breaths. "I took her to the playground with my son. They were playing. And that boy from across the street was there. I was talking to some of the other Moms and when I looked around Lettie wasn't there. I panicked. I started searching, and then I saw that boy from across the street, he was leading Lettie up the steps to his house. I ran over and got her back, just before he took her inside."

Vic was on his feet, Liz staring at him.

"Where is Lettie now?" Vic asked, the cold anger of his words surprising even himself. It was as if a door opened to the day Dannie disappeared, to those feelings.

"I have her here. At my house."

"Stay there, I'm on my way." He ended the call.

Liz stood. "You want me to come?"

Vic snagged his jacket from its hangar. "No, but log me out, okay?"

He fast-walked to the car and shot through the rush hour traffic, fighting down his rage. Twenty minutes later he pulled to the curb in front of the house where the boy lived, across from the playground. He took the steps two at a time to the front door. Yanked open the storm door and pounded on the wood with the heel of his fist.

The door swung open perhaps six inches and Vic looked into the face of the boy's father, the one who warned him off. Vic put his shoulder to the door and rammed it open, the force pushing the man backwards into the house.

"Explain this." Vic stepped right up to the man, inches from his face. "Your son walked my granddaughter to your house. He wanted to bring her inside. I want to know one thing. Did you tell him to do it? Did you try and get my granddaughter inside your house?" Vic's mind flashed to the bedroom door in North Dakota, the deadbolt on the outside of that door, the interior where Dannie was kept prisoner. He fought his rage. "Did you tell your son to bring my granddaughter here? For you? You slimy piece of shit?"

The man opened his mouth and closed it, opened it again. "Get out of my house."

Vic snagged his badge from his belt and held it to the man's face. "I'll ask the questions, and I'll tell you what to do. Right now, I'm investigating a crime. Yours."

Sweat broke out along the man's forehead, but Vic had an odd sensation. It was the silence, how it felt like a held breath. He backed up a step and glanced around. They were standing just inside the front door at the edge of the living room, but there was no living room furniture. Just desks with computers on them. People sitting at the computers. Everyone was staring at him. He looked through into what would normally be the dining room. The scene repeated itself, although most of the desks were unoccupied. Spread across the computer screens were websites.

"Explain what happened to my granddaughter," Vic said carefully, struggling to compose himself. Scared by his own tunnel vision.

The man shifted back half a step. "You're the girl's grandfather?" he asked.

247

"Yes. And like I said, your son tried to walk her into your house today. But someone stopped him."

He nodded, hard, as if he wanted to make a point of agreeing. "Right. I didn't know about it until that lady ran up on my porch and grabbed her. Lettie, right?"

"How do you know her name?" Two of the people at their desks were staring at their computers as if they were working, but Vic didn't see anyone typing.

"My son told me when I asked him about it. I'm sorry, I didn't know anything until it happened."

"Didn't you? And what did happen?"

"Look, my son and I moved up here from Atlanta a few years ago. My ex-wife is still there, and she has custody of our daughter. She's about Lettie's age. He misses her. They used to play together all the time. That's all. He just wanted to be friends with her."

As the man talked, Vic let his gaze drift from computer screen to computer screen. Slowly, it dawned on him what he was looking at. "Okay," he said slowly, shifting his attention back to the man. "And did you or did you not put your son up to it? Ask him to bring Lettie here?"

"Why would I do that?" He swung his arm at the desks and computers. "We're working here."

"Yes," Vic said, an idea organizing itself in his head. "About that. Maybe we could talk somewhere else?"

The man blinked twice, rapidly. He glanced about. Vic was fairly sure he wouldn't want to continue the conversation in front of his employees, or coworkers, whichever they were. "Sure. Follow me."

The man led Vic down the hall to the kitchen at the back of the house. One counter held an industrial-sized coffee maker and a tray of well-picked-over bagels.

"What's your name?" Vic asked.

The man licked his lips. "Arlen Toombs."

"Okay, Arlen. You and I are going to reach an agreement, and then we'll both go away happy. You understand me?"

CHAPTER FORTY-FOUR

Arlen just stared at him.

"Do you understand me?" Vic repeated.

"Yes," Arlen croaked.

"First. Tell your son, Lettie stays with whoever is watching her on the playground. She does not leave the playground. We good on that?"

He nodded sharply. "Yes." Relief bloomed in his eyes.

"Second. You own this house, right?"

Arlen frowned slightly. "Yes."

"I saw the computers out there. You own your house, and are you also the owner of the Newsburgh website?"

He turned a shade paler and didn't answer.

"Yes or no question," Vic goaded.

"Yes," he said finally.

"And the people working out there are your employees?"

"Contractors. Not totally employees."

"Right, now, I want you to tell me your source for the articles you've been publishing about the DA's office."

Arlen stepped back and puffed up his chest. "I'm not telling you my source."

Vic noted his use of the singular case. One source. "Let's make sure we understand one another. First, you need me to forget I was ever in this house. Your house. Because if I remember I was here, I'll tell the local authorities you're running a for-profit business in an area zoned residential only. And they will come in here and shut you down. The question is simple, do you want me to remember I was here, or completely forget?"

Arlen shifted from one foot to the other.

"And to be clear, Arlen, I don't want you to *tell* me who your source was. That's bad for journalistic integrity." Vic slid his notebook from his pocket. "I want you to write it down. In here. And sign it."

Vic put the notebook on the counter next to the tray of demolished bagels. He placed a pen next to it.

Arlen stared at the notebook as if it were radioactive.

Vic waited, letting the seconds tick by. Finally, he said, "Can you afford to be shut down?"

Arlen let out a slow breath. He rolled his eyes. "Not with my damn alimony."

"And I'm guessing that if you slip on your alimony payments, then your custody arrangements collapse. And your son goes back to Atlanta."

"You're a piece of shit." Arlen grabbed the notebook and pen, flipped to a blank page, and wrote something down. He signed the bottom with a scrawl. He held out the notebook.

Vic skimmed the lines, closed the notebook, and put it back in his pocket. "So, you'll talk to your son?"

"I will."

"Good, and I'm going to go pick up Lettie and forget I was ever here. And Arlen, let's make sure this doesn't happen again."

Chapter Forty-Five

This was Vic's first meeting in Hana's office, and the only major difference he could spot was the desk. It was smaller than the ancient wooden monstrosity the previous DA preferred. Vic had a feeling Hana didn't like how the larger desk might have swamped her smaller stature, making it look as if the desk was overwhelming her. He thought she was probably selling herself short. The other differences were a spider plant on the windowsill and what looked like a Civil War-era saber with two faded gold tassels hanging on the wall. He was dying to ask about it but hadn't found a good way to work it into the conversation. Hana seemed happy to just leave it where it was, hanging over everyone.

Hana studied Vic. "And this Aaron Holt, or David Zielinski, or Aaron Varelli, he'll be able to stand trial?"

Carter Lee spoke before Vic could respond. "Concussion and a separated shoulder, plus a nasty stab wound in his arm. He'll be good to go in a few weeks."

"Okay. That gives us time to get our evidence lined up. Your report mentioned a letter you found in Vincent Lombardo's safe? It explained the set-up between Zielinski and Varelli and itemized what was in the storage unit?"

"It did. There was almost one-hundred and fifty thousand dollars in cash, and that's missing, but we know who has it."

"His mistress?"

Vic nodded. "When we talked to Aaron's wife she told us about her. Terri Cleevis, a waitress at one of Bandini's restaurants. Apparently, Aaron's wife

251

was sick of his sleeping around and was in the process of getting divorce papers written up. This will speed things along. We're guessing Terri was the same one who gave the spiked coffee to Mike Turcelli and helped Aaron exchange cars after the Varelli murder. But she's taken off with the money."

"And the preliminary DNA proves Aaron is Geno Varelli's son."

Vic nodded again. "It does."

"How utterly sad," Hana said slowly. She took a long breath.

Vic wondered if the saber might have something to say, but it remained silent.

Hana collected herself and shifted her gaze back to Vic. "We have him on suicide watch?"

Vic recognized Hana's turn back to practicalities. "We did. But I went to see him a couple of days ago and I think he's come to terms with the real identity of his father. The person who buried Geno Varelli actually bought two plots. The second was for Aaron's mother, he always felt that she and Geno should be together. I explained that to Aaron and he gave permission for his mother's body to be moved up here from Florida and buried next to Geno. I let the guy who bought the plot know. Then I got a psychologist to interview Aaron, and he cleared him off suicide watch."

"We'll still need a psych evaluation on him. His defense lawyer will trot one out, you can be sure of it. And this Mary Monahan, Bandini's daughter, you know her, right?" Hana's tone sharpened.

"Yes, I do know Mary," Vic answered.

"Do we charge her with assault?"

Vic shook his head. "She'd just been coerced at gunpoint into signing a contract and was under imminent threat of kidnapping. I don't know about you, but I think we could look the other way."

Hana sat back. "Nice work, Vic. I read your report but I wanted to hear it from you in person. Pass my thanks on to Liz as well."

"I will." Vic stole a glance at the saber, wondering if this might be the right time.

"And maybe this will get that damn Newsburgh off our back, finally."

Vic reached into his shirt pocket and produced a sheet of paper torn from this notebook. "I think they'll leave us alone." He passed the paper to Hana.

Hana skimmed it and looked up, staring at no one in particular. She didn't say anything for a moment, then turned to her computer and typed out a short email. When it was sent she turned back to Vic.

"How did you get that?"

"Right place, right time. But Arlen Toombs is the owner and editor of Newsburgh. It's authentic."

She frowned slightly and passed the sheet to Carter. "What do you think, Carter?"

Carter skimmed the note and flushed. "This is bullshit. Press doesn't reveal its sources. They're constitutionally protected."

Hana didn't say anything. Vic studied the saber.

"You can't actually believe I'm the source?" Carter finally huffed out.

Hana tapped her fingernails on her desktop. "It does explain a few things. Like you always counseling me not to respond, to let it play out, how quick you were to blame Gabe Chilton."

"I don't think it was Gabe," Vic interjected. "I talked to him, and for what it's worth, I believe him when he says it wasn't him."

"Carter," Hana said quickly, "If I asked you to surrender your cell phone and home computer, would we find evidence of you talking to Arlen Toombs?"

"You're putting me under investigation?" Carter shot back, his heel tapping a staccato on the carpeted floor.

"I just asked you a question." Hana smiled at Carter. Vic had seen more friendliness in a hornet swarm protecting its hive.

Before Carter could answer a soft knock came on the door. Hana called for the person to enter, and a uniformed and armed county sheriff stepped into the room.

"Answer the question, Carter," Hana said. Her voice was the same steel as the saber.

Carter shifted back and forth in his chair. "Screw you. I'd make a better DA. I've got fifteen years in major crimes with the FBI. I could run this office with my eyes closed. I have a law degree I got at night school."

Hana didn't move a muscle, except to speak. "Carter, the sheriff here will take you to your desk so you can recover your personal belongings. He will then escort you from the premises. You'll have a letter from HR tomorrow confirming your termination for cause." She nodded to the sheriff, who stepped next to Carter.

Carter shot out of his chair. "Better than working in this backwater." He turned and headed for the door, the sheriff following.

Vic and Hana sat in silence for a few seconds. A flush spread over Hana's face, and Vic decided they needed to change the topic. "Why the saber? It's killing me not knowing."

Hana looked at it as if she was seeing it for the first time. "Oh that. Family heirloom. My great great grandfather's. Pennsylvania cavalry during the Civil War. He was at Gettysburg. As was the saber."

"Impressive."

Hana smiled. "Speaking of which. You're off to a good start, Vic. Both you and Liz."

"So would this be a good time to ask a favor?"

"I'm not a pushover, Vic."

"I think I know that. But hear me out. There's a guy in the crime scene investigation group, Craig Luntz. Before that, he was in tech at the Bureau of Police. His dad was a Pittsburgh cop and my first commander. I'm wondering if we could bring him on board."

"Has he passed his detective exam?"

"No, but I was thinking he could work with us while he studies. He's smart, I don't think it will be a problem for him. He was the one who came up with the lead that got us to Bandini in the storage unit. Probably saved Bandini's life. I think he's a natural."

"Does he want to be a detective?"

"I don't know. I could ask."

Hana sat back. "Then ask. I'm sure we can figure something out. We seem to be short-staffed in your department right now." She gave him a small smile. "It's always interesting with you Vic. And are you going to Thuds' funeral this afternoon?"

"I am."

"Okay, then. And now back to work. Let me know about Craig." She stood and Vic did the same. They shook hands over the smaller desk. As Vic headed to the door Hana called after him. "And thanks for straightening out that Newsburgh thing. It was a royal pain in my you know what."

Chapter Forty-Six

The Days to Come

The headaches were the worst. They came, they went. He was a master of headaches, now. The sharp biting one, like a stiletto through his ear. The hard, dull, throbbing ones, as relentless as time. Those were the ones that made it impossible to look toward a window, forced him to cringe away from any kind of light. The grousing, troubling ones that wouldn't just finally go away.

And this man who came sometimes. Who talked to him. Asked him about his father, the feel of the gun in his hand, spoke endlessly about guilt and sorrow.

That man was an idiot. Whenever he sat next to his bed, it was as if the man's fingertips moved through his hair, pressing on the hard outer surface of his skull, searching for a way in. He wouldn't give him one. He answered the man's questions. Had already learned the responses that brought the tiniest of smiles to the corners of the man's lips. He would feed him those lies until he left for good, sated by his own ignorance.

And on the bedside table, that small photograph in the faded frame. He knew who put it there. That detective, Lenoski. It returned his stare. His mother, that child. Him. Suspended weightless in the air between his mother and unseen father, like a promise.

A truth so real even secrets couldn't hide it.

Restrained in the bed, he could only gaze at it. Eyes wet. His mother's singing voice shimmering in his mind as they drove through the darkness.

At least now his mother would lie beside the man she loved. That thought was the only thing that beat back the headaches.

All *he* had left to lose was himself, when the time was right. When the courts were finished. The cell door closed.

And he would welcome it.

Chapter Forty-Seven

Vic and Liz arrived at Allegheny Cemetery a few minutes before the service was to begin. Thuds' coffin sat on brass rails above its final resting place. Bandini was there, standing between Mary and Mike Turcelli, the three of them surrounded by a collection of people Vic assumed worked in Bandini's businesses. Justin Day was there as well, looking as if he desperately needed a cigarette. Even Andrew Mendelbaum was there. But it was the tall, elderly man standing near the coffin that caught Vic's attention. He leaned close to Liz.

"That's Priest. I did not expect him to come back here."

"You were too god-damned nice to him," Liz shot back.

Priest spotted Vic and gave him a slight nod. Then he opened his oversized Bible and started the service.

It was afterwards, as everyone ebbed away, after Justin Day came over and reminded Liz and Vic he was owed first shot at the Aaron Holt story, that Bandini ambled over. He was still pale, and more slouched than Vic remembered. He shook both their hands.

"When I'm feeling a bit better I'd like to take you two to dinner. This is twice you got Maria out of a tight jamb."

Vic caught Mary's eye. "I think this time she got herself out of it."

Bandini turned to her. "I heard. That's my girl." He smiled at her and Vic could have sworn that Mary Monahan, toughest businessperson in the city, blushed a little.

Finally, it was just Vic and Liz, and Priest, who still stood beside the coffin, his head bowed.

When Priest raised his head, Vic asked, "Need a ride to the airport?"

Priest gave a small nod. "I was hoping you would ask. But perhaps in a couple of days. I have someone to bury tomorrow, next to Geno. Geno Varelli and Mary Twail, together at last. Thanks for arranging that, Detective Lenoski." He turned to Liz. "I'm John Jefferson." He held out his hand.

Liz shook it. "Liz Timmons. And I know who you are, Priest."

"A priest," he corrected.

"Did you know Thuds well?" Vic asked, fighting back a smile.

Priest turned back to the coffin. "I did."

Vic waited, used to Priest's pauses.

Priest closed and opened his eyes. "Have you ever heard of the Cannonball Baker Sea-to-Shining-Sea Memorial Trophy Dash?"

"Yeah." Vic frowned, dredging up the memory. "Road race from New York to LA. Whoever gets there fastest wins."

"Right. It was invented by a man named Brock Yates. People still run it today. No rules. And Vincent Lombardo, that boy could drive. Geno and I, we called him Brock Yates Junior. Best driver in Pennsylvania, maybe the whole east coast."

Vic stared at him, the meaning of what Priest said sinking into him. "Thuds was your wheelman? For you and Geno?"

Priest smiled. "Wouldn't have anyone else. Part of the reason no one ever got caught. And he was the house."

Vic hadn't heard the term. Liz cocked her head in confusion.

Priest smiled. "I'm not saying we pulled any jobs, but if we had, we'd have someone we trusted hold the money. That way no one gets funny ideas about taking it. And Vince, he was always the house. Honest as the day is long."

"We figured out the honest part," Liz said quietly.

"Yes. That matters whatever business you're in." Priest looked out over the cemetery and took a deep breath, as if this was a place he wanted to remember. He turned to Vic. "Vic, something else, before that drive to the airport, I'd like to say a few words over your daughter's grave. If you don't mind."

259

Vic stared at him, glad in a way he hadn't felt in a long time. He smiled. "I'd like that, Priest. I'd like that very much."

Acknowledgements

How novels are formulated, written, and published is a miraculous and painful alchemy, redeemed only by the amnesia that strikes when I first hold the new book in my hands. Somehow, with that physical touch, the strain of producing the novel is lost forever. Afterwards, when asked, I will say the book was fun to write, or perhaps that it surprised me. I have no idea if those comments are true, but they may be, because the actual process of writing is forgotten.

With two exceptions.

Invariably, with each book I produce, I remember the idea, story, or humorous aside that pulsed in my mind and told me a novel was waiting to be written.

This book, *The Things That Secrets Cannot Hide*, is unusual, because there were two such moments. The first happened during a lunch with Verena Rose, my eternally patient and supportive editor at Level Best Books, who asked me if I could transform my three Vic Lenoski mysteries into a series. It wasn't a light question. Those first three novels were specifically written as a trilogy. The last book ended with Vic jobless and unsure if he could bring himself to work in law enforcement again.

Verena's question shook me out of my lethargy, and I fell back on an old marketing tactic. I turned the weakness of Vic's joblessness into a strength, using it as a stepping-stone to land him a new job with more responsibility and broader jurisdiction.

From there, I combined elements of two crimes that actually occurred in Pittsburgh: the 2019 shooting of an elderly man in his car outside a cemetery (it turned out the victim once served time in the 1980s for his involvement in a string of contract killings), and a 1980s spree of highly successful armed

261

robberies around Pittsburgh. The money from those robberies was never recovered, the thieves never caught.

With that I was off and running.

The second exception to my amnesia is that I can't forget the people who help bring my novels to publication. I am indebted to them, given the time, support and effort they give to my projects. They include critique group members Sylvia Adams, Jen Collins, Barb D'Souza, Howie Ehrlichman, Caren Knoyer, Janet McClintock, and Steve Sharpnack, who all read various chapters of the novel and helped me streamline, tighten and clarify the prose and storyline. A second critique group of established and successful mystery writers—Jeff Boarts, Annette Dashofy and Mary Sutton (better known under the pen name Liz Milliron)—read the entire novel and commented thoughtfully on the plot and characters, while reminding me throughout that I really needed to get the police procedural aspects of Vic's job correct. That they continue to put up with my penchant for repeating words and mixing up character names is astounding.

The complete manuscript was then read and commented on by Sono, my wife, who is always the first and most dedicated reader of my finished novels, my son, Jason, an established humor and satire writer in his own right, and Steven Hastings, a long-time friend whose judgement I absolutely trust. Only then did I submit the manuscript to Level Best Books, to be edited by Verena Rose and Shawn Reilly Simmons.

Afterwards, I waited for the final copy of the book, to touch it, and for the blissful wave of amnesia that makes it so much easier for me to start the entire process over and write my next book.

About the Author

Peter W. J. Hayes is a recovered marketing executive and author of the Silver-Falchion nominated Vic Lenoski mystery series. His short stories have won the Pennwriter's short story award and been finalists for Derringer and Al Blanchard awards. An early novel was a finalist for the Crime Writers Association (CWA) Debut Dagger Award.

SOCIAL MEDIA HANDLES:
    Facebook: Peter W. J. Hayes
    Twitter: @PeterWJHayes
    Instagram: Peter W. J. Hayes

AUTHOR WEBSITE:
    www.peterwjhayes.com

Also by Peter W. J. Hayes

The Things That Aren't There

The Things That Are Different

The Things That Last Forever